PENGUIN BOOKS

WIDEBOY

Simon Bye was born in Burgess Hill, Sussex, in 195?. He moved to London and has had a variety of jobs. He has translated books on ... Wagner, Marson and ... ... His first novel, Flint Reckoning Gridly, was published as a Penguin Original in 1998, and he turned it into a TV sitcom of the same title.

SIMON NYE

WIDEBOY

PENGUIN BOOKS

PENGUIN BOOKS

Published by the Penguin Group
Penguin Books Ltd, 27 Wrights Lane, London W8 5TZ, England
Penguin Books USA Inc., 375 Hudson Street, New York, New York 10014, USA
Penguin Books Australia Ltd, Ringwood, Victoria, Australia
Penguin Books Canada Ltd, 10 Alcorn Avenue, Toronto, Ontario, Canada M4V 3B2
Penguin Books (NZ) Ltd, 182–190 Wairau Road, Auckland 10, New Zealand

Penguin Books Ltd, Registered Offices: Harmondsworth, Middlesex, England

First published by Viking 1991
Published in Penguin Books 1992
10 9 8 7 6 5 4 3 2

Penguin Film and TV Tie-in edition published 1993

The moral right of the author has been asserted

Printed in England by Clays Ltd, St Ives plc

6059516

For my mother
and in memory of my father

Contents

Office   1

Is it a Boy, or What?   22

Handling People   26

Slime   31

Barbara Windsor   34

The Big Armchair   43

Rock-hard Tomatoes   48

School   55

Sex   62

Music – Celebrities – Acrobats   74

Prosperous Friendly   81

The O'Briens   88

Wes and Wendell   95

Invitations   103

Diane   113

Look at Yourself   122

Ambition   130

Frank Sinatra   137

Easy Ride Chauffeur Hire   145

Irritation and Disappointment   156

Everyone Can be Queen   167

Party   176

Tory Party Rules   186

Confidence   193

Stella   216

Safe   238

■ Office

Frank Stubbs wanted to know if the postman had been.

He picked up the telephone. 'Janice.'

'Yes, Frank?' she said in that typical way she had of speaking.

'Janice.'

'Mm-hmm?' she said, a little less confidently.

'Has the postman come?'

'How would I know?'

'Letters. You can tell by there being letters lying under the slot in the door. Letters and parcels and postcards.'

'I've only just arrived.' She had a harsh voice, but Frank didn't mind a harsh voice if it came out of a soft mouth. She went on, 'He may have come this way but not had anything for us.'

'You have a point. You're sharp, Janice.' She laughed out loud and Frank could hear her through the office wall they shared, as well as down the wire. 'I have another question. Has my son been in? Has he poked his head round the door at all?'

'No.'

'Janice, you're an attractive woman. I'm going to ask you again. Has my son been in, poked his head round the door and said "Janice, don't tell the old man I've been in"?'

'I would have remembered,' she said.

There was a silence at her end of the line and then she erupted into screams so loud that Frank had to put the listening end of the receiver inside his jacket for a moment.

'Letters,' she was screaming excitedly. 'Coming through the door.'

He joined her in her office as she tiptoed to the front door in her pencil skirt. Frank could see now: it was called a pencil skirt because there was no room for even a pencil inside her skirt, which was full of her legs. Even he could see that she had set the women's movement back about ninety years, simply by dressing that way.

'All right, calm down. Let's pace ourselves. Let's not use up the day's excitement over such a small item,' he said as he strolled towards Janice, who was now crouching over the pile of stationery on the mat.

'I love getting letters,' she said, suddenly subdued. She held them up in wonder. 'But I never get any.'

'I'll tell you what. You can open these.'

She was a new secretary. The morning before, he had telephoned a secretarial agency and asked for a receptionist. He wasn't sure where the misunderstanding had occurred but half an hour later a man walked in, asked where he should sit and where the typewriter was. The man explained equal opportunities legislation for a couple of minutes and then Frank threw him out. He rang a different agency and asked for a woman. 'It has to be a woman,' he explained, 'because the kind of man I deal with expects a female receptionist. He doesn't feel at ease with a male receptionist. If it was up to me I'd be totally *chuffed* to have a male receptionist, but my kind of client, my type of associate, unfortunately, is a man – or a woman – who likes to see a bare knee or two peeping out from under the desk. Do you know what I'm saying?'

They had weighed Frank Stubbs in the balance and found him Janice.

Frank was going straight.

'You can't be a wide boy all your life,' he told his partner Archie.

'You have though,' Archie reminded him. 'Mind you, as wide boys go, you've been narrow.'

Frank had known people who had broken thumbs in order to expedite an invoice, arranged for a truck of unsolicited manure to be dumped in an open-top car and paid someone to sleep with a business rival's young daughter.

'I don't touch those sorts of business persuader,' he had told his son.

'Why's that?' Jason asked.

'If I want supplementary questions, Jason, I'll buy myself the *Daily Mirror Quiz Book*.'

In recent months Frank had been wondering what he should do now. He thought of something he did better than anyone else he knew. But there was no money in touching the end of your nose with the tip of your tongue.

He had asked his mother and she suggested a whelk stall. Sometimes Frank felt she was losing her way.

His sister Petra was fortunately in closer touch with the present shape of the world. She could be brusque, and sometimes Frank had the impression that he embarrassed her. They had not been in regular contact since she married an estate agent, but he rang her and they shared a forthright conversation while in the background her husband played on his Yamaha organ.

'What are you good for, Frank? Three-card tricks on windy street corners. You're the man who bought at twenty and sold at five.'

'Hey, what brought this on? I could buy you out tomorrow. Behave. I have cash coming out of my navel.'

'So why aren't you legitimate, why – wait a moment.' Frank heard his sister swivel on her chair and shout at her husband, who was struggling over *Für Elise*, 'Honey, honey – Colin, for Christ's sake try out some of the black notes. We paid good money for those black notes and you never even use them.' She returned to Frank. 'Jesus, I'm going to have to take that thing right out of his hands and burn it in front of him. What was I saying?'

'Legitimate how? I don't want to get involved in paying tax, love. I don't *move* in tax-paying circles.'

'So Al Capone lives on in Hackney.'

'I once bought a television licence, came out in a rash in the Post Office.'

'How unusual.'

'How about estate agency?'

'Frank, you're too old to be moving into big-time extortion.'

'Was that a joke?'

'A joke is when you hear me laughing. Otherwise it's advice.'

The conversation had been of little help to Frank, and on the debit side he had hummed the white-note version of *Für Elise* for a week. (Then he heard *I'm Gonna Wash That Man Right Out of My Hair* in a lift and hummed that for a week, until he realized that the lyrics were not right for him.) Nevertheless, the idea of crossing the line that divided a tout from a businessman had already grown large in his mind.

*

The letters were all open and Janice was sitting with a look of high expectation on her face.

Knowing he was about to spoil her expression, Frank slitted his eyes in an imitation of someone weighing up pros and cons and said 'I was thinking, for one, and don't take this the wrong way, that you ought to call me Mr Stubbs.'

The brightness left her cheeks and eyes and her lipstick dulled before the sentence was out of his throat and half way across the carpet.

'Why?' she breathed.

'It's my name, love. I wouldn't ask you to call me Mr Stubbs if it wasn't strictly my name. Business is business.'

'But we were getting along so well. And now you'll have to call me Miss Wiggins.' And she lowered her eyelids until they touched her cheeks.

'Now hold on here a moment. I didn't say anything about your name.'

'It will have to be Miss Wiggins,' she persisted.

'No, listen.' He came and sat on the corner of her desk and leaned forward, breaking into her perfumed airspace. 'The relationship I'm going for,' he said calmly, trying not to show his irritation, 'the mood I'm trying to create is one of trust, certainly, mutual respect, by all means, but above all it is a relationship, Janice –'

'Miss Wiggins,' she said quietly.

'Janice.'

'Wiggins.'

'JANICE.'

'WIGGINS.'

'– a relationship of inequality and total obedience. Do I make myself clear?'

Frank Stubbs smiled and Janice Wiggins chewed the side of her mouth. Frank was already coming to know Janice's state of mind from what she was chewing. When she gnawed her lower lip it was because she was perplexed, if she nibbled the top lip it was a sign of indecision and if she chewed her hair it was because she was hungry.

The door swung open and there was Frank's son Jason, as large as life but, as Frank put it, 'not as interesting'.

'Dad, you old bastard,' he said, grinning and walking over.

Frank hit him across the back of the head.

'That's not the kind of talk I want to hear in this office. Where have you been?'

'Out.'

'Out, he says. Well you've made a mediocre start, my boy, that's all I can say. A day and a bit late is bad going in anybody's book, isn't that so, Miss Wiggins?'

'I believe so,' she agreed with a demure smile. 'A day and a bit – well.' She pursed her lips and sucked in. 'It's got to be.' She shook her head and tutted a little. 'I mean, it's certainly on the late side,' she said and re-pursed her lips, put her head on one side and nodded gently for a while. They were both watching her now, expressionlessly. 'Late, well, yes.' A pause set hard.

'Who's the woman?' Jason asked.

'That doesn't matter now. I got her from an agency.'

'Can I have one?'

Most schools in the area encouraged their pupils to stay on and go to college, but Jason's school allowed him to melt away from them by the age of thirteen. It went against the prevailing orthodoxy but it was much easier. He had picked up his education in supermarket car parks and under railway bridges, wherever his friends gathered together to misbehave. Frank had hoped his son would be one of those people who became smart by living on the street, but instead Jason was splashed by lorries and knocked over by cyclists. He had been an attractive boy, but he lost a lot of his good looks when he crashed through puberty one night after touching his first girlfriend in the underpass.

Frank and his wife Diane watched Jason change from being a cheeky tyke into an awkward young man, as though knowledge of a woman had disturbed his balance.

'Jason, you've got the charm of a box of spanners,' Frank told him. 'I reckon we'd do better swapping you for a couple of Jack Russells, now that you're old enough not to take it too hard.'

'Jack Russells – they're dogs, aren't they?' Jason asked.

'Frank, leave him alone,' Diane said wearily. It was thankless work, correcting her husband's heavy-handedness. Frank didn't see that she needed to. He regarded what he said as vigorous, fatherly and good-humoured.

'And your Jack Russell, see,' Frank went on, 'goes nicely in a hold-all if you have to take one on a bus or away for the weekend.'

A few weeks after this conversation, Jason found another girlfriend and their lives changed quickly and alarmingly. Now Jason was eighteen, lived on his own and spent much of the time in bed, watching his sheets grow greyer and furrier from day to day and relying on his father for money because he had difficulty understanding the Social Security forms. Frank looked after Jason, but muscularly and without sentimentality. To his way of thinking, Jason was still young, and if you were young you were already playing with a very full pack.

'Dad, me old mate, how can I help?' He was jumping around suddenly like two kids at a football match.

'Bring in the letters.'

'What, these letters?'

'Just do it, Jason.'

'They've been opened. Do they deliver them already opened or has somebody been tampering with our mail?' Jason thought he was on to something.

Frank walked towards his office, dragging his feet through the tangerine carpet with a heavy heart. 'Just bring in the letters.'

'Catch you for lunch maybe,' Frank heard Jason say to Janice. 'I know a pub near here where they do loads of different kinds of crisps.'

'Jason,' Frank called out, 'I want you in here where I can see you.'

Frank Stubbs was not a naturally gifted salesman, but he had worked on his technique. At first he used to make the mistake of *insisting* that people buy, even if they were not keen. He would remonstrate with them and grab their wrists, which was unsightly and unethical. ('I tell you you *need* this, I'm not fucking about here, this is absolutely what you need, I'll tell you what I'll do, no, I'll tell you what I'll do. I'll throw in my cuff links too, no, wait, no, come back here, come *back* here.' And the little ten-year-old girl would come back with tears in her eyes and she would buy that ironing board or that plastic washing-up bowl from Frank Stubbs with the last of her pocket-money.)

He was not helped by the way he looked. His small, squared-off face was dominated by heavy eyebrows that were high towards the temples but angled in aggressively towards the top of the nose. His delicate hands were used economically. His tallness supported a sharp, deep, loud voice. He had a knack for wearing his hair at the most unfashionable length; if thin ties were in Frank wore fat ties, and not as a matter of policy.

Fortunately a few years earlier Frank had stumbled on a selling job he was right for. He was walking past a theatre when a man in a sheepskin coat said something to him that he could not quite catch. Retracing his steps, Frank heard the man ticking very quietly to himself: *tcks, tcks, tcks.* After a while he began to enlarge this into a mantra. 'Tickets, tickets. I'm buying, I'm buying, I'm selling, I'm buying. Let's 'ave your spare, I'm buying spare, let's 'ave your spare.' Frank took his eye off the man in the sheep for a moment and when he turned back money was exchanging hands between a wealthy-looking couple and the man who was interested in spare. The ticket tout added a fist of notes to a roll.

Frank liked the size of the man's bundle of notes and he enjoyed his way of speaking out of the side of his mouth, a sure sign that money was in the equation. Above all, Frank liked his own life to be touched with glamour, and here, suddenly, was showbusiness. Never mind that most punters spoke like they had something stuck to the roofs of their mouths. Or that they were Swedes who could be sold cloakroom tickets and would not notice until halfway through the show, when they started to wonder about all the coats and umbrellas. He himself was a self-confessed lowbrow and considered Bernard Breslaw's performance in *Carry on Camping* probably unsurpassable in any branch of the arts.

Frank was impressed enough to stay around watching the tout operating, to see whether it looked like a line of business he could make worthwhile money in. It looked as though it was, from the way the man's roll put on weight like a dog in a butcher's. Five minutes before the performance he sold his last ticket and walked up to Frank.

'Have I got something you want,' he asked, 'or have you got something I want, or is my dick hanging out?'

'Police,' Frank said. One of his specialities was pretending to be a plainclothes policeman. 'I've decided to let it go on this occasion, but don't let it happen again.' He had learnt that if you wanted to imitate a policeman properly you had to speak within certain parameters.

'I don't recognize you, as it happens,' the man persisted.

'If I was in the recognition business I'd be wearing a flashing blue light and rollerskates.'

'You boys in blue are some of my best customers. I could get you two tickets for any Bill Ball from here to there.'

'Oh really? Actually I'm not interested, since I'm not a policeman.' It was easy to pretend to be a policeman but it became boring after a while. 'I'm thinking of branching out into the ticket market myself and I wanted to watch an operator.'

'Well, night school is now over. I'll call you if I want my shirt lifted.'

Frank couldn't understand why the man thought he was a homosexual. 'Yeah, yeah, yeah,' he said.

The man in the sheepskin coat turned out to be called Archie. Frank came to see a lot of him and eventually they knew so much about each other that they formed a loose alliance. By and by the alliance grew stronger (not that they liked each other particularly), and it was only a matter of years before they both felt ready to enter into an informal association, which developed, after much thought and a good deal of testing of the water on both sides, into a semi-official coalition, whereby one partner might go so far (say) as to look after some of the other's money if the other was feeling vulnerable because he had a mile of notes in his pocket. And now, after a good number of years, they had joined together in a formal and official partnership, in which they could be totally Frank and completely Archie with each other and weld, link by link, a bond of trust and mutual concern between them.

'What I want to know,' Frank now said, welding, welding, 'is where that cunt Archie is.'

The office consisted of two rooms – a small back office with two high square windows you had to stand on a chair to see out of (and even then you climbed down disappointed), and the larger front room containing Janice, an old desk and chair and a small safe, vaguely hidden under a blanket. This was to be the reception area (bright, roomy, plants, umbrella holder), which was to contrast instructively with the back room (intimate, confidential, a room for making deals) where Frank and Jason sat on rickety chairs separated by a baize-covered card table with a damp-stain in one corner.

Frank had rented the office a week earlier, but had done little so far other than have the telephones put in.

'That's all you need to make money nowadays, a telephone,' he told the engineer, who was playing with thin strands of coloured wire.

'How does that work?' the man asked.

'Percentages,' Frank answered, casual, confident.

'What about things? Making things and selling them.'

'Sure, you can do it that way too, if you've got the time,' Frank agreed. 'I'm just saying all you need is a telephone.'

'And a pad to write messages down on,' the engineer said, tearing off some plastic sheathing with his teeth.

'You're right,' Frank said, his face clouding. 'I'd better get one of those.'

He was looking forward to the office being busier, the sharingness, the oneness of premises and the sense of achievement at the end of the day, the warm goodnights.

They had not planned exhaustively what they were going to do with the *business space*, as they had once heard it called by an estate agent. Technically, he was not an estate agent but a broad-shouldered man called Moss they had met in a pub. They had got talking one evening after Jason knocked the man's packet of crisps on to the floor on his way back from robbing the condom machine in the gents. Moss took it very well but insisted that Jason buy him a triple vodka and tonic by way of restitution.

'In the same glass?' Jason asked Moss.

'No, in a biscuit tin,' he answered.

When Jason arrived back at the bar and explained to Frank and Archie what had happened, Frank refused to pay for the drink and went over to talk to Moss, who was sitting placidly with a newspaper, doing the crossword. He had answered three clues and had only achieved that by putting two letters in some of the squares. They exchanged words across the lager-drenched table but by sleight of hand Moss finished up with more words than Frank. When the rift was healed (they reached a compromise – Jason would just buy Moss the large vodka without the tonic, but would also wash Moss's car the next morning) Moss was invited over to join the men at the bar.

'Moss – is that your surname or your first name?' Archie asked.

'It just came about,' he replied sharply. 'Listen, don't

shout what I have to say around the place, but I've got this office to let.'

'Oh really?' Frank said quickly.

'What do you think of that bird over there?'

'Shut it, Jason, I'm interested in what he has to say about an office,' Frank said.

'I think she's giving me the eye.'

'Jason, you're talking through your cock again and in the middle of a business meeting,' Frank decided to say.

'We don't need an office.'

'Jason, Jason,' Moss said, 'everyone needs offices. Where do you transact business otherwise?'

'In the front room. Call-boxes.'

'I don't think you'll find the Saatchis and Murdochs of this planet working out of their sitting rooms, Jason,' Moss explained convincingly.

'He's a boy, Moss, you can safely ignore him.'

'I don't see Tiny Rowland popping down to the payphone all that often.'

'Tiny who?' Jason asked.

Frank was standing quietly at the bar with his elbow in an ashtray. He was already making plans. To a man like himself the word office had the kind of exoticism other people find in longer and more foreign words – *homunculus*, *Caracas*, *gecko*, *office*.

'This office,' Frank joined in. 'This office you have to let.'

'Tiny *who*?' Jason still wanted to know.

'It's actually a suite of rooms, Frank. To call it an office is to be misleading. It's available. I can't say much more than that at this stage, except that it's available.'

'You say it's actually a suite? That would be more expensive, would it?'

'I'll say this much at this stage, lads. Yes, it will be more expensive, being a suite rather than an office. Don't press me too hard at this junction.'

Moss successfully fostered the illusion that he was not just letting out a couple of shabby rooms to three men he had met in the pub. It was shit-hot fostering.

They went to see the premises the next day, after Jason had cleaned and polished Moss's BMW until it gleamed. The lessor started to introduce an element of reality into his description of the accommodation as they approached it.

'The carpet may need a Hoover running over it,' he said when they were halfway there. 'I chose the curtains myself,' he clarified when he had his key in the door. 'You can't get this wallpaper any more,' he said as they took the full force of the decor.

Archie wasn't convinced that the office was a good idea, but Frank could already see the slant of light filtering through Venetian blinds and cigar smoke curling into a chrome air-extractor. His senses were full of the possibility of secretaries in ankle-breaking stilettos and improbable cosmetics, carrying documents this way and that and eager to park the twin moons of their bottoms on his lap on Friday afternoons.

'Jason,' he said quietly, 'run down to the offy and get two bottles of the best pooh and a can of Coke for yourself, there's a smart boy.'

'Daaaaaaaaaad,' he whined.

'Here's £15. I want change.'

'Daaaayyyyaaaad.'

'You're riding for a fall, my boy Jason, if you carry on whining. And I'll make sure you fall on your head.'

Frank and Archie discussed the deal, standing on one side in the office. Archie looked doubtful. He was prone to worry, most recently about whether the universe was really expanding and whether the Woolworths in Hackney was really cheaper than the Woolworths in Islington.

'Why do we want an office, Frank?' he asked.

'Why did the chicken cross the road? Why are there three coins in the fountain?' he answered. 'Do you know what I'm saying?'

'Those are goodish answers, Frank.'

'I mean, Archie. I mean.'

'I've an idea what you're saying.'

Jason had gone down to the off-licence. He would be some time. Frank found it useful to decide how much time it would take the average person to do a certain errand and then multiply that time by about eight to arrive at how long it would take Jason.

'*Do* you know what I'm saying, Archie?'

'Don't play games with me, Frank.'

'I mean, are you for giving this a tumble or are we going to spend the rest of our lives out in the rain?'

'I think we should tread carefully,' Archie added, narrowing his eyes.

'Why are you narrowing your eyes?'

'Was I doing that?'

They were standing in the middle of the office, with Moss out of earshot, waiting to be called back and told of their decision.

'Hey, lads, I haven't got all day,' he said, coming over.

'Nor have we,' Frank said. 'I've got other offices to look at.' He was being cunning.

'You won't find offices like this this side of Canvey Island.'

'I'm not saying it's not a bitch of an office,' Archie said.

'But?'

'I mean,' said Archie, stubbornly, 'it's not perfect, that's all I'm saying.'

'In what way short of perfect?'

They debated awkwardly for some minutes. One of them would say *I'm not saying* something and would then proceed to say exactly that; the other would then reply, querying what the other man had not said. Archie was not saying the office was overpriced and shabby. Moss eventually lost his temper with Archie.

'Frank, Archie doesn't have your vision.'

'Don't listen to him, Frank. I've got your vision all right. I've got your vision, and vision over. So fuck you, Mr Real Estate.'

At that moment Jason came panting through the door with two bottles of Maltese sherry. 'It's like champagne,' he said, putting the bottles in his father's hands and backing away.

'In what way like champagne?' his father asked, his lips stretched tightly across his teeth. 'As like champagne as champagne, or not quite as much?'

'How should I know?' Jason asked.

'And where's my change?'

'I dropped it down a grate.'

'Oh, give over. What am I, simple?' He walked up to his son and stood on his foot. 'I'm not going to get off your foot until you tell me what has happened to the fifteen, all right?' Jason enjoyed these games, Frank knew he did. Father and son, horsing around.

'I lost it on the Mastermind machine in Playtime.' Jason was a compulsive gambler and machine player. He was an obsessive emptier of his own pockets.

'You're the last person who should be playing that game, Jason. You don't even know how many beans make five,' Frank shouted from two inches away. 'You had less chance of getting money out of that machine than I have of sleeping with Linda Lusardi.'

'Can we progress on a little here?' Moss was asking.

'My associates and I have decided to take it,' Frank said suddenly, turning to Moss. 'That's why I've bought these to celebrate,' he added, holding up the two bottles of Maltese sherry.

'You've got style, Frank Stubbs,' Moss answered.

Frank handed over £900 cash as advance rental and commission. When they arrived the following morning to re-arrange the furniture and organize themselves on their new premises they found a group of people there already, standing around in some embarrassment, thumping walls in anger and turning this way and that. Between them, they were jingling eight sets of keys. Frank looked at his own set and said 'I'm going to find that prick. I'm going to push his head back down his neck and drag it out through his arse.'

A few weeks later they found their present office through legitimate channels.

'We've arrived, Archie,' Frank said, looking around at the shabby interior.

'We're here, if that's what you mean.'

'Feels like . . . I've come home,' Frank went on, trying to express his sense of challenge and awe. He was feeling untypically soulful.

'Don't be young in the head, Frank. You wouldn't make your home in this place even if it came with an *au pair* and a fridge of beer.'

*

Eventually Frank heard the front door open. He heard Janice say cheerfully 'What can I do for you, sir?'

'Shut your eyes.' There was a quiet moment, presumably while Janice did what he asked. 'Think of a number. Double it. Add three. Divide by eight. Take all your clothes off.'

Another moment of silence, before Janice tutted loudly enough for Frank to hear her yards away.

'Relax, darling. I'm Archie.'

Archie was small and rotund. Smaller than a man would choose to be if it were up to him. As he once told Frank, he put it down to spending all his school dinner-money on food for a dog that he had found in the street, which his mother refused to feed. The dog had died and Archie was left with no dog and no height to speak of. If he could have his time again, he said, he would turf out the dog and take the protein. Frank often felt sorry for Archie because although he was vain (for no reason anyone could think of, and Frank had asked around) he was also moody and often depressed.

'I've got more worry-lines than Big Ben,' he once confided to Frank over a great deal of lager.

But Frank and Archie said a lot of odd things when they were very, very relaxed.

'What's your name, darling?' Archie was saying to Janice.

'Wiggins,' she said defiantly.

'You free for lunch?' he asked.

From the back office, Frank cut in: 'Come on in, Archie.'

Archie grew up in a tiny house in a stub of a road. There was even a school of thought (Frank) that Archie himself was short because he came from such a house in such a road. 'Nature can do that kind of shit,' Frank said. Archie had described his past to Frank with the style and detail of a fairy tale. He was the only child of a single parent but there was someone who lived in the house called Uncle Jim, who used to tell his mother terrible jokes in the middle of the night which made her whimper and terrifying stories that made her scream and moan. Times were as hard as nails during his childhood. Archie came home from school one lunchtime to feed his dog and found another uncle, Uncle Jack, lying on his mother to keep her warm because she had run out of clothes. The house, which Archie had lived in alone since his mother was taken off to Australia by Uncle Shane in 1969, backed on to Hackney Marshes. The wind whipped across the marshes all through the winter, as though a large door had been left open somewhere.

Archie had made two improvements to the house over the years. He started by installing stone-cladding over the front of the house, then round the back. Then he had the front wall clad and the coal bunker, and then tried to persuade his neighbours Mr and Mrs Bairstow to have their own property done (but apparently they were devoted to pebble-dashing). Two years later his mother found out about the cladding from her bungalow in Melbourne and wrote to Archie ordering him to have it removed. That was the second improvement.

'I'm afraid I'm not free for lunch, actually,' Janice said.

'Frank's told me all about you.'

'He didn't know I was Miss Wiggins until this morning,' she said sulkily. 'I think you men are taking me for granted.'

'If you say so, darling.'

'I do say so.'

'If you say so.'

'I do say so.'

Frank opened the door and shouted, 'Are you going to have a proper conversation or am I going to have to smack arses? Archie, where have you been?'

'Around and about, up and down.'

'Here and there?'

'You could say that.'

'That's good, Archie. Grafting, eh?' Frank looked over his shoulder and said to Jason 'I wish you'd do some of that, earn your keep. It's about time you put something back into the pot.'

'Where's the pot?' Jason asked morosely.

'Not a real pot, Jason. Not a pot in that sense,' he said, shaking his head.

Archie turned to Janice. 'You'll like Jason. He says two kinds of things. Wrong things and stupid things.'

'So why are you late for our meeting?' Frank asked tartly, turning back suddenly to Archie. 'I was beginning to think you'd had to go back for your bus pass.'

'I don't need to give you reasons, Frank, you know that.'

Frank leant against the door jamb. Archie sat on the edge of Janice's desk. Janice chewed the side of her mouth. Frank envied Janice because she didn't have any responsibilities and could just sit there gnawing harmlessly on bits of her own body until the moment came to go home at the end of the day.

'The time has come for a bit of a natter,' Frank explained, moving to the centre of the room.

'Right,' Archie said.

Janice started chewing her thumbnail.

'Hey gorgeous, you know what you need?' Frank asked. 'Calcium supplements,' Frank answered.

'I was only chewing my nail.'

She stopped for a moment and then started very quietly to suck a tooth.

Frank cleared his throat. 'I want you all to look very

closely at some documents. They're important. They actually came in the post this morning.' Frank clicked his fingers twice. After a few seconds, when nothing had happened, Jason hadn't moved, Frank went into the back office and brought in the brochures himself.

Frank spread them out on the mildewed card table.

'This is the way I see it. You'll have your own opportunities to contribute after I've said a few words.' He interlaced his fingers and rested his chin on them. 'You've got your melamine and you've got your Formica. As far as I can see, melamine *looks* good, it's hard-wearing and it would stand up well to some of the heavy use we'll be demanding of it. And you've got your Formica, which is a name everybody knows. It's bound to inspire trust for that very reason. In a moment I'll pass the leaflets among you. And then you've got your teak finish. You might be surprised to hear me say this but I'm going to float this one out to you. I'm tempted by that teakette.'

Archie shook his head slowly and looked at the picture of the teak-finish table next to the Formica table. He held the two up to the light, then he picked up the third brochure and held that up. One of the glossy leaves slipped from his fingers and he mumbled an apology, gathered it up again and held the three options at a different angle of light, where he might do proper justice to the richness of the colour reproductions.

'Does it matter?' he asked.

Is it a Boy, or What?

Over the years, Frank's mother had described the circumstances of his early life, filling in the big gap between birth and memory.

He was born on VE night. His mother wanted to be on the street with the celebrating crowds but instead she saw the evening in indoors, listening to the news on the radio and trying to push Frank out of his swimming pool on to the rubberized sheet. Frank's father was the worse for wear by early evening, but he managed to struggle up the stairs twice to tell her what a time they were all having.

'I'll be down shortly,' she assured him from behind her thighs, confused by her throes.

The red-haired midwife wanted to be out on the street too, kissing sailors, but she made do with opening the front bedroom window and shouting down, 'Can we have a bit of hush please, some of us are trying to have a baby up here.'

Frank's mother later described giving birth as 'a little painful'. She had never been a controversial figure; Frank was a twelve-pound baby and some people felt that she might have tried to be a little more descriptive on this occasion. She was disappointed not to be there cheering among the bomb sites and the khaki swirl, but the next morning, when she was the only adult for miles around not to have a head like an open sore, she was glad that she had stayed indoors with her feet up. It was a mystery to her where they had got the alcohol to celebrate, because there was a war on.

In 1943 she had been mistaken for Vera Lynn by a bomb-disposal man and she always recreated that glistening moment when the general drabness made her want to cry. When the compliment was made they were sheltering down on the tube platform and the light had not been very good. But that was the war for you, she explained to Frank, always dark.

Frank was her insurance for the future, but she had about fifteen years of premiums to pay before she got any money back, by which time she realized that she would look like Vera Lynn's mother, or her grandmother at the present rate of hardship. She wanted Frank to have the things they had gone without in those difficult years: she would get him bananas. And eventually he would provide for her, small tokens at first, like three new tiles to replace the broken ones above the sink, and then larger and more ambitious offerings, like a house with a drainpipe running down the outside in a neat vertical. There was a thirst for order and symmetry in those days, and Frank's mother saw the future as a time when old, zigzagging plumbing would be torn away.

'Is it a boy, or what?' Frank's father asked the next morning.

Frank still had some of his baby-clothes, and if he had been small enough he would have climbed back into them sometimes and tied up the tiny little bows. Frank had a strong sense of the past, but it only just kept pace with his desire to be seen embracing the future. He usually ended up settling for the day before yesterday. Baby-clothes had been a

difficult issue when he and his young wife Diane were bringing up Jason. She found a piece of desiccated, twenty-year-
old food caught between the filaments of Frank's old shawl
and insisted that everything be burned: the yellow bootees,
the little green shorts with the perished waistband, the match-
ing green shirt that no longer matched because it had been
exposed to sunlight on the top of a wardrobe between 1953
and 1961, the tiny cardigans made of wool from long-dead
sheep. Frank escaped from the house with his baby-clothes
and hid them in the boot of his car until Diane was ready to
be mellower on the subject.

His mother's name was Grace. Frank felt his grandparents
must have had a certain delicacy to come up with such a
name.

'I would have liked to know them properly,' Frank said to
his mother. 'They look a bit of a laugh in these brown
photos.'

'Not really. They kept themselves to themselves.'

'Well they would, wouldn't they, if they had to go down
to the shops in those stiff collars and crazy old boots.'

'They dressed up especially for the photograph,' his mother
said drily. 'It was a big event.'

'Who's the bloke with one arm?'

His mother quickly removed her glasses and stared more
closely. 'I've never noticed him before. Maybe it was a friend
of the photographer.'

Recently Frank had been able to move further back in
time. When he was twenty his earliest memories were of the
time he had his first cigarette, when he was eight. He had
swallowed the smoke and worried that it would swarm for
weeks in his stomach, creating terrible purple cancers. At the
age of thirty the earliest incident he could recall was when as

a five-year-old he was sick trying to eat whalemeat, the housewife's friend. Now he was in his forties he was almost certain he could remember rolling off the kitchen table at a very young age. His mother thought he was probably one and a half, but her memories of the fall were clouded by worries that the social services would hear and take Frank into care, even at this late stage.

He had been lying on the table while Grace scrubbed at the sink with her red hands, standing a few inches away from the chipped stone rim because she was pregnant with Petra. Occasionally she would put her hands back on her hips and straighten out her spine. The atmosphere was dense with washing soda and somewhere a damp corset with tired pink straps hung like a shed skin. The table had been painted lime-green, but patches of wood showed through. Frank shared it with a pile of clothes-pegs, two empty milk bottles and a bicycle pump that always, no matter how many times you pumped it, contained stale air. Frank landed on his side and rolled across the floor towards his mother at the sink. Irrationally she spent some moments trying to find a cloth to dry her hands before she gathered Frank up in her arms which, as she had predicted, had already lost some of the bloom of the war years.

There was no purpose to these flashbacks; they did not comfort Frank. He feared that he would crawl so far down the black tube of his past that he would push his head out of the other side and suddenly there he would be, at his own conception. And knowing his father there would be a copy of the *Sporting Life* propped up against the headboard, which Frank senior would be studying as he rocked to and fro over the young Mrs Stubbs.

■ Handling People

'Have you considered smoked glass?' Janice asked.

Frank found Janice wife-leavingly attractive. Perhaps she would not have been considered pretty all over the world, but in their part of it she was the kind of woman men abandoned their homes for. They walked away from their wives, their cars, their home beer-making kits. The only thing they would not leave would be a forwarding address. It was an Oriental sort of beauty in the sense that it lost much of its power when Janice and women like her went west of the Aldwych, like hedgehogs stepping out of the undergrowth and into the road. Frank saw this peculiarly eastern charm as *perkiness*. It showed in her hair, which was highlighted in blonde and teased into perky stiffness, and in her body. Frank could not be sure what lay beneath her blue blouse and her taupe tights but he was pretty sure it would be perky.

'Smoked glass, Janice? Tell me more.'

Frank stole a look at Archie. His belly was asking for extra performance from his shirt buttons, his trouser belt was a tourniquet, his clothes a harness. Archie was an optimist when it came to tailoring, forever cramming, making the shape of his clothes dictate the precise swells of his body.

This wasn't fashion, it was taxidermy.

'Hey, aren't there other things we should be doing?' Jason said.

'You just have no idea, do you, Jason,' Frank said, tearing his eyes away from Archie's chest hair, which poked out above his top button like three-day-old cress. 'What is the difference between the successful businessman and the old geezer selling wet matches in the street?'

'Blindness, usually,' Janice answered for Jason.

'Lack of foresight, certainly,' Frank said. He was impressed with the width of her understanding and the depth of it.

'Matchsellers are usually blind,' Janice pushed on.

'Now you've spoilt it,' Frank muttered.

Archie stepped in to say, 'Unlike successful businessmen, I don't know any big blind dealers. Although there's the little guy with the eye-patch who runs that tight little bookies' in Stepney.'

Jason had not finished either. 'I don't know why they let the blind sell matches when they're so dangerous. They could go up at any moment.' There was a pause. 'Whoosh,' he added.

'I have to be a special kind of stupid to listen to you, don't I,' Frank said heavily. 'The difference, if you can remember what I was talking about, is *presentation*. If we can get the office looking right we are halfway there.'

'Halfway where?' Archie said.

Frank decided that, although he was surrounded by dwarves, he would nevertheless show some understanding.

'Shall I go over our strategy for the future again? Would that make anyone happier and a bit less ignorant?'

Jason and Janice nodded, Archie just watched. Frank got

to his feet and walked around. He thought about starting 'I have a dream', but you can only use a good idea once. Then he toyed with 'I have a vision', but he *knew* that Jason would think it was some kind of car, a Vauxhall Vision. Allowances had to be made constantly.

'I see myself,' he started, 'as "Frank Stubbs Entertainments".' He allowed that to sink into the carpet and curtains. 'Don't get me wrong. To my friends I will always be plain Frank. Nothing will change on that level, you can sleep easy.' Jason's attention span had already been exceeded. He started to try out some kind of dance step. Frank was used to this and carried on, concentrating on Janice. 'No offence to Archie, who will be looking after the ticket side of the business from these premises, but you don't make a splash nowadays by touting around a few tickets outside the Palladium. Archie and I know what that gets you.'

'Varicose veins. Arrested,' Archie confirmed.

'OK, so it might be worth a few bob. I wouldn't have twenty-eight big ones now in the safe if I'd been selling lettuces.' They all looked over towards the safe under its blanket, then, one by one, they turned back to Frank's small face. 'So I'm moving in a new direction. Archie and I share overheads, pool resources, and when I start to make money it all goes back into the company.'

'Yeah, yeah,' Jason said. Archie looked sceptical.

'Where's all the money nowadays, Janice?' Frank asked, breezily.

'In the safe,' she suggested.

'No. Well, yes,' he conceded. 'But I'm talking about management. People handling other people and getting paid for it. There's very few people actually doing much work. We're going to be handling people, basically.'

'Who?' grunted Jason. Frank had no real alternative this time but to slap him across the temple.

'That's for pretending to take an interest,' his father told him. 'Janice, I haven't told you who we're going to be involved with yet.'

He started to sing in a low voice, *shoom shoom de doob doob my baby's got* (and then in a higher voice, out of his range by two or three octaves) *styyyyle* (and then low again) *shoom shoom*. There was a pause which was in a way more frightening than Frank's singing.

'Does that ring any bells, Janice?'

'Was it –' she searched for the right word '– a song?'

'What if I say this to you: Nobody Can Dance Like You Can Do It.'

'You'll have to help her out,' Archie said.

Frank was becoming impatient. 'Aren't you *interested* in pop music, darling? I thought everyone your age was. You must have heard of the O'Brien Brothers. Help me out here, Archie, what was the name of their other hit single?'

'I don't think there was another one, was there?'

Frank didn't like the way Archie was almost smiling.

'It wasn't as huge as *Nobody Can Dance Like You Can Do It*, but how could it have been?'

Janice and Jason had fallen silent. Frank watched them for the slightest signs of smiling at his expense, but they seemed genuinely cowed.

'Of course, we're talking about 1972, '73. They were huge then.'

'My mum might have heard of them. She used to have, you know, platform soles.'

'Thanks, Janice. Anyway, I've managed to sign them up, against stiff opposition. In the music business it's all ebbs and flows. One minute it's the Tremeloes, then it's the O'Briens, and then, hey presto, it's the O'Brien Brothers again.'

'Who are the Tremeloes?' Janice asked.

■ **Slime**

Before long Frank could not help but realize that the man who lived in their house was his father. His mother tried to keep it from him until he was strong.

His father was a spiv, a reputable white-collar job immediately after the war. It was a time when average citizens were in a mood to tolerate rule-breaking and to do a bit themselves. So many people were stepping out of line that it was no longer possible to remember where the line was, where rectitude became merely ridiculous. Only so many clothing coupons could be totted up, only so much whalemeat eaten before patience ran out. And when it did a lot of people had a friend who had a friend who knew Frank's father.

Frank was told that his father was a *businessman*, which was so close to the truth that for years nobody was philosopher enough to try to explain the difference to the boy.

The query against Mr Stubbs' moral health did not in any case centre on his choice of commercial career; it was the way he failed to distribute the company profits that caused such resentment. The shareholders – Grace, little Frank, Petra and Grant – received their only substantial dividend in 1948 in the form of a new second-hand cooker, although Frank's mother then had to find something to cook in it.

Frank remembered his parents' conversations, which had

the shuddering bitterness of the Nuremberg trials without the promise of a thumping good hanging at the end of it all. They only ever talked about money, even though it was the subject they disagreed about most. They never discussed the three children except tangentially, as consumers of shoes, a three-headed Cerberus guarding the gates of affluence.

Frank's father said several times 'I don't give you money so you can *spend* it.'

Other sayings from his father's domestic lexicon floated through to Frank when he took the time to look back:

'What do you think I am, *made* of underwear?'

'*Too right* I'll be asking you for receipts next, gorblimey yes.'

'One day *I'll* fall off the back of a lorry and then you won't know what hit you.'

And so on. All of it nonsense.

He clearly had more money than he revealed. Frank's mother reacted stoically when that dawned on her, after she had thrown at her husband one final pitchfork of accusations that clattered around her kitchen. She gathered her children about her dolefully, like a bag-lady with three special bags, and gave up her job as a wife in order to become a full-time mother.

On Frank's first day at school his father left the family house for good. His last words to his eldest son were typically off-colour: 'I don't want you sitting down in those new trousers and wearing the backside off them.'

Nobody tried to persuade him to come back to the family he had relinquished, and contact was limited to a series of notes exchanged some years later, mainly by solicitors, which sealed the divorce. Frank had thought about inquiring into his father's whereabouts but gave up after a couple of phone calls. As his mother said in a rare aphorism, 'You can't trace slime. It just washes away.'

Frank wondered about the slime. When he thought about his life he did not pretend that some had not rubbed off on him. After all, he had some slimy friends. He too had betrayed his wife. So now, the more he remembered of his father, the faster he moved in the opposite direction, into the respectable world of office furniture and international entertainment.

Barbara Windsor

'Dave?' Frank shouted down the telephone.

'I can hardly hear you.'

'Is that Dave?' Frank said.

'I can't – is that Gerry?'

'Dave, it's Frank.'

'Gerry, you old tosser.'

'No. It's Frank, Dave.'

The line went quiet, apart from the noise.

'Gerry?' the voice repeated.

'No, no, it's *Frank*, Dave.'

Frank put his hand over the receiver and turned to Archie. 'Eleven hundred pounds he paid for that phone.'

'That much?'

'For decent carphones nowadays we are really talking telephone numbers.'

The noise of the road continued in his ear. Dave seemed to have hung the telephone out of the car window.

'Where's your telephone, Archie?' Frank asked idly, while he was waiting for something to happen.

'In the hall.'

'Mine's in the hall too.'

The line suddenly went dead.

'He's a hard man to catch on the telephone,' Frank said.

'You're not bullshitting.'

Janice and Jason had gone into the front office. He didn't trust his son not to put his hand on Janice's bottom as they walked across the room together. He would be sued by the agency for sexual malpractice and they would have the *Hackney Gazette* jumping on their necks.

Archie and Frank sat quietly. Frank was alert and upright but Archie was slumped, as if he had heard that points would later be awarded for inertia and slobbery. Frank was alert with good reason: he was planning a big party for later that day. If he could get hold of the likes of Dave Giddings and other big players like Ted Nuttall then it would almost be an occasion. He was just hesitating over whether to invite his sister Petra. She had a history of plain-speaking, which didn't always go down well at parties.

He dialled Petra's number and she took an age to answer.

'Hey babe, what took you so long?'

'Is this my brother Frank?' she said thinly.

'As far as I know.'

'I'm in the middle of something.'

'Essex.'

'Don't try too hard, Frank. I've got three-quarters of a migraine as it is.'

'Petra, I'm having a party.'

'Why?' She always sounded blasé. It would have been nice if once in a while she could rummage around for some enthusiasm.

'It's a gathering, actually.'

'I never gather on a Tuesday. And my gathering frock is at the cleaner's.'

'I want you to be there to meet some important business

associates. There'll be food and drink.' Frank made a mental note to arrange food and drink.

'I've got Dawn at home.' This was her fifteen-year-old daughter.

'So bring her. Why isn't she at school?'

'She tried it but doesn't like it.'

'She and Jason would make a team.'

'If I want Dawn in a team I'll find her a pair of huskies. What are you launching? Some kind of boat?'

'Not as such. Do you remember I talked about a business venture?'

'You have lots of ideas, Frank. It seems to me you re-invent the wheel every other week.'

'This is totally kosher, Petra. Frank Stubbs Entertainments, a leisure combine. Big names will be present.'

'I think you probably mean *long* names.'

'Yeah, well, don't push it, Petra. Your invite is hanging in the balance right now.' Archie was nodding at this. 'I may have to reallocate your space on the cocktail floor to Barbara Windsor.'

She was dying to come, Frank thought, but it was a long way. She would have to get the Audi out of the double garage (mind the paintwork). Her husband Colin would have to relearn how to work the microwave if she wasn't there to press the right buttons herself. Frank could imagine Colin panicking on his own in the Mars-age kitchen, trying to activate a prawn curry by running it through the dish-washer. Colin was slow-thinking, which normally saved him from doing too much damage too quickly. He needed five or six hours to blow the place up, by which time some-one had usually returned to sit him in an armchair again and reset the dials. As far as Frank could see, Colin had spent his life shedding the sense he was born with, cell by cell.

'I won't be able to stay long. What time shall I be there and where is there?'

He told her. 'Hey, if you arrive early you can help stick the cheese in the grapefruit.'

'Sounds like a classy do,' she said in a headachey voice, and hung up.

That was more like it. Today would be like rolling a smooth boulder: he had to start slowly, that was all.

Frank had a lot of telephoning to get through. He preferred to transact his business and generally make his mark face to face, where he could use his tallness. The telephone made everybody the same. Frank resented the way a little man with a deep voice could just as easily be a tall man on the telephone. It was cheaper than a height operation. He could be as ugly and mean as February but if he had a good voice and a full set of verbs suddenly he was a top-of-the-range businessman, saying phrases like *I'll have a word with my people.*

Archie continued to sit.

'Is that Ted Nuttall's number?' Frank said into the telephone.

The woman on the other end snorted. 'No, it's his wife. Ted's out.'

'Isn't he just,' he said. 'Know what I mean?'

'No.' Nor did Frank.

'I'll tell you what.' This was one of the things Frank said. Frank admitted to himself that it really needed a good friend of his (or a language coach, and there weren't too many of those in Frank's neighbourhood) to tell him when he was creating a banal speech environment. 'Why don't you tell me where he is?'

'How should I know? You could try the market.'

'Why don't I do that?' Frank had once met Brenda Nuttall out with Ted in Sainsbury's. Frank only remembered the occasion because the Nuttalls had brought their dog into the shop. They made it down one and a half aisles before the animal was spotted by a member of staff. An argument escalated as Frank looked on. Brenda fought long and hard for the right to go shopping with her chihuahua, but the only way she could comply with the law was to pretend to be blind, which she did with the help of her husband's sunglasses, laughing raucously as the little dog pulled her towards the till.

'I'm going to the market,' Frank said.

Archie asked 'What shall I do?'

'You're a dynamic little bleeder this morning. Did you die in the night or something?'

'That's about it.'

'Yeah, well, you can call your own ambulance.' Frank put on his jacket and went to the door. He changed his mind and walked back towards Archie. 'This is supposed to be a partnership, or didn't I tell you? Janice doesn't pay for herself, you know. Office furniture doesn't grow on trees.'

'Not the stuff you're getting,' Archie said quietly.

'Did you say something?' Frank shouted at him. 'Look at me, you're making me get red in the face.'

Archie sat his ground, a blob of trussed body. Frank had nothing against *ampleness* if it were carried with panache, like a heavy vase with well-turned handles. Frank had recently had an affair with an ample woman, following on from a lover who had ribs you could bash out a tune on. She lay passively on the mattress in a way that, in a thin woman, would have looked like boredom, whereas with her it seemed like voluptuous repose. Her bones played under a series of dense convex surfaces. Frank compared her attraction to the beauty of thick snow covering the fuss of a city street, where a caved-in dustbin becomes a pure bright mound and next-door's aborted rockery turns into a majestic dune. There were drawbacks: Frank had to think twice before he allowed her on top (in the harsh winter of 1963, he remembered, weight of snow had brought down the new flat roof of the local primary school); he was used to having what he wanted in the palm of one hand rather than welling over two.

Archie had developed from being merely physically disadvantaged into being a bonsai sumo-wrestler. He used to bounce about where the money was, outside theatres, applying his skills to the milling couples.

'Don't you think the lady deserves good tickets?' he would say, creating a mood. 'I think she does, or are you too shy to tell her you don't want to go out with her any more?' His selling methodology was based on humiliation. 'You're right, why don't you just buy her a bag of chips and put your money in the post office?'

He spread an aura of recklessness that encouraged well-off couples (the kind who looked like they owned lawnmowers you sat on) to pay over the odds, for a laugh. I am the picturesque working class, he seemed to be saying to the unpicturesque middle class. I am a pearly king (Lord luv you, sir), he suggested to Americans.

'*Cockney*,' Germans would say to each other as they listened to Archie's idea of a sentence, '*so wie der Kevin Keegan.*'

It was like a fringe meeting of the United Nations outside the shows, as South Americans jostled with Japanese in search of the complete English evening: a pizza meal, tickets for a German opera conducted by a Hungarian and then being refused half a pint of warm beer at two minutes past eleven by a barmaid from Sydney. Archie was part of that panorama. He was a street entertainer who would sell twelve pound's worth of entertainment to anyone who put £90 in his hat.

'Those were the days, literally,' Frank had said only the week before, showing his usual respect for the language. 'You could have sold peep-hole panties to the Salvation Army in those days.'

'Easy,' Archie had agreed.

'You could have sold things like, I don't know, mud, or leaves, anything.'

'Yeah. I could have done that. I probably could have managed to sell leaves.'

Perhaps the truth was that Archie operated best on his own. Some did. Frank did. His appetite for making money had lost its edge when he first had to share it with his wife, however much he loved her. It became utterly blunted when he had to provide for his small but already irritating son. Jason, who dirtied or dribbled on the articles bought with the little money Frank earned, who broke everything that was put before him and sabotaged the quiet hours of the evening with his toy vocal chords. I am working for *that*, the purpose is *this*? Frank became as listless then as Archie was now.

'I'm going out to look for Ted Nuttall,' he told Archie.

'What should I do, boss?'

'Stop calling me boss.' He turned away. 'Lose some weight.'

'Up yours.'

Frank stopped at Janice's desk on the way out. She was

picking the mascara out of her eyelashes. Her eyes and mouth were open wide.

'You have no idea how attractive you look like that,' he said.

'Oh yes I do,' she replied, smiling.

He came round behind her chair intimidatingly and then faced her again.

'I'd like to invite you out to lunch today.'

'Do we have time?' she asked. 'It sounds like we have a busy day lined up.' She was still picking away at her eyes.

'This will be a working lunch. You might like to bring your shorthand notebook.'

'I don't do shorthand, I'm afraid. I could never cope with the Ss.'

'I want –'

'Or the Ps and Bs,' Janice added.

'You do type though, don't you?'

She laughed. 'Of course. I'm a secretary, stupid.'

'I want you to keep an eye on my partner. He's acting strange.'

'I don't like the sound of that.'

Little pieces of mascara and an eyelash had fallen on to her desk. Frank looked up and scanned the room. On the floor against a wall sat an old manual typewriter he had picked up from a friend in exchange for a racing tip. The horse came in fifth, or, as his friend put it, last. A naked bulb shined a yellow light, and swayed gently whenever a door was opened. Frank noticed a cobweb in a high corner, picked up Janice's small English dictionary and threw it at the angle of walls and ceiling. He hit the right spot and the dictionary rebounded to the floor, wrapped in a dull skein.

Janice said 'Well, really.'

Two nails poked out of expanses of mottled wall. Beneath each nail were pallid rectangles where pictures had once hung. On the back of the door that went through to the room where Archie sat slumped like liver, two plastic stick-on hooks had sheared off, leaving nowhere for anyone to hang their coats. Frank walked over to the metal-framed window. He focused on the pitted frame and ploughed a finger through the condensation that beaded the edge of the window. The street below was crowded with traffic. There were no vehicles any more; there was only traffic. Frank watched a mother thread her way across the road through stationary cars, steering her child in front of her by his head. Behind him, Frank heard Janice totter across to gather her dictionary from the carpet.

'Sorry,' Frank breathed into the window. The office suddenly depressed him. He turned and said 'I'm going out for a walk. If anyone rings –' Janice looked at the telephone '– tell them I'm out with a client.'

'Out with a client,' she mouthed slowly as she wrote the words on a piece of paper.

They didn't think you were a serious person unless you were in a meeting. Availability in a businessman was as much use as a period on a wedding night. Frank knew he would have to start dancing to a new set of tunes. He would have to start shimmying and sidestepping like a businessman.

'No, fuck it,' he said. He would start to be a businessman after lunch. 'Tell them I've gone out for a walk.'

The Big Armchair

Frank survived the disappearance of his father and became the man of the house at the age of five. He was not the only boy at his school without a father, but most of his friends' dads had been killed in the war, which gave them moral ascendancy over Frank. On the way home from school he was once asked where he had lost his father, and he had had to say 'Mum says he was last spotted by neighbours on the corner of Greenwood Road.' After that he started to say Burma.

Some of the older children had lost mothers as well in the bombing and lived with relatives or neighbours. If Frank could have lived with anyone he would have chosen the Cloughs two doors down, because they had a bird-table. His own family struggled to make ends meet; Frank and his sister Petra would pull on one end while his mother and little brother Grant tugged on the other, but still the ends had trouble meeting. But they managed – with the help of the welfare state, a network of forgiving local shopkeepers and a 'friend' of Frank's mother whom she 'did' for once or twice a week for a number of years until he apparently told her that he had found another woman who 'did more' for him.

In spite of the hardships of the early years they generally spent a fortnight on the Kent coast in the summer. Much of the East End went hop-picking inland in the dewy Kent countryside, but Frank's mother objected to beer-making on ideological grounds. The Stubbses could not normally afford an ideology, but luckily Grace had kept in touch with a schoolfriend called Ethel who ran a guesthouse. They lodged free in one room in exchange for help around the house in the morning. Frank helped by disappearing after breakfast and coming back just in time for lunch.

He could remember the dining room where they all sat in paralysed silence. It was a 'theme' room ahead of its time, heavy with nautical motifs and encrusted seashells. Even in the busy season a table was set aside, like an altar, and on it were arranged a selection from Ethel's treasure trove of interesting items – a fishing net, a deckchair ticket, a card-mounted article from the local newspaper about the benefits of bathing, a pile of fascinating pebbles, a sou'wester with a cigarette burn on it. The big attraction was a model of HMS *Victory*, until Frank ruined it one afternoon by pushing pieces of leftover carrot and fish through the portholes. He was unable to explain why he did it. Ethel described the episode as 'saddening'.

The holiday involved frequent walks along the promenade, with Frank darting off all the time to kick pebbles in his crepe-soled sandals. He would rush on ahead, read the smutty postcards and not understand. The family used to sit and watch the Punch and Judy show, but as the years went by Frank's heckling became more and more unruly, until one summer the man burst out of his tent, still wearing the Policeman on his left hand (the children pointed their sticky hands and laughed), tore off one of Frank's sandals and threw it into the sea. But most of the time they just sat on the beach, where it cost nothing.

Frank did not make his mother's life easy on the beach.

'Mum?'

'Mm.'

Sometimes he would hold the conversation like this, leaving it hanging there, blocking out the sun. Grace Stubbs would be lying on a threadbare towel, wearing a heavy swimsuit that took three days to dry out. Petra would be sitting apart, trying even at that age to distance herself from her family and their habits. Grant would be lolling in the sand, or eating it.

'Why are men hairier than women?'

'I don't know, dear.'

'No, why?'

'God wants it that way.'

Frank might break off to ponder his mother's reply, to decide whether it was worthy to be inscribed in his list of truths.

'No, why?' he said.

'Nobody knows.'

'Is it because –'

'Don't make any silly guesses now, Frank.' His mother was often scared of what he would say. She knew that silly guesses were a special area for Frank. He knew they were too.

'Is it because . . .' And he would leave the start of his suggestion pinned up in the air again, giving everyone a headache. Just as the memory of the half-finished silly guess began to efface itself Frank might well decide to top up the tension by saying again: 'Is it because . . .'

Sometimes his mother tried to arrange a game to keep them occupied.

'I spy with my little eye something beginning with S,' she said.

'Vagina,' Frank had little hesitation in saying, because that was the kind of boy he was.

Seeing that he was the oldest man in the house, Frank realized that this gave him privileges. His mother never hit him, as though she sensed he would hit her back harder, like a good patriarch. She let him sit in the big armchair that his father used to occupy. Frank had the intelligence to understand what the armchair meant and, with the proprietorial instincts that children show more brazenly than adults, placed it out of bounds to his brother and sister.

Not that Frank neglected the duties that came with the rights. He observed that his mother – made strangely colourless and numb by the pressure of bringing up three children on her own – needed help. He assumed responsibilities he could cope with, like persuading door-to-door salesmen that not only could his family not afford to buy anything, they positively needed to be given things. The men had just started to feel pleased with themselves for getting their foot in the door when they realized that the ten-year-old boy had shut the door behind them and was rummaging through their bag of wares and samples for something that appealed to him.

The holidays were a mixed pleasure for Frank, who was happy enough playing around in derelict buildings with his friends in London. He wasn't sure he liked to be exposed to his family most of the day and all of the night. His mother's idea of play was for them to sit in the shelter on the promenade and count the people on the beach; his was to throw stones in their direction.

When Frank looked back now, they were happy days, all of them. Teaching Petra to swim by throwing her off the groyne, watching the sun go down behind the power station, listening to his mother snore herself awake in the middle of the night. This period was well-documented with photographs, taken inexpertly and often at a slight angle. They were developed by Ethel's husband in his darkroom under the eaves, grainy prints on dull cream paper with irregular borders.

Frank wondered what the name of Ethel's husband was. He was the kind of marginal figure who cropped up again and again in Frank's mother's photograph album. If a group photograph was taken of all the participants in Frank's life – and that would not be such a bad idea, he thought, if someone could see their way clear to arranging it – Ethel's husband would be right at the back and to one end, blurred, smiling muzzily, his eyes red from staying too long in the darkroom again. He would be standing between the boy in Frank's class at school who died of blood poisoning – what was *his* name? – and the woman who served in the corner shop in 1953 and 1954 and never said thank you. They were shadows in Frank's life, as he was in theirs. Somewhere, Frank hoped, they might be wondering what Frank's name was.

Rock-hard Tomatoes

The day was bright and the air sharp. Frank walked down the street in his loose-limbed style, his feet pointing slightly apart like a ballet dancer's. He was energized by the sunlight into feeling he could do anything he wanted. Wrongs need righting? He could do that.

The shops had always changed, but the pace of change had quickened recently. The eel-and-pie place was still there but the pie-and-mash restaurant had turned into a hamburger bar. Too many pies, market forces. There was hardly a shop on the street now that didn't have a great flat plastic sign to announce itself. Before, there had been paint on glass or wood; calm-looking men straddled across ladders would stand and paint colours between finely drawn guidelines. They probably used to be members of a guild of signwriters or at least a union of decorators and insignists, now disbanded. It was the kind of trade Frank would have tried to interest Jason in once upon a time, but now he suspected that you had to be a plastics expert to get anywhere in that field. You needed qualifications just to live and breathe in the late twentieth century.

Frank accepted the need for change and tried to be positive. 'Look at smallpox,' he recently explained to Archie. 'You can't get that now even if you *want* it.'

'Naa, I rather liked smallpox,' Archie said, who was opposed to change. 'And what did we get instead? Aids, Alzheimer's. And that's just the As. You've shown one disease the door and another six have already come in the bathroom window.'

'You're as bad as those old stagers I used to have to listen to as a kid, rattling on about how you used to be able to go out for the evening and end up with more money than you started with.'

'Well, they're not wrong there,' Archie insisted.

Even so, Frank wished they had kept some of those signs and some of the old shops. Did they really need another hamburger joint? Nobody liked hamburgers anyway. They *tolerated* them. And the old folk were right about something else. No amount of money could buy a proper fishcake these days.

Frank saw his reflection in the shop windows, a tall figure with a small head. The smallness of his head in relation to his body had cost him a lot of worry over the years. There wasn't much he could do about it, except wear a hat and hope that the material of the hat would be misconstrued as head. But, in any case, he still had a full head of hair, thick and dark brown, hair to be shown. Barbers often mentioned it as they circled. His ears hugged his head tightly behind his temples and his chin protruded a little. The length of his neck suggested that he was keeping some back.

Nevertheless, Frank could walk down the street as he was now and be sure that at least one or two people were impressed enough to alter the angle of their eyes in order to follow his movements. That was all the encouragement anybody needed.

He turned into the road that contained the weekday market. Vegetables were at this end, household items in the

middle and everything else at the other end, including Len
Worthington's famous knicker stall.

'*Annaaaarr!*'

The ancient newspaper seller on the corner was limbering
up. His first edition *Evening Standard*s had not arrived yet
but he was getting in some early practice. He had had a
solitary tooth in his mouth for ten years or more, a frangible
orange post. Out of a sense of tidiness and pity Frank wanted
to reach into his mouth and snap it off.

Coming alongside, Frank said 'Hallo, Tom. What's happening?' He got a nod and smile for a reply.

Frank had been listening to Tom's selling cry since the
mid-1960s. He started off back then with whole words
('*Ev'ning Standard, Ev'ning News!*') but by the early seventies
he was down to '*Staaannaa, Eeev Nooo!*' He maintained that
level of articulation until the *Evening News* disappeared in
the late seventies, when he had honed his delivery down to
its present rousing, life-asserting '*Annaaaarr!*' For a few
months in the mid-eighties, when there were suddenly three
titles to sell, he had a worried look and shouted out 'Paper,
paper,' rather hesitantly.

Frank moved on, going carefully now on ground strewn
with stems and bruised fruit. The noise and colour were
welcome after the staleness of the office and the new difficulty
over Archie. Frank had worked here for years and knew a lot
of the men and women on the stalls. He had watched as the
stallholders' children grew up and took over their pitches.
Sons and daughters inherited their parents' cries: three gener-
ations of greengrocers, the Douglas family from Bow, had
shouted '*Rock 'ard tomatoes!*' on the stall in front of the
bagel bakery. The tomatoes didn't even have to be rock-
hard, they just shouted it anyway. Sometimes they also

balled out: '*Laaaahhhhhvverly tomatoes!*' Frank said hallo to Arthur Douglas.

'Morning, Frank. We don't see much of you, recent times.'

'Nah. I've got a bit of business on. I don't suppose you've seen –'

'*Rock 'ard tomatoes!* Sorry, what?'

'Never mind.'

He moved on. Further down on the left was Les Bone, well known for being the rudest man in the market, and it was a market of rude men.

'Well, if it isn't Frank Stubbs coming down the garden path,' he called out. He broke off to say 'Don't squeeze those avocados or I'll fucking squeeze you,' to a nun.

Frank walked on. There was no sign of Ted Nuttall, not that he worked there regularly any more. Now he had a few of his own operators who did all the work for him. Others got up in the dark and hauled produce into vans and brought it to market. Ted strolled around and supervised and did the odd bit of arranging. Frank wanted to be like that. He had always known who to learn from – ticket touting from Archie, business logistics from Ted, pet care and courtesy from his brother Grant.

Ahead of him Frank saw Sue, one of his new clients, chatting to another woman in the middle of the crowded thoroughfare. They were holding people up. Sue's friend, whoever she was, had been heavy with her makeup, as if she had a purple birthmark to hide or a large quantity of makeup to get rid of quickly. Sue was looking rather tired and unmade but anyone who knew her lifestyle as Frank did would be surprised she did not look tireder.

'Sue,' he said into the knot of people who were trying to get round her and her friend.

She was almost as tall as Frank and her long face was framed by dyed black hair. Apart from her sentences, everything about Sue was long – her teeth, her hair, her legs.

'Frank.' She abandoned her friend immediately as though she had been trying to get away since last Tuesday. The crowd parted. 'All these bloody people. There isn't room to wipe your arse.' Sue hadn't been to finishing school.

Her skirt almost reached her ankles but it didn't fool Frank, who had seen her thighs, knees and calves. She needed them in her branch of work.

'How was last night?' he asked.

'How is it always? I shook it around a bit and then I stopped.'

'Have you thought about what I said to you?'

'What, about my tits looking like –'

'No, no. My business proposition.'

Sue used to work with doves but they flew away. Frank had seen her working in a pub one Sunday lunchtime. Some-one at the bar said it was as erotic as a packet of biscuits, but that wasn't how it looked from where Frank was standing, trying to master his trousers. Anyway, this was strictly busi-ness. The way he saw it Sue could do better than a pub with a flooded toilet where the height of sophistication was not spitting in your Babycham. She probably wasn't ready for the Albert Hall yet but she could play tinselly cabaret venues and the better Rotary clubs where they didn't expect her to turn herself inside out. She looked good in clothes, good out of them and she took them off convincingly, as though she really wanted to be rid of them.

'Who handles you at the moment?' he had asked.

'Everybody,' she replied. 'It's that kind of business. I've

had more hands in my underwear than Marks and Spencer.'

'You need an agent.'

'I don't need anyone interfering,' she had said as she changed in the back room of the pub. Her only concession to modesty had been to turn her back on him, but in a naked, bending woman that was hard to class as modesty.

'You do. Who answers your phone when you're out? Who negotiates your fees?'

'If you want to do it properly, do it yourself.'

'Looks like it's working for you,' he said, looking around him, at the burst sofa and peeling walls. 'Carry on doing it yourself, Layla.'

She laughed. 'That's a stage device, honey, grow up. You know, like Chloe and Mitzi and all those other slaggy names. Call me Sue.'

'I can get you bookings in dance-halls.'

'Dance-halls. Where have you been for the last thousand years?'

'Call it what you want. I have friends who have openings.' It was going to be difficult to be Mr Twenty Per Cent if he always met with this amount of resistance.

'I'll think about it.'

'You're doing the right thing.'

'I said I'd think about it.'

'I know where to find you.'

That was last week and now here she was. Frank had been thinking about her and had decided that she fitted well into his portfolio of all-stars, alongside the O'Brien Brothers and the footballer Nobby Spicer, the recently retired master of the short, tight ball who Frank had signed up to open supermarkets.

'So let's have a business talk, shall we?'

'If that's what you want. My flat's only just round the corner, we can talk there.'

Frank liked the sound of that.

■ School

Abbott, Kenny	Hacking, John
Baker, Len	Harknett, Brian
Ball, Peter	Harknett, Keith
Bence, Gary	Harknett, Denzil
Blagden, Arthur	Kite, Arnold
Chubb, Neville	Loomes, Jack
Coppins, Terry	Malone, Andy
Croucher, William	Murty, Winston
Eades, Ronnie	Neighbour, Mike
English, Gavin	O'Connor, Nogger
Flaxman, Sid	Ptaszynski, Tommy
Fox, George	Singh, Nadir
Funnell, Frank	Stubbs, Frank
Glover, Stanley	Teeling, Alf
Gumbel, Alan	Warren, Clive
Guthrie, Dick	Wibberley, Roy

Frank had never planned to stay long at his secondary school. A couple of days, enough time to steal a few pencils. The first work they did at big school was to write out the names of everyone in the class, and for some reason Frank had kept the piece of paper. It was the only memento he had from his schooldays, apart from a fret-work penguin he made in woodwork class, which his mother still had in her bathroom, next to his brother's.

He had written the list in blue ink that had turned brown over the years. The handwriting was terrible even for an eleven-year-old, and this was the fourth version. It was always a surprise to see his own name there, staring back at him under the Singh boy, who was soon to be taken away from school because he had been victimized for being Asian. Stanley Glover was also bullied, for having thin wrists. Being different was worse than being unintelligent or poor. They all wore shorts in the first year except Roy Wibberley. Gavin English's blazer was a different shade of blue to everyone else's. Alan Gumbel was the only boy who failed the eye-test in the first term and came to school the following week in heavy glasses. Frank could still picture Alan Gumbel walking into class with his new glasses and that was all he could remember about him.

His friends were the Harknett triplets and Andy Malone. That was enough friends. The others were lacking in some way: Gary Bence still went to Sunday school, Winston Murty was a diabetic and had to bring in special food in jam jars, Tommy Ptaszynski sat too close to the teacher. Clive Warren was too small and thin, and Alf Teeling was too fat. Nogger O'Connor had a stupid name. George Fox's mother was rumoured to be on the game (a rumour was often all it took). Neville Chubb and Terry Coppins always sat together and were regarded as suspicious for that reason.

Dick Guthrie was clever and eventually went on to Warwick University to study metal. He should have gone to grammar school but his mother wanted him to be able to come home for lunch and the grammar school was too far away. Frank saw him once or twice out of school because he used to clean windows down his street at weekends. Not only is he fantastically clever, Frank thought at the time, he's also a perfectly adequate window-cleaner. It seemed an incredible combination. He always had the generosity to admire people with skills he didn't have. Frank got on well with Dick in spite of the academic gulf between them, firing off questions in playtime like a quizmaster:

'Dick, how many Chinese are there?'

'I should think there's . . . eleven, twelve million.'

'How come you know so much, Dick?'

'My dad gets these science magazines and I read them.'

'How do refrigerators work?'

Frank just wanted to do his time and then leave. He really had no interest in how many Chinese there were, not for more than three or four seconds, enough time to ask a question but not to listen to the answer. He wanted to be out on the street.

They would stand around in the yard at lunchtime, flicking cigarette cards against the wall, telling outrageous lies. They were physical, pulling each other off the wall (especially Clive Warren, whose skinny body could be bent into a thousand positions) and scuffling haphazardly.

A lot of boys had an undeniable urge to damage each other. Frank had the urge, Mike Neighbour had the urge, Keith Harknett had the urge. Jack Loomes may have had it, Frank couldn't remember, and Kenny Abbott had it for a while and then appeared to lose it. Frank didn't want to hurt anyone permanently but he liked to assert himself. It wasn't difficult to find something to fight about. Football, the precise workings and structure of the female body. Whether Stanley Glover's gag should be loosened slightly. When Frank found he was not managing to get his point across he did sometimes lift other boys up and drop them, but only because shows of strength were the only playground currency there was.

In class they played out the everlasting games – authority was mocked, notes were passed, ink was abused. Frank felt these activities were expected; he was no more interested in tying Stanley Glover to the school railings upside down, in fact, than he was in the population of China. But it was on some unofficial curriculum that had to be obeyed.

Frank was interested in the subject of discipline and persuasion. He watched his teachers carefully to see how they handled the class, whether they used their power well. He felt that somebody should have had a word with Mr Meacher, who often seemed close to tears.

'Simmer down, simmer down,' he said over and over again, his cheeks reddening and his grey hair boiling up into a wild froth.

What you do is this, Frank could have told him: first you don't wear that kind of jacket because it's got *can't cope* written all over it, front and back. You bring the wicked kids up to the front and menace them systematically. You don't just confiscate Keith Harknett's flick-knife – you hold the point under his chin; you tell Andy Malone he's got a girl's hands, Andy really hates that. Be a bully (but not to Stanley Glover – he's already close to breaking point). And get rid of the beard.

Inevitably, Frank was stronger in some areas than others. He was good at maths as long as they dealt in figures. In English he could write a forceful and imaginative story but had difficulty judging the work of others; he was marked down for preferring Denzil Harknett's essay on how to steal from a bread van to Rudyard Kipling's *Kim*. Geography made him dizzy; he was perturbed and disoriented by the vastness of the world after his capsular upbringing in a tight network of streets. He had only recently come to terms with

Kent. When they later touched on astronomy he became genuinely nauseous.

He was interested in history when they studied battles but was confused by any attempt to view the past sociologically.

'How did the common man earn his living in the thirteenth century, Frank?' he was asked by his modern teacher, in a moment of rare quiet.

Shit, a question. 'Doing this and that,' he said, playing for time.

'What would your father have done in those days, for example?' A titter went round the class. Frank made a mental note of the titterers.

'Ten years?' There was general laughter. Frank forgave his titterers.

His teacher had the breadth of vision to ignore intrusions of that sort. 'He would have been a serf, almost certainly, working for an all-powerful master. Some people say we still have that system today.' Tommy Ptaszynski told his father about this comment and others like it, and Mr Tozer was subsequently asked by the headmaster to 'tone it down'.

Frank resisted the challenge to become politicized. He stood on the everyone-for-themselves ticket, the oh-dear-here-comes-a-policeman school of economic thought. His wife Diane, the daughter of a Labour councillor who had once gone down to Brick Lane and thrown a chair at Sir Oswald Mosley, later called it selfishness. Frank called it independence. Diane asked him if he knew anything about Clause 4 and he said 'Is that another sequel to *Claws*?'

There was only one episode from Frank's schooldays that he didn't like to think about.

He fell in love with Keith Harknett.

Keith was a pretty boy with blond hair and a tanned,

cheeky face. He and his brothers Brian and Denzil were technically identical, but it was an approximate identicalness. Keith was good at sport, whereas his brothers, like Frank, thought a cricket box was where you kept your cricket racquets. On the football field Keith made others look foolish, ungainly, and he maintained this superiority in the shower. Frank found himself wanting to be with Keith all the time and hated it when he had to settle for anyone else's company. He wasn't sure what he was going to do with Keith when he got him alone. He had no real desire to take Keith's clothes off. The attraction went beyond his understanding.

It was a relief when Frank realized that his hero had feet of clay, was, in fact, mainly clay. All Keith did was to return some of Frank's affection, say one ignorant thing too many, and Frank began to be able to cope again. Keith never knew, and nobody must tell him.

That first class stayed together for a year and then there was a reshuffle. Neville Chubb and Terry Coppins were victims of this minor diaspora, but they were often seen together in the schoolyard and were still regarded as suspicious. Alf Teeling lost a lot of weight in the second year but put it all back on again two years later after somebody told him he looked better when he was fat. Len Baker (or was it Alan Gumbel?) was caned in front of the class for exposing himself to the headmaster's daughter in a moment of forgetfulness. Frank Stubbs threw away his shorts.

Frank did not judge his schooldays. He had never wondered if they were a good or a bad time, an education or an emptiness. They certainly didn't translate into paper qualifications, unless you counted his cycling proficiency certificate. All he could be sure of was that the 1950s had ended.

He met Keith Harknett again by chance, out shopping,

when they were both in their early twenties. Keith was wearing black-rimmed glasses and the sleek golden face he remembered had rounded out into a pale circle.

'It's Frank, isn't it?' he asked.

All Frank could find to say was 'Keith, you've got yourself some glasses.'

'It was either that or not see where I was going!'

Lord, Frank thought.

■ Sex

Sue and Frank threaded themselves through the boxes and strewn vegetables in the market, down two streets and up the front steps to her flat. Sue had a long stride. They didn't say a word to each other on the way, as if they had agreed some time in the past that conversation was a waste of time. The corridor smelt of old mail, with an insinuation of unwashed and uncollected milk bottles.

Frank watched the folds of her skirt sway this way and that as she walked ahead of him up the stairs. Sue's flat was heavily scented with air freshener. On the coffee table he could see the globe of slatted plastic containing the fragrant green disc. It disappointed Frank, who liked the smell of people. In the living room there was a white, wade-through carpet and some furniture that looked new.

'Nice place,' he said.

'It comes out of a catalogue.'

They went through into the kitchen. Sue took her coat off and switched on the electric kettle with one movement. She leaned back against the fridge, leaving Frank standing in the middle of the room in his coat.

'Take your coat off.' She said it with a simple authority, but the way she was leaning back against the fridge with her arms crossed gave the words a certain disdain.

'Don't mind if I do,' Frank said brightly, trying to loosen the stiff atmosphere. It was turning out to be awkward. As the water started to heat up he added 'You've got one of those new kettles.'

She said nothing. What a bitch to say nothing. Frank leaned back against the cooker.

They took their coffee through to the living room. She raised the temperature above zero by saying 'Let's get business over first.' She was sitting on the sofa with her knees slightly apart so that some of the material of her skirt fell between her thighs. Frank sat in an armchair so soft and low and deep that he anticipated problems getting up.

He settled back to outline his ideas. It didn't take very long because he didn't have many ideas. Sue nodded twice. He explained about his office facilities and successfully used the word *infrastructure*. Janice was glamorized as 'the invaluable Miss Wiggins', Jason as 'my son. What a tearaway!' He almost called Archie his personal assistant but felt that that would be going too far.

Looking levelly at Frank, she drew her legs up on to the sofa and said 'Sounds good. Secretary. Offices.'

'I'll be getting a photocopier. Maybe two.' If that doesn't clinch it, Frank thought, then she doesn't *deserve* representation.

'Sure. Let's do it. Perhaps I do need a little help. You know what it's like for a woman alone.'

Frank relaxed and smiled. 'I'd have to imagine.'

'It's like being a man alone, only you get followed home.'

'You're not attached then.'

'My husband went away.'

'He must have been crazy.' Frank felt so charming it made him ill.

'No. He just went away.' She had kicked off her shoes and was showing him ankle. Frank was laying odds that he and Sue were about to go to bed together. If he could get out of the armchair his chances looked better than even.

'Must have been mad.'

'All right, you said that.' Three to one against and drifting.

'I've lived on my own for a couple of years,' he said.

'Like it?' She produced a cigarette from nowhere and lit it.

'Sometimes I find it rather –'

'Lonely?' She sucked in enough smoke to fill a barrel.

'Fun,' he lied.

'Sure, it can be fun. What do you do for sex?' Now she exhaled her funnel of brown air. Betting had closed.

Frank smiled but she didn't smile back. She didn't seem the sort of person who ever needed to.

He said 'I rub up against trees. What do you do?'

Frank first had sex at the age of seventeen. They met at a dance in a scout hut with a wooden floor that bounced up and down during the dancing. He was wearing his smart jacket and was not in a mood to dawdle, broadcasting looks that said: *if not now, when?* and *sex machine*. Denise had come with a boyfriend but he danced like a man with a poor personality. Frank went up to her when the boyfriend was in the toilet.

'Hallo there,' he shouted above Frank Ifield.

'I've got a boyfriend,' she shouted back, jumping straight to the point at issue.

'Is *that* what it was?'

He had had a few shandies, so he pulled her towards him and kissed her on the lips.

'Come outside for some fresh air,' he said into her ear.

'What about my boyfriend?'

'Let's try it with just the two of us first.'

Nobody was more surprised than Frank when she took his hand and moved towards the door.

'Where are we going?' he said, following her. Ask, he thought, and it shall be given.

When they were outside, wedged between two closely parked Ford Prefects, she said 'I don't know, I'm just in the mood.' She kissed him on the mouth for twenty seconds. One of her hands was massaging his shoulder and the other had pulled his shirt out of the back of his trousers.

'What for?' he asked.

'The bedroom's through there.' Sue hadn't moved. Frank knew what to do, but not how to do it. 'It's up to you,' she said, picking fluff off her skirt. What had she done with her cigarette? That was all they needed, a blaze at a time like this.

Her coolness made him queasy. Suddenly, for the first time in his life, he wondered whether it was worth taking his clothes off only to have to put them back on later. He didn't care that she was out of the top drawer and generally built for sex, she was doing this all wrong.

Frank and Denise did not make love that night. It was the early 1960s and there had to be negotiations, a visit to the chemist. Denise wanted to keep her boyfriend because he had a car and his mother could get them into the Odeon free. Besides, it was better if she and Frank could make love in a warm and soothing environment rather than lying down between two Ford Prefects. But Frank liked what he had done so far: felt a woman. Years later he could still recall the exact feel of wet woman under a wisp of cloth, the spring of hair between their two skins that first time. He only wished he had cut his fingernails. She had actually been willing. A woman could be willing to let a man do these things to her, without persuasion, without clearance from the authorities, even without necessarily saying *What do you think YOU'RE doing?* This was the great, big, exciting, new, startling truth.

Frank lost his virginity in Denise's bedroom a week later while her parents were out and her boyfriend was attending his Double-entry Bookkeeping evening class.

'Have you got the doodah?' she asked after a moment of deep breathing in the hall.

'I've got a packet.'

'Christ, a packet.'

'We don't have to use them all.' He was shaking.

She leapt up at his mouth. 'Everyone's out. I've fed the cat and dog.' They kissed again. 'To keep them quiet.' They grappled in the semi-darkness. 'Christ, a whole packet.'

They ran up the stairs. Denise had Frank by the hand and pulled him into her childish bedroom with its signed photo of Adam Faith, releasing him to undo a necklace of plastic beads. She threw herself down on the bed and her flouncy skirt rose up. Of the six buttons on his white nylon shirt Frank pulled off four in his urgent need to be naked.

Sue – or was it Layla? – ripped the edge off the little silver packet with her teeth. They were both sitting on the edge of her bed, Frank rather gracelessly. Neither was saying anything. She leaned across and smoothed the condom over him with firm movements of her hand. It felt as though she had done this many times before.

'Feel OK?' she asked him, as she swung round to lie back on the bed. Her breasts parted.

'Sure.'

'How would you like me?'

Frank wondered if she might like to moan a little? If she started, he would join in.

'You're fine as you are.' Frank convinced himself not to be too sensitive about this. Even when sex was bad it was better than reading the paper.

'That's good,' she said as Frank edged into her.

'Umm.'

They carried on in silence until the telephone rang.

'Umm,' Frank said.

'Umm.' Denise.

'Umm.'

'Umm.'

'Umm.'

Frank was amazed when she answered the telephone with him still plugged inside her. She put her finger up to her lips to warn him to keep quiet. Gently she unlocked her ankles from his kidneys and lowered them.

'Speaking,' she said. She was breathing completely normally.

Frank rested on his forearms, gasping a little. There was a tinny voice coming out of the phone. He couldn't decide whether to slip out of her, tuck himself back inside his trousers and make his excuses.

'No! Really!' Sue was saying.

What was correct procedure on answering the telephone during sex? Maybe he was old-fashioned, but Frank had always let it ring. (He now had the impression that Sue would be prepared to *make* a telephone call during sex.) On the only occasion he had practised telephone-induced coitus interruptus, padding to the hall with his laden penis drying out in the central heating, the phone had stopped as he reached it. By the time he returned his wife had already put her knickers on and gone back to stripping the bedroom wallpaper.

'Look, I'd better go,' Sue now said into the phone. She avoided looking at Frank.

'Oh, for God's sake,' Frank said under his breath. Sue looked at him with a sudden fierce disapproval. He shifted position. What time was it? Eleven, half past? What was he doing here?

Sue replaced the receiver by stretching out her right hand. She circled Frank again with her legs.

'Sorry to keep you,' she said.

The young Frank's trousers had finished up on Denise's dressing-table, where they had knocked over and smashed a bottle of perfume. Denise's heavy bra had ended up dangling from the window catch, where it titillated an eagle-eyed passenger on the 18.48 from Liverpool Street to Gidea Park. Other items of clothing were scattered all around. Frank was still panting, and he had been finished for five minutes. Denise's eyes were bulging.

'That was ... the best ever,' she said, fanning her face with her hand.

'It was, it was.'

Frank was not going to tell her it had been his first time. He hoped Denise had interpreted his lack of experience as an understandable wildness, his clumsiness as frenzy.

'I get so excited,' she said in a small, surprised voice.

Frank came away from her. The twin-backed creature split down the middle, revealing two soft and sweating bellies. He laid a hand on her breast.

'When are your parents getting back?'

Sue had lit up a cigarette and was smoking it with small, urgent puffs. The two of them were sitting bolt upright in her bed.

'Who was that on the phone?' he asked. He couldn't bear the silence and coldness any more.

'Just a friend.'

'Did you have to answer it?'

'It rang, didn't it?'

There was a pause. Frank wasn't sure what to say but there seemed to be an important statement waiting in the top of his head.

'Sex used to be something special. God, but I was a horny kid,' he said eventually.

'Do you want to talk about it?'

'I'm talking about it. What's that supposed to mean? I am talking about it.'

'I'm afraid I'm going to have to ask you for a, you know, retainer.' She stubbed the cigarette out in a cut glass ashtray with a gold rim. Frank had seen them on sale down at the market: £1.75.

'What?'

'A fee, you know.'

Frank thought about this.

'A kind of fee,' she said.

'Yeah, yeah. I heard you. A fee, a fee, a retainer. What for?'

'Services, business.'

Frank was tempted to get out of bed and leave right then.

'What for? For screwing? Are you trying to tell me something?'

'I've got outgoings,' she said, lighting up another cigarette. 'Call it an advance on the business we're going to do together.'

'You must be fucking joking, honey. Frank Stubbs doesn't pay to have his bell rung.' He was getting warmed up. On the other side of the bed Sue was still staring straight ahead. 'There's two things I don't buy. One of them's sex.'

'What's the other?'

'Muesli.'

They just sat there. Frank wanted her to cover her chest up.

'Fucking Swiss crap for breakfast.'

Sue swung her legs out of the sheets and got up. Frank refused to watch her go.

'Fifty quid, or there's no deal,' she said.

'Oh, unbe-bleeding-lievable. I think I'm taking on a high-class act and it turns out she's a working girl.'

She turned on him. 'What are you, religious?'

'I wish I was. I wish I bloody was,' he shouted straight back.

'Well, it's up to you,' she said as she went towards the bathroom.

That was just what Frank didn't want this early in the day. An ethical dilemma.

'No wonder they don't tell kids about this,' Denise said, coming round, her chest still heaving.

'Want to do it again?' Frank asked.

'Nah, I'm feeling a bit sore. How many do you get in a packet?'

'We've run out. I'd have to use an old one.' Frank lay back on his side of the narrow bed. There was a question that was bothering him. 'Why don't you let your boyfriend do it to you?' he asked.

'He's never asked.'

'Is he right in the head?' Frank had asked almost all the girls he knew. One had said yes but she changed her mind when she heard his zip going down.

'He's just a bit shy.'

He never managed to persuade Denise to give up her boyfriend. For three months afterwards she continued to enjoy sex, with Frank, in a way that he had seldom seen since, but she needed her boyfriend too, with his car and standing offer of marriage. Where was *she* now, with her little gasps? Maybe he should take a trip down to her house next week and ask her what she'd done with her life. She couldn't have changed that much in twenty-five years.

After Denise's fear of discovery got the better of her ('Frank, Frank, was that the door? I think that's the front door. Oh *no*, Frank, stop, stop. All right, but quick'), he had had to wait six months before he could enlarge on his experience. The sexually permissive age had not yet arrived – except for Frank, who permitted everything. He would have given totally strange women a completely free hand. He believed he was probably the most permissive man in the country.

His next girlfriend, Sandy, was two years older than Frank. He met her in a queue at Jack's Fish. He could still remember her order: 'Just a piece of fish, please, with a light sprinkling of vinegar.' You could be thrown out of places in Bethnal Green for using that kind of language.

Sandy had a middle-class background that was alien to

Frank. Perversely, it made him feel more sure of himself. She was a student, living on her own. Frank never asked her what she was studying and she didn't tell him. He did not introduce her to his friends or family because he couldn't trust her not to do or say something that would illustrate how different they were. Sometimes they would go to a pub together and sit quietly in the corner. He had banned her from going to the bar since she frightened the publican by asking for a drink with a French name. Nor did he have any illusions about mixing in her world – they were happy just the way they were, hanging around on her bed most evenings, talking occasionally, with long pauses.

'How did you get that little scar on your thigh, Frank?'

'Scar shop, Kingsland High Street.' His sense of humour baffled her.

Frank was only eighteen and liked to put the heater full on, kick the blankets to the end of the bed, and look at her freckly body. She was unsure at first but soon became accustomed to his anatomist's attention.

'Why are you looking at me like that?' she asked as his eyes hovered around the tops of her thighs.

Sandy was Frank's sexual education. Unlike most of his friends, Frank didn't have to make love in cars or in derelict buildings, although he believed he might have enjoyed that as well. From Denise he had learned the power and freneticism of lust, while Sandy had taught him the pleasure of lying around in bed, Sunday morning every night of the week.

'I want to see how it all works,' he said, staring.

'It's embarrassing.'

'What's this bit for?'

He enjoyed these moments away from the strains of the

family home. His sister Petra had taken to isolating herself – 'Leave me alone,' she said from inside her bedroom. 'Leave my food outside the door.' Grant, his younger brother, was heavy going and the next-door neighbour's son had been given a saxophone for Christmas, and was playing it. The only concern Sandy and Frank had in that little room was to have enough coins for the two-bar electric heater. Late one evening they ran out of change and Frank's hand, which had been above the covers, had to be defrosted in the morning between Sandy's warm thighs.

'Frank, stop staring at it. Look it up in a book.'

'Where could I get a book like that?'

They went on like this for hours and days, and then the days turned into months and the autumn turned into Christmas, when Frank met his wife Diane.

Music – Celebrities – Acrobats

Frank walked back to the market on his own. He was thinking about Sue and about the £50 he had given her for sleeping with him. The last time he spent that much money and felt this disgruntled he had just paid Jason's fine for urinating in a Royal Park. To show that he didn't need her kind of glamour he had not invited her to his party later that day. He would prefer it if she weren't there at the door handing out a price list.

Within a couple of minutes he had found Ted Nuttall, standing in the sun with a cheese roll in his hand.

'Ted, I've been looking for you.'

'And now you've found me, am I right?'

'I'm having a do.'

'He's having a do, he says. That's nice. Am I invited?'

'I could hardly have a party without you, now could I?'

'You could, strictly speaking.'

He bit into his roll, leaving a great crescent. Ted was in his late fifties. He wore a flat cap and visible braces. It was for the Revenue's benefit, he said. 'Let Johnny Taxman see you wearing a suit with buttons and all and you'd be better off dead.' Ted wiped his mouth.

'I've taken some of your advice,' Frank said.

'Was it good advice?'

'I hope so.'

'Some of it's shit, you know,' Ted said. 'Do you always know what you're talking about?'

'No,' Frank said, immediately.

'I fucking don't, I can tell you.' He laughed.

Frank laughed, catching up with Ted.

'I've got myself some premises,' Frank said.

'No kidding.'

'I'm running an entertainment agency.'

'No kidding.'

'Showbusiness,' Frank said, nodding.

'Showbusiness sort of thing?' Ted said, also nodding by now.

'That's it.'

Ted cackled again, took another bite out of his roll and threw the rest on the ground.

'I'll still be selling the odd ticket, Wimbledon, Glyndebourne,' Frank said, trying to steal back some of the initiative lost through Ted's cackle. 'Well, Archie will.'

'Funny you should say that, as it happens.'

'Why?'

'As it happens.'

'Why's that?'

Ted took Frank's arm and walked him three feet to one side. He looked all around and then at Frank, whose face was now six inches away.

Frank said 'Is this confidential or do you just want to sniff my aftershave?'

'Dave Giddings let slip they've just opened a new booking period for *Bitch of Broadway*.'

Frank was annoyed. He had a network of contacts in the box-office business and nobody had tipped him off. He would have to slap Dusty the Walrus and Big Glenda's heads for them.

'Thanks for the nod,' he said. 'I'd better get some in.'

'I think this deserves ten best pairs, don't you, for the tip-off?'

'Do me a favour, Ted. That's a monkey, house price.'

'Frank, Frank, be a gentleman for once in your life.'

'What is this, charity week? I'll give you a couple of stalls and that'll do you.'

Ted seemed to accept this, for the time being. They had moved apart and were talking normally again.

Frank said 'I'd better be getting on, actually.'

'Yeah, bollocks.'

'Here's my card with the office address on it.' Frank had had two thousand printed – a thousand with his name and five hundred each marked Jason Stubbs and Archie Nash. 'Oh, the telephone number's wrong, by the way.' Frank took a pen and wrote in the correct number. 'Dickhead printers.'

'What say I turn up late-ish and we play a bit of poker?' Ted said, pocketing the card.

Frank didn't like card games, although he sometimes got lucky like everybody else.

'We'll see.'

'Right. Be lucky.'

Frank spent the short walk back to his office wondering how much money to sink into *Bitch of Broadway*. Frank hadn't seen the show but Archie's view was that it 'crapped on *Phantom of the Opera*'.

He climbed up the narrow staircase to his office. A typed notice had appeared on the internal door above the letter-box, saying

Welcome to FRANK STUBS Entertainments
Music – Celebrities – Acrobats

Frank came in saying 'What's all this about acrobats?'

Janice had hauled the typewriter on to her desk and was sitting there with a piece of paper in it and a strand of hair in her mouth. Jason was sitting on the other chair, which he had positioned against the wall. He had his feet high up against the wall and was singing along to the music coming through his earphones. 'Waahah waahah.'

Janice looked up and said 'No acrobats?'

'Not yet,' Frank said as he walked over to Jason and turned up his Walkman.

Jason was instantly in pain. 'That's dangerous,' he shouted, ripping off his headphones. 'You could have burst my ears.'

'He's right,' Janice said, tutting.

'And Stubbs is spelt with two Bs, Janice,' Frank said, ignoring her but walking in her direction. 'NO acrobats. TWO Bs. Now, let's do some business. Jason come over here. Stop whining.'

'What? I can't hear you,' Jason said.

'Just shut up and come over here.'

'You'll have to speak up, someone's just broken my hearing,' Jason persisted from his corner of the room.

Frank stormed back over to his son. When he reached Jason he changed his mind, put a gentle arm round him and steered him across the room. Before starting, Frank checked that Archie wasn't in the room.

'I want to give you a lesson in touting, Jason, so be a good boy, don't spoil it for yourself and for me by being a complete wanker.'

'It's a big one, is it? Hey, let's deal,' Jason said.

'Sit down on the chair. Janice, you can listen in.'

Janice chose that moment to open her handbag, take out a stick of lipstick and smear it on her lips.

'Right, Jason. I'm about to send you out to buy a batch of tickets for the hottest show in the West End. If you cock it up, your ears will be the least of your worries, know what I mean? Janice, if I want your face painted I'll call in a decorator, OK love?'

'Rude,' she said, clicking the tube shut tartly.

Frank sat on Janice's unlovely desk and talked.

'What are we doing? We're buying and selling tickets. Why can we feel proud of this? Because we're laying our balls on the line, pardon my plain speaking, Janice, and putting in our own money – straight, I might say, into the pockets of some shyster theatrical producer with a tiny dick and a big car. There's a lot of people – *busy* people, visiting diplomats, German tennis players, Liz Taylor, bless her – who don't like to wait for three years to see a show, unlike the average dozy punter down Surrey way, so they come to me.'

'Anybody ready for lunch?' Jason interrupted.

'God's bum, Jason, any chance of you not being a prat for a fraction of a second?'

'Sure,' he said.

'So this is the age of the self-made man. Sometimes you've got to put all your chips on one square or you'll be a toe-rag all your life. And you've got to hustle, because there's a lot of people that want what you want. You've got to be smart or you only get the empty bowl to lick out. For once in your life Jason I'm going to pay you the favour of letting you use your loaf.'

'No problem.'

'I'm going to give you two and a half grand to buy one hundred top-price tickets for *Bitch of Broadway* at the Prince Albert Theatre, different nights, preferably weekends. I don't care how you do it but you keep the money buttoned in your shirt until you're inside that theatre foyer, OK? Now, you might find they don't want to sell so many tickets to one punter. What do you do?'

Jason considered. 'Tell them to blow it out their arse?'

'No,' Frank said patiently. 'You buy twenty at a time. You go away and come back. And go away and come back. And go away and come back. You maybe wait for a different ticket clerk to come on. Get the picture?'

'Piece of piss.'

'You tell them a story. You work for a hospital social club.'

'Knockout.'

'Or for a children's home. If they rumble you then you find a kid, tip him a pony for his trouble and get him to buy them for you.'

'Find a kid, okey-dokey.'

'Righto. Repeat, what's the name of the theatre?'

'Prince Albert. What's in it for me, when I've made all this money for you?'

Frank stopped and stared at his son. He exploded briefly. 'I leave your *balls* on, that what's in it for *you*. I give you enough already. Don't push me, I've got a busy day, OK?'

Frank went to the safe in the corner. Five of them had had to move it from his house the day before. They agreed that it was the worst job in the world. Bending down, he removed the money he needed.

'I don't know why,' he said as he gave the bundled notes

to Jason, 'but I think you're going to do all right on this little job.'

'Course he will,' Janice said, straightening the piece of paper in the typewriter.

'Hey, who changed your straw?' Frank said.

'I'm sure you under-estimate that boy.'

'I've tried it, Janice. Can't be done.' But he was touched by her motherliness. Perhaps he ought to tell her that she was an attractive woman. Or had he already done that?

'Yeah!' Jason said.

'And don't hang around in Soho. I want you back here passing drinks around.'

Jason shuffled out of the door in his training shoes. Maybe I'm too harsh and cold with him, Frank wondered. If you tell someone they're unintelligent enough times they end up believing you.

'Do I give him a hard time, do you reckon?' he asked Janice after Jason had gone.

She looked up from the blank sheet of paper and folded her arms. 'You can't help the way you are,' she said.

'He could have done with a spell in the army. I tried to put his name down for the Falklands.'

'Lovely,' she said, aimlessly.

'What he really needs, though, is hard work.'

Janice put her head on one side and pulled a strand of hair into her mouth.

'Mining?' she suggested.

Prosperous Friendly

Before Denise, before Sandy and Diane, but some years after Keith Harknett, Frank had tried his hand at working behind a desk.

As a prelude to leaving school he had a talk with the careers adviser. Mr Astley-Rushton was totally bald on top but had long, luxuriant hair over his ears.

'What would you like to do with your life, ideally?' he asked. They were surrounded by pamphlets. Frank could see one entitled *A career in the merchant navy: It's plain sailing!*

'I'm already working on a stall in the market.'

'Ever thought of bettering yourself?'

Frank had heard this expression before. He didn't know what it meant. 'We sell household goods, pots and pans. You should come down one Saturday and have a nose around.'

Mr Astley-Rushton smiled politely and sadly. 'Unfortunately I live in Basildon. Have you thought about a trade? Plumbing, joinery?'

'I wondered about photography.'

'I don't think I have a leaflet about that.'

'Oh, shame.'

Mr Astley-Rushton leaned back in his chair and took off his glasses. Frank had nothing against him personally but he still wanted to stamp on his glasses.

Frank's school record was lying on the table. His adviser picked it up and glanced at page two with a glimmer of interest.

'Your mathematics teacher says you have a certain facility with figures on the isolated occasions in which your interest is engaged.'

'Come again?'

'You can add up.'

'It's not so difficult.'

Astley-Rushton looked up from the sheets of paper. Frank wasn't paying attention to him, he was wondering how a man can come to have all his hair on either side of his head and none on the top. Where was the sense? 'So he is prepared to recommend your name to the Prosperous Friendly insurance company as a junior clerk. Posts of this kind are extremely hard to obtain for boys of your background, I hardly need add.'

Frank had heard this and didn't like it. 'For *myself*,' he explained edgily, 'I'm an outdoor kind of person.' The careers adviser didn't seem to understand. More desperately, Frank added 'I don't like the feel of paper.'

Pressure was applied. His mother took it dramatically, saying he might as well stab her to death there and then if he didn't take the job, because the disappointment would kill her anyway. Mr Astley-Rushton told him he would be letting down himself, his maths teacher, his school, his community and God. Frank weighed up both sides and initially decided to stab his mother. Eventually, however, he caved in.

On the day he joined he was introduced to Barry, who would be supervising him until he knew what he was doing. Barry was only in his mid-twenties but nervousness, national service and a lopsided ginger moustache made him look ten years older.

'Pleased to make your acquaintance. May I call you Frank? I hope you have a long and prosperous career with the firm.'

'Cheers, Bazza, like your whistle.'

Frank's suit was one of his father's old ones. It was double-breasted and there was enough material in the legs to cover a three-piece suite with some left over for a couple of cushions, but at that time Frank thought fashion was for Italians.

Barry, a bachelor, was set in his ways. He tried to convey to Frank the sensuality of routine:

'I like coming in in the morning and knowing exactly what is going to happen. Sudden movements and unexpected developments make me feel tense and affect my appetite. Your starting here has caused me a lot of worry because it has disrupted the established pattern. The world is full of confusion, except here.'

'Dry up, Baz.'

Frank was only fifteen, but working in the market had taught him confidence. Not having a father had hardened him. In his head Frank was twenty-nine. Physically he had two inches to go until he levelled off, by which time his father's suit showed the top of his shins when he sat down. At fifteen in Prosperous Friendly you were considered so junior you needed to have even your yellow dockets countersigned! The pressure to conform was heavy. The whole weight of the organization bore down on Frank, but still he carried his head as lightly on his shoulders as if it were a balloon.

'Ever get bored?' he asked Barry when he had been working there two and a half days.

'Only boring people get bored, as my grandmother used to say.'

'Sounds a bit of a card, your gran, bit of a wild old bird.'

'Not at all.'

'What if –' and Frank paused to think. 'Supposing she was locked up in the dark in a small room for, say, ten years, on her own. I reckon if she *wasn't* bored by then she'd be pretty boring, no?'

'I, I don't know.' Barry went back to his work with a worried expression on his face.

Frank's job was to check figures. The figures he was checking had already been checked by Barry, who never made any mistakes. There was a rumour going round the office that he made an error back in 1957, but Barry said he had been on holiday when it happened. There were four of them in the same small office. Frank sat facing Barry, next to Peter, who sat opposite Doris. Doris was a middle-aged secretary who had a respiratory problem. She had to sniff all the time, or said she had to. Peter was the same age as Barry and shared his pleasantness, but he talked too much about his wife and child.

'Have you seen this photograph of my wife Pam, Frank?'

Barry and Doris looked away. Frank took it from Peter's perpetually damp hand. 'Nice legs,' he said.

'Where?' Peter snatched the photograph back. 'No, that's her friend Deirdre.' Relieved, he started to smile again hesitantly and gave the snap back to Frank. 'Pam's the one wearing the calf-length socks.'

'I don't think you'll have any trouble with her,' was all he found to say.

'Pam and I have been married for four years.'

'Suits you, does it?'

'Oh, yes. I think a person really develops within a marriage. I know we have.'

'What have you developed into?'

'We think we've become more understanding and sensitive. And now there's our little baby.'

'And Deirdre. What does she do at weekends?'

Doris was more hostile. She always took off her glasses before she spoke, so whenever Frank saw her reaching to take them off her ears he would start a long sentence and try to make it last until five o'clock. When she got a word in it was to tell Frank off.

'You talk too much, my boy,' she snapped one day.

Frank had taken everything she threw at him for several days, but now decided it had to stop.

'I'll stop talking as soon as you stop being an ugly old bag.'

Peter squirmed and Barry looked as though he had suddenly found he had only two minutes to live.

'I think an apology is in order,' Doris said, putting her spectacles back menacingly in front of her rheumy eyes.

'Why, what did I say?' Frank said, showing his palms.

Before long Frank ran into discipline problems. He started walking the corridor for excitement and girls of his own age. Barry had to bring him back. Frank went off again, further this time, down to the staff car park to have a cigarette, up to the senior-managers' toilet on the third floor. It was a tired old office building with a red linoleum floor that was disintegrating in places. The rooms were small, cupboards were dark. If employees moved at all from one small office to another on essential errands, they did it hurriedly and with rabbity glances up and down the corridor. There was an atmosphere of curfew. Frank noticed the tang of something, a quivery apprehension among the staff, but he never worried, he merely felt squeezed and bored. When Barry found him asleep in a roomful of old files Frank didn't worry. He told Barry to relax as he was herded back into the little office, where Peter was telling Doris that his wife was an autumn person.

'I have the unpleasant duty of reprimanding you officially,' Barry said. He sounded upset. Frank was sorry about that.

'OK by me,' he said, to reassure Barry.

His supervisor sighed sadly and dropped into his chair. 'The last fellow who worked here, Tom, he loved doing your job. He was heartbroken when he left.'

'So why did he leave?'

'He was seventy-three. Wrote a marvellous memo.' He looked across at Frank, appealing to him. 'Gosh, nobody minds the occasional joke.'

'I like a joke every now and then,' Peter volunteered. He grinned to show how humour was very much a part of his life. 'I enjoy a joke, absolutely.'

Frank sat in solemn silence for a moment. 'There's two one-legged men hopping up the A1 – '

'Maybe not just now, Frank,' Barry intervened.

Frank did the little he could to join the weft of the corporate fabric, but he still stood out like a Hawaiian shirt at a funeral. Some of his friends were having a better time than he was and they were earning enough to think about owning two suits. And Frank's body was telling him to meet women. He absented himself from the office for long periods to go and sit in a toilet cubicle and throw darts against a hand-drawn target on the door. Barry no longer came to look for him.

Two months after he had joined, Frank looked around him and did not like the way things had worked out.

'Baz?' There was no reply. Frank remembered, Barry and Doris had sent him to Coventry on Monday.

'Peter?'

'What?'

'Listen to this.'

'I'm listening.'

'You know, all this talk about the terrific future I'm supposed to have if I sit here long enough, even if I don't enjoy it today. I've been sitting here and thinking – the future's just a load of todays, isn't it, one after the other?'

'I really don't know.'

'No, think about it.'

Frank felt a lot more cheerful by eleven o'clock, when his head cleared. At lunchtime he took his sandwiches out to the nearby square as usual, ate them on his customary bench and then walked quickly and quietly away from the Prosperous Friendly for ever.

The O'Briens

'Dave Giddings speaking.'

Frank thought: here we go, he's in his bloody car again.

'Dave, it's Frank.'

'Hank? Hank! Where've you been all my life?'

'Get a grip, man. It's Frank Stubbs.' Dave sounded as though he had the roof down and was driving at mach two through a power station.

'Frank. You're breaking up.'

'No, *you're* breaking up. Don't tell *me* I'm breaking up.'

'All right, cool off. I'm on the – whoooa –'

The line went quieter.

'Are you OK there Dave. Dave?'

'It's all right . . . I've got it back. Life in the fast lane, eh?'

'Sounds like you were on the hard shoulder there.'

'What? Sorry, you're breaking up.'

'I'm having an office party.'

'Fish bar?'

'No, OFFICE PARTY,' Frank shouted.

'Ring me later, Frank. You're crackling.'

'I'm not crackling, you fucking big-shot bastard,' he said loudly, but Dave had already hung up, or rolled his car over.

Frank put the receiver down and looked at Janice.

'I thought you wanted to buy some office furniture,' she said. 'And you can't have a party without food and drink.'

'Don't rush me. We'll do that this afternoon.'

'It is this afternoon.'

'In that case we're late. Get your handbag, Janice.'

While Janice posed and postured in front of her little handbag mirror Frank looked around and wondered what could be done to improve the look of the place by that evening.

'Where's Archie?' he asked.

Janice was rolling her lips round a piece of tissue, leaving a perfect red kiss. First they put the stuff on, then they immediately took it off.

'He left just after you did,' she said, running her tongue over her fine top teeth. 'He didn't seem as chirpy as when he came in this morning.'

Frank said nothing but tore the paper out of the typewriter, wrote *Archie – back after lunch. Start preparations for party, streamers, nuts, etc., without me*, and left the note in the middle of the floor, near Archie's centre of gravity. He grabbed Janice's cool hand and walked her quickly to the door, because it was a good excuse to touch her and they were late anyway.

Back on the street the sun was still shining. Frank hung on to her hand and she struggled to keep up with him. She caught up by running for a few strides, slipped behind again, caught up again, slipped behind. Whenever her handbag slid from her shoulder she would hike it back.

'Slow down, my stockings are slipping.'

'Stockings, eh? What are you trying to do to me?'

'They're more hygienic,' she said in a breathless voice.

'It's funny, isn't it,' Frank said, stopping Janice on the

pavement in the busy street. 'A man starts talking about his underwear, he gets looked at like he's a pervert. In a woman it's, like, earthy and sexy.'

'That's you talking,' Janice said. She was hanging on to the sleeve of his coat as she emptied a stone out of her shoe. Frank saw her toes flexing at the bottom of their tube of beige nylon and enjoyed the intimacy of her hand on his arm.

They drew up to the Sad Harry and went in. There weren't many people inside – a barman wiping a glass, two or three drinkers and a man in cowboy boots feeding a fruit machine.

'What would you like, love?' Frank asked when they reached the bar.

'Ooh, let me think,' she said, and pondered, standing first on one leg and then the other.

'Large martini and lemonade, please mate,' Frank said after a short while. 'And a pint of best.'

'Is that Extra Best or Special Best?' the barman asked.

'Tell you what,' Frank said, as Janice continued to think, 'let me have a pint of Super, in a jug.'

'Duggan's Super or normal Super?'

'No, as you were, make that Special Best.' Frank turned away from the bar and looked around.

'I'll have a medium sherry, please,' Janice said.

'Too late, love, I've ordered.'

Janice sighed.

Frank turned to the barman. 'You're new here, aren't you?'

'I was once.'

'What's your name?'

'Stan.'

'Thanks, Stan.' Frank liked to know people's names, in case he needed to refer to them. 'Gerry O'Brien been in yet?'

'Singer, is he? Let's hope he's been held up.'

' 'Preciate your sense of humour, Stan.'

They took the drinks to a quiet corner. Two couples and three individuals came in in the time it took Janice to take off her coat and settle.

'The O'Briens should be here soon,' he told Janice as they sipped their drinks. 'Little Gerry, he's not actually in the band, he'll be playing his geetar.' Frank liked pronouncing it *gee-tar*. 'The others'll be coming too for a bevvy and a chat. They should be here already.'

Janice scooped the ice cubes out of her glass and put them in the ashtray.

'This is an Irish pub,' Frank said. He didn't like silence and usually tried to fill it. 'Lot of Irish in here. A few non-Irish. Lot of people with names beginning with O, you know. O'this and O'that.'

'O'Wiggins,' Janice suggested.

'Yeah. Nah.' A few more minutes went by. 'O, O'Shaunessey,' he added. More minutes. 'Tell me about your family.'

'Well –' she started.

'Stop, stop. Sorry, love, they've arrived.'

Three slight men with curly hair came in, looking around them for a familiar face.

'Over here, lads,' Frank called out, standing up immediately. 'What'll you have?'

'I'll have the young lady sitting next to you if that's all right with you,' said Michael, who looked the oldest. Frank couldn't make himself laugh, even though Janice successfully smiled. Two brothers sat down close to Janice. Gerry went to the small raised platform next to the bar to set up his guitar and small amplifier. Frank went to the bar.

'Stan, my man, get me another large martini, a jug of your best Special Best, pint of Brunnsteiner –'

'We've stopped doing that. I can do you Niederdorfer.'

Frank shouted across to Michael 'Niederdorfer do you?' He nodded. Frank wanted Michael to sit less close to Janice. If they'd been sitting any closer they would have been making love. 'In a straight glass, please, Stanley.' Stan hadn't heard him. He pursued him – 'Straight glass, straight glass. Ta. *Another* pint of Special with a squirt. And half a Guinness.' Stan stood there pouring, staring at the door. 'One for yourself?'

'Scotch.'

The youngest O'Brien didn't take long to set up his equipment. He arranged a few wires and said 'Testing'. Frank sensed a ripple of something go around the bar as he did so. Tension, fear.

'Been working here long?' Frank asked.

'Fifteen minutes longer than when you last asked.'

'Sorry, mate. I've got my mind full.' That was the kind of detail of memory Frank knew he would have to start to get right.

As Frank ferried the drinks across, Gerry O'Brien was saying to his audience 'A little late starting, I'm afraid, owing to a bit of trouble with the van.'

'Clear a space.' Frank sat down heavily in the small gap between Janice and Michael O'Brien.

'You're sitting on my leg,' Janice said gently.

'Bugger, I forgot to say no ice,' he said to himself and to her.

Frank wasn't a great fan of Gerry O'Brien. He was the kid you often got in artistic families, the one nobody knows what to do with.

'Ever thought of having Gerry in the band?' Frank asked Liam.

'No.'

People were leaving, but they may have been going anyway. 'Chirpy chirpy cheep cheep,' Gerry sang into the flimsy microphone. 'Chirpy, chirpy chirpy cheep cheep, chirpy, chirpy cheep cheep, chirp.' Verse.

'Where's Neil?' Frank inquired. He was the third O'Brien, the one who, in his heyday, received most of the underwear sent in by female fans. Liam also used to get a fair share and Michael had told Frank that even he was once sent a slightly greying bra.

'He's helping a mate out in the Railway Arms.'

'Look, boys,' Frank said, even though they were his age or older, 'that's bad business. Don't let your public see you doing stuff like bartending. They shouldn't see you out doing activities that they do, shopping. That's bad.'

'Frank –'

'Honest, you're selling yourself short.'

'How much are you selling little Janice here for?' Michael asked. He and his brother smirked and Janice again managed an approximate smile.

'That's enough of that,' Frank heard himself say, a little too sharply to pass unnoticed. Maybe, he thought, they've been deceived by her snug skirt. 'Anyway, I'm here to give your act the little tickle it needs.'

Liam spoke into his beer. 'It needs more than a frigging tickle, I can tell you.'

'It's just a bad patch. We've had them before,' Michael said. Frank could see that he was the brighter of the two but that was like being the better trampolinist of two dinosaurs. Not that he made any claims of his own to being the biggest intellectual on page 47 of the A–Z.

Meanwhile, Gerry had moved on. *Let it be, let it be, let it be, let it be.* He seemed to like songs with words that went round and round.

'Have you told your manager you're not renewing?'

Liam said 'Oh yes.'

'What did he say?'

'No, I haven't told him. When the contract's up we'll just shoot off and you can start doing the business.'

'And don't you worry about that side,' Frank said, gradually relaxing. The bitter was starting to work. 'We run a smooth show. Tell them how smooth it is, Janice.' She looked baffled for a moment. 'Go on, tell them.'

'We run a smooth show,' she said very deliberately, as though she were learning to speak again.

'There,' Frank said, rubbing his hands together. 'Now let's do some drinking.'

Wes and Wendell

Wes and Wendell Harris were a big noise when Frank met them. They were introduced by his friend Doug.

'Wes, this is Frank Stubbs, a friend of mine.'

'Fuck off, kid, I'm having a quiet drink.'

'Sure, OK, Wes.'

Of the two of them, Wendell was taller and meaner and had the more dangerous look in each eye. The Krays had a round-the-clock watch on the Harris twins, or so it went. Frank was eighteen and it was a time of rumour. (He'd also just met Diane and word was reaching Frank that in bed she exploded and fizzed like an epileptic.) The Harrises were rough. They blew their noses with their fingers. Wendell Harris, it was said, had broken Toni Spavoni's hand and elbow during an arm-wrestling match. He had done it with the leg of a chair. Wes had a few mental problems and it was rumoured that when he was fifteen he had drowned a boy in the River Lea for looking at his girlfriend. Now they lived from protection rackets, boosted by a series of raids on sub post offices which had started the day after Wes and Wendell's mother was overcharged for a postal order. There was even a rumour about Wes and Wendell's sister Molly: that she had got Wes to tattoo a lover who had jilted her on the back with the words *I'll remember Molly till I die*. They were a close family.

Doug and Frank sat down again in their corner of the flatly lit pub, Frank feeling bewildered as to why Doug had wanted to talk to them in the first place, Doug saying 'I picked a bad moment.'

'I reckon,' Frank agreed. 'If your timing had been any worse we'd be taking bits of glass out of our face.'

'Yeah. Wes Harris probably likes a quiet drink.'

The two brothers were sitting on stools at the bar. Behind them, gathered round a table, sat three henchmen waiting for instructions.

'How come you know them?' Frank whispered.

'Don't whisper. They don't like that.'

'Christ.'

'My brother was lookout when they did over the soup factory in Clapton.'

'What did he want to do that for?'

'They told him to.'

'So he did it?'

'You don't say no.'

'What if you do?'

'Say no?'

'Yeah.'

'You don't.'

Frank wanted to leave right away, but it already seemed that right away was too late. Wendell was peering round his brother from the bar.

'Hey, kid, come here a minute.'

Frank thought: oh dear. Two minutes earlier his friend had wanted to talk but now Frank didn't think he felt the same way. It was the difference between having the apple on your head or the crossbow in your hand. Doug hadn't moved. Wes had also turned his head, very slowly, and so had the seedy entourage of three.

'Don't be shy,' Wendell went on. 'We're not shy.'

Doug walked. Frank heard Wes start 'You're Benny's little brother, aren't you?'

That was enough. Frank made himself into a small, quiet creature and left the pub. Sometimes it was good to get involved. At other times it was shrewder and safer to lose all identity and disappear.

Two weeks later Frank was sitting with Doug in a stolen Ford Popular in a quiet street near Epping Forest. It was raining.

'How dark does it have to be, for Christ's sake?' Frank asked.

'Darker than this. This is light.'

'How can you *say* that? I can't even see the bleeding windscreen.'

'We might as well wait a bit longer,' Doug said.

'I'm out of pocket on this trip, do you realize that? Next time, nick a car with a pint or two of juice already in the tank, will you? Fucking car's leaking. "Wes, this is Frank Stubbs." I can't believe you *really* said that. That has to be the most ignorant, thick-arse thing you've ever ... "Wes, this is Frank Stubbs." What was *your game*?'

'Don't raise your voice. There may be someone out walking their dog.'

'I hope so, and I hope it's a copper with an Alsatian and a list of stolen fucking cars in his pocket, so we can get away with a month or two for car-stealing instead of five years for burglary. Look at me, Doug – do you know how many women you can have in five years?'

Frank could feel the water gathering around the soles of his shoes.

'Let's go and do it,' Doug said.

Wes and Wendell Harris had given them a little help – Wes

had written down on a beer-mat the address of the house they were supposed to burgle. 'I'm sorry, kids, but someone's got to do it,' Wes had told Doug. 'And you'd better get that weaselly friend of yours that's just slipped out of the pub to help you, all right?' Frank didn't know whether to believe that Wes had really called him weaselly, but he had been asking around the market about the Harrises, *casually*, and he'd had a few things confirmed.

'Wendell Harris? Mad as buggery,' Norman Doaks said as he weighed out parsnips. 'Friend of mine heard he cut the end of some bloke's nose off.'

'Shit, somebody's nose.'

'It's just skin, see?' Norman put his fingers on the end of his nose and waggled it.

Sam Taplin thought for a while after Frank asked him. Leaning on the arm of his pushcart, he said 'Wasn't it one of the Harris twins who set fire to that kid a couple of years back?'

'*Isn't that illegal*?' Frank said, hardly able to control his voice.

Sam carried on leaning for a moment, then he said 'Now that I *don't* know,' and wandered off.

Frank realized what his choice was: he could either lie low for seven or eight years, maybe buy a hat with a low brim, or he could do the burglary.

Frank didn't make a move to leave the small wet car, even though Doug had already opened the driver's door an inch or two. Cold air came in.

'Let's think about this,' Frank said. Lying low might not be so bad. It might be underrated.

'No. Let's just do it.'

'I'd like to think about it.'

'You wanted to go ahead and do it just now,' Doug said.

'I was wrong, you were right. It's got to be much, much darker. I'm not moving until that house is so dark it looks like . . . a hole.'

The owner of the house was George Podd, a former business associate of the Harrises. The twins apparently didn't like the largeness of his house or the width of his garden. From the little Frank could learn from Doug – who hadn't been told much – the Harrises did not like flashy money. They were less amused by a house with a walled garden than by the idea of sending out two kids they hardly knew to rob and scare George Podd.

'Let's go.'

'Shut the door, you're letting in air.'

'So what's your idea, the first drive-in burglary?'

'Listen, wait, listen, what happens if old George pads down in his pyjamas with his knob dangling out the flap and a shooter in his hand?'

'What's he going to do, call the filth? Man like that's probably got a record as long as a snake's arse as it is.'

'That's supposed to cheer me up? So we get sat on afterwards by a tough nut with previous if we manage to blag a couple of his fire-tongs and a dodgy silver teapot. And we get our faces cut by the Harrises if we stay in the motor. And if, just if, we get caught there and then on the stairs by George or some screwy bandit butler he keeps on the premises we get kicked in by everyone.'

'My brother did his job all right.'

'Doug, I don't give a monkey's about your brother. I don't care two turds about any of your relatives, to be honest. How does that sound?'

'Sounds fair to me, Frank. I'm just saying he did what they asked and the Harrises left him alone.'

'Until the next time they ask him. What does he say then? Sorry boys I'm busy for the rest of my life?'

Frank distinguished in his mind between illegality and criminality. 'I don't mind fingering the law but don't ask me to screw around with it,' he told Doug. He didn't want to be put away. Cells scared him. Claustrophobia, aggravated by homophobia: he did not want to live in a building full of men. Already at eighteen his only definition of bad business was business that carried a custodial sentence. Doug had interfered with his principles. Now he would have to sit there and argue it out.

'You see, Doug my son, some of us think we should stand up to the men of violence. Don't you think we should do that, that little thing, really? Douggie?' It was hard for Frank, talking to someone he couldn't even see.

'Go into hiding, you're saying?'

'Right. And if we *do* happen to meet the Harrises out and about, we simply –'

'Tell them –' They were feeling their way.

'We're still . . . at the planning stage.'

'Planning stage.'

'We're still planning the best way to –'

'Do . . .'

'Do the job.'

'In the best way.'

'Yeah, that should do it,' Frank told himself.

'You don't think we'll be, like, *bleeding* already by that stage?'

'Wait, I've got it,' Frank said. 'We'll say we were caught with our hands in the, I don't know –'

'In the silver, in the –'

'That's it, George interrupted us so we gave him a good going over, showed him the front ends of our boots, and then left.'

'By the front door.'

'That's a good touch, by the front door. We'll use that.'

Now they were cruising. Talking helped a great deal. For a moment they sat in silence, satisfied. The water at Frank's feet had seeped up into his socks, which now had his ankles in a cold, wet, sucking embrace.

'What if –'

'*Leeeave* it out,' Frank whined.

'No, listen. What if the twins question George Podd about getting his backside kicked in?' Doug asked. 'He says "What, Who, Eh? Don't get your drift, Wes," that kind of thing.'

'So?' Frank had decided definitely to stay in the car.

'Well I'd say that leaves us worse off than when we started out.'

'We say: well he *would* say that. That's what he *would* say, we say. Nobody likes to admit to a kicking.'

'Not an arse-kicking.'

'Right.'

Frank was tired but Doug kept him arguing for two more hours, until the sky started to lighten. Doug hot-wired the car into motion and drove it back to the outskirts of London, where milk-floats had just come on to the streets. Abandoning the Ford, they took the bus straight to the market and went to work looking like death.

Frank and Doug didn't go out much for several months, until Wendell killed Wes Harris one night by headbutting him over the balcony of their mother's new high-rise council flat. Frank felt even better later that year when Wendell was officially described as criminally insane and put away.

That evening Frank and Doug went for a celebratory drink to the pub where the Harrises had been sitting on their stools all those months ago, before the authorities had had to scrape Wes's face up off the tarmac with a pallet knife. There was a man standing at the bar with a head like a bullet and a fat scar across the back of his neck. As Doug ordered two pints of bitter the man leaned across to him and Frank heard him say in a voice like concrete 'Aren't you Benny's little brother?'

Taking the words out of Frank's mouth, Doug said: 'Who's Benny?'

■ Invitations

Frank was back at the bar, but only just.

'Five pints of beer and a martinade and lemoninini. Please.'

'Beer? What kind of beer? Bitter, pale ale, non-alcoholic?'

'Stan, my man –'

'Brown ale, lager in a bottle, in a can, Guinness with a twist of lime?'

'Dan –'

'Stan.'

'Stan, don't be a smart-arse, no, no, you're a lovely man, lovely man, what'll you have, come here.' Frank put his arm round Stan's neck and brought his head towards his own. Stan tried to pull away but Frank was full of love.

Frank closed his eyes and tried to concentrate. 'Fuck me,' he said. 'Look, just give me what I had the last time.'

'With the chasers?'

'Don't, look, don't compliment the material, don't.'

'I'm not with you.'

'Don't complicate.' Frank stopped and just stared at the barman. Summoning up an effort, he said slowly 'Give me what I had before.'

Stan said 'Sure,' and started pouring.

Frank could hear Janice giggling behind him. He swept his

head round and saw her and the O'Briens at the end of his tunnel of vision. He wanted to go up to Janice and say: Janice, I . . . I . . . What was it he wanted to say?

'Anything else?' Stan was asking. Frank turned back. His head seemed to take longer than the rest of him to centre again in front of the bar.

He should get some food inside him. To soak up what he had drunk he needed ten buckets of sand.

'Peanuts?' Frank didn't mean it as a question.

'Dry roasted, ready salted, honey roast, cashew mix –'

'One of every. And a packet for your own.'

The O'Briens, what great guys! Michael, Gerry, Barry, and Neville, no, Larry, no, Liam. And Neil. Whoever! Here they were, with Janice. Frank made his way towards them with a pint in each hand and two whisky chasers under each arm. He lost a couple of the whiskys on the way. Somehow he hadn't thought he would make it without losing something. He was having spells of mental and physical confusion – no problem! – but he knew he had a robust enough body to cope.

'Hey, Frankie's made it back,' one of them said.

'Mr Stubbs to you!' Janice hooted. 'Only I can call him Frank, can't I, Frank?'

'I want you to know you can say anything you want to me.' He was trying to put his warmth into words. 'You're the fucking top of the milk, Janice, I want you to know that. You're too good for this world.'

'Have another pint, Frank,' somebody said, making a lot of people laugh. He joined in and was still laughing when Janice said 'You're *drunk*' in a happy, swooping squawk.

Frank sobered up when anybody said that. Prickings of shame. Now he noticed details: Liam had fallen asleep with his mouth open and Michael was dropping peanuts into it, Janice had the top button of her blouse undone, Gerry had his arm along the back of her chair . . .

Frank took a long pull on his latest pint, which set him back a little into the land of drunken confusion.

'Dusty Springfield,' he blurted. 'You must have worked with some performers, Engelbert Humperdinck, the fat blind guy with the skinny whatsit, woman.'

'We shared a taxi with Dean Martin once, did you know that?' one of them said.

'No kidding, what was he like?' Frank asked.

'Actually he got out when he saw we'd got in after him.'

'Fucking rednose,' Michael said.

'What about . . . Nana Mouskouri. What's she *really* like?'

Michael said 'She's a bloody gent, Nana.'

'Russ Conway, tell me about Russ.'

Liam woke up suddenly and choked on his peanuts.

'There wasn't much you could tell *him* about a piano,' Frank added, still slurred, phasing in and out of control.

'I'm getting a headache,' Janice said. 'I've had too many drinks.'

'You've only had one drink, love. It's just that you've had a lot of glasses of it,' Gerry said.

She had stopped smiling but her button was still undone. Frank could see the top of her bra. He had a quick image of her steering and smoothing herself into the two white cups that morning. Frank tried to imagine what it felt like to put a bra on but he couldn't do it.

'One thing I can't understand,' Frank said, 'is how Liberace played his old joanna with all those rings on. Did you ever, you know, get a, you know, *insight* into that?'

They had started to ignore him. What a pathetic mess

their little party was in. Deciding to tidy up, Frank reached across the table, which had enough glass on it to glaze a cathedral, and brought the two halves of Janice's blouse together again. The mother-of-pearl button kept slipping through his fingers, which felt too big for his hands. Janice just looked down at Frank's knuckles as though it were none of her business. Her flushed skin felt warm over the bony spars of her ribs.

'There,' Frank said.

Liam's mouth had fallen open again and his upper body was seeking the horizontal. Gerry and Michael had heavy-looking eyes. Janice appeared content to say, do and think nothing at all for a few hours.

'I think the showbusiness party in the corner should get some fresh air,' Stan said in a semi-public voice as he massaged glasses with a cloth.

'OK, fresh air all round, straight glasses,' Frank said, getting up mechanically, remembering he had a whole day ahead of him and only half a day to do it in.

He went to the toilet, put his fingers down his throat and made four convulsive fountains. What was it about men's urinals that persuaded him that hell might look like this? The bars of the window were covered in brown furry dust and the window opened on to an enclave, a shaft of damp masonry lined with moss-covered putrescence. Although the window was open, the toilet smelt like one hundred ferment-ing corpses. Pipes cavorted this way and that up and down the walls, each joint dribbling and crusted with some kind of orangey-bluey-green coral. The outflow from the urinal sprouted the bloated butts of cigarettes. The air was cold and wet and used. Just so, Frank thought – it's a toilet, how could it be any other way.

Wiping his feet on the carpet, he made his way to their suddenly sad table. He swilled his mouth out with one of Janice's four untouched martinis and said 'What are we, all set?'

Gerry was already struggling to put his microphone stand back in its case, trying to get the fat end down the thin end.

'Me and Janice had better scoot,' Frank said. 'I'll see you lads later tonight. Put on some decent clobber for the ladies and gentlemen, won't you, men?' They looked a bit less like pedigree performers to Frank now that he felt more himself again. It was true that they had worked with Dana. But who hadn't?

Frank felt the love he had had half an hour ago dying. Which was more real, the way he felt now, or then? Where was the bottom of all this?

'How you feeling, love?' he asked Janice as they walked along the pavement.

'Much better, thanks.'

'You were great in there.'

'I didn't do anything.'

'You were a queen in there, don't argue. What were you?'

On her pointy heels Janice had to look carefully where she was going. Still looking down, she said in a subdued voice 'A queen.'

'Come on, let's hear it properly.'

She stopped and looked at him. He stopped. 'All right,' she raised her voice to say. 'I was a queen, a queen. OK now?'

'Sorry,' Frank answered, taken aback, as they stood there. 'Just trying to pump it up a bit.' It's true, he thought – you always hurt the ones you fancy.

Janice turned, her mouth tight-looking. They moved off again. The sun had gone in, changing the light in the street from yellow to an ashen shade of white.

After two minutes walking along it was Frank's turn to stop. 'Look,' he said, 'I wasn't trying anything on.'

As her face softened, the fullness of her lips emerged again. 'It's not that,' she said. She had quietened down.

'So what's wrong? Bonce still giving you gip?'

'You're just, I don't know, a bit of a bully sometimes.' She ran her hand through her hair, seemingly embarrassed.

Frank stood and pondered. He put his hands deep into his coat pockets and trailed his tongue all the way across his top front teeth. 'A bully?' he said, mildly. He was shocked to hear it from her.

'You were bullying me just then.'

'Was I?'

'You don't even know that you're doing it when you *are* doing it.'

'Oh?'

'You bully Archie and you bully Jason all the time. I bet you probably bullied your wife and brothers and sisters.'

'So you're saying I'm, what, a bully?'

'Well, I don't know. Yes.' There it was again, that passing of her hand through her hair. She had found the courage to look into his face.

Now Frank scratched the back of his head. The two of them were a mass of gestures.

'So you reckon bullying's a possibility, do you?' he asked.

'Yes.'

'Fancy,' he said as they walked on again. 'I suppose I'd better do something about that.'

It took a woman, didn't it (he felt), to alert one to these

things. On the alerting front you could do a lot worse than a woman.

Back at the office Janice threw herself into her chair as Frank called out 'Hallo, Archie, how you doing?' into the other room. Frank looked at Janice with an innocent questioning smile, as if to say 'Did you hear the generosity in that?'

Archie replied a muffled 'Piss off' through the half-open door from the other office. From the crunched-up timbre of his voice it sounded as though he had his feet up.

'I'm just going to invite some people to tonight's party,' Frank shouted through the door again. With the headache he was starting to have he wondered how he was managing to be so patient. It was wasted on Janice, who had her head in her hands. He went on deliberately 'I'm picking up the phone now. Maybe while I'm doing this you'd like to go out and arrange the booze for our do?' Silence from Archie. 'Maybe you'd enjoy doing that?'

As Frank dialled the first number Archie bowled through the office and left, banging the door.

'Who's this? Ron?'

'Who'm I talking to?'

'You're a tight bastard, Ron, won't even give your name out without a receipt.'

'I've got enemies, Frank. Know what it's like to have those?'

'Nope. Must be one more thing I don't know.'

The trouble with Ron Rumsby was that he thought he was in a film all the time, that was Frank's opinion. Worse, when he forgot to be self-dramatizing he tended to be equally foolish. His line was buying and selling, and he didn't mind what. Ron had a whole series of lock-up garages and none of them had cars inside.

'Is there anyone in the room there with you, Frank?'

'Why?'

'You know better than to ask that.'

'Can we get on, please, Ron, I've got about fifty more people to talk to in the next half hour and they're all more interesting than you.'

'So talk.'

'Come on over, I'm having a party, eight o'clock, my new office address.'

'I'll be there. Any big names be present?'

Frank considered using his sister's joke about there only being long names (it had better have been a joke, otherwise it amounted to rudeness) but instead he said 'I don't think you'll be disappointed.' It didn't matter what you said to Ron, he always came back with something lame anyway.

'Well, let's not run before we can walk, eh?'

'Bye, Ron.'

Frank took another look in the broken-down old notebook where he kept his numbers. In the next few hours he had a great deal of phoning to get through and a heavy buying programme – furniture, food, drink, balloons.

'Is that Mimi Dickson's office?' he asked in his business voice. It was like his normal voice except it had a few extra Hs thrown in.

'That is correct. How can I help you?' Mimi Dickson, superstar. She had had a show of her own in the late seventies, in which she sat on a quantity of high stools and sang duets with Val Doonican and people like Val Doonican. And she was a personal friend of Frank's, a rather special person.

'I'd like a barney with Mimi, please, babe. This is Frank Stubbs.'

'I'll see if Ms Dickson can come to the telephone.' In the

silence that followed, Frank put his hand over the mouthpiece and said to Janice, whose head was now resting on the table, 'I reckon we're going to have a – Hallo?'

'Hallo?' There she was.

'Mimi, this is Frank Stubbs.'

She paused. That was how she was, very composed.

'Who?' she said.

'I sold you some tickets a few months ago.'

She was still taking her time. 'Did you?'

'You were having trouble getting into *Angel Melon* at the Plaza.'

'Ah yes.'

Frank pressed on, though he was losing confidence. 'I wondered whether you'd like to come to the launch of my new entertainment venture this evening.'

'No, I don't actually –'

'Oh, there'll be drinks. I thought you might like to, you know, give something back to your public.'

'Thank you, no,' she said in that prissy way she had, as if light entertainment couldn't get by without her.

'Listen here –' Frank started but she put the telephone down. He held the receiver out at arms length and shook it for a moment with rage. 'I don't get that kind of shit from Liza Minnelli,' he balled down the dead wire. Janice Wiggins raised her head to find out what the noise was all about, heard Frank tell her 'Any case – she couldn't carry a tune if she had it in her handbag,' and hid her face again under her arms.

So she thought Frank was too small-time for her. Sometimes he was glad he had stayed in the East End, where people didn't put the phone down on you 'just because you haven't ever sung *Puff the Magic fucking Dragon* with Rolf Harris'.

It was a relief for Frank to turn to another page in his Book of Numbers and find the name Nobby Spicer.

'Frank, I was hoping you might call me,' Nobby said. Life had been problematic for Nobby since he ended his football career. He had been drinking too much. Too much for ten. He ran a sports shop, but the last time Frank had gone visiting there had been hardly anything on the shelves.

Nobby had been a hero of Frank's and he wasn't going to let him down.

'I want you to meet some people, Nobby.'

'You reckon you might have something for me?'

'Sure,' Frank said. 'I'll have you opening supermarkets before you can say banana.'

'Thanks, Frank.'

'No problem.'

◼ **Diane**

Frank had had to let go of Sandy, his freckled girlfriend, when Diane came into his world.

Diane was petite and had dark shoulder-length hair. Her features had something foxy about them, like Frank's, but her nose was prettier and her teeth were far more orderly than his, which were like a shed-full of old tusks. He had his first glimpse of her in the distance as he worked his stall in the market.

'Hey, Norm, who's the new girl?'

Norman the Mormon, they called him, because he was a Jehovah's Witness. He looked down the line of stalls.

'That's Cheryl. She's not new.'

'No, behind her, on the other side.'

'What, Annie? Don't get interested, kid. She's got one of those disappearing bottoms.' He wasn't a very good Witness but he was a good witness.

'No, you big stiff, in front of her.' Frank completely agreed with Norman about Annie – her legs started where her back ended. She shouldn't rightly have been able to walk.

'I don't know. Maybe she's new.'

'Thanks, Norm, keep in touch.'

Frank spent a few days looking for an opportunity to talk to her. He found out her name – Daphne. Well, that was wrong for a start. The simplest thing to do, Norman said, was for Frank to buy something from her.

'Can I have two pounds of grapes, please, love, my name's Frank, I've seen you around.'

'Two pounds of grapes?' she said, frowning. Frank loved her face. Dark, with bright eyes.

'That's right. They're the small purple things next to those long curvy yellow ones.'

As she weighed them, she said to Frank 'Didn't anybody tell you it was rude to stare?'

'No. Were they supposed to have?'

'You've been staring over at me for days.' There was a good reply to this, if Frank could only remember it.

'I don't know, the label's come off,' he said. Hell, *no*, that was what you said after 'What are you staring at?'

She looked at him as though he were mad, handed the grapes over and took his money.

'Like it here?' he asked.

'Yes thanks,' she said curtly. 'Next.'

'Pound of rhubarb.' It was Frank again. He needed more time to think.

As she wrapped the pink stalks in the racing results Diane said 'Can you order them together next time, it's quicker that way.'

This time he asked 'Are you free anytime this week?'

She hesitated for a while and then said 'No'. Then she said 'And pack in staring.'

After three months of buying fruit of all kinds and coming to work in his best clothes, Frank received the answer he wanted.

From their first date together (26 October 1963) for more than twenty years, Frank loved Diane wholly and unthinkingly. He had offers from other women but he turned them down. More than that, he actively defended the institution of marriage all through the late sixties and seventies, when there were so many piles of car keys on so many tables, even the tables down Frank and Diane's street. Sometimes it felt as though everybody – except Frank and Diane Stubbs – was sleeping with everybody else, but Frank could bear that thought.

Soon after their first date Frank went to Diane's house for Sunday tea. Her family were highly political and Frank had some difficulty keeping up with the conversation.

'Are you in a union, Frank?' Diane's mother asked.

'Mum, don't start,' Diane said. She had put aside her politics that day for Frank's benefit.

'There isn't one,' he said, tucking his serviette under his chin. He didn't want to lose Diane by letting jam drip down his shirtfront.

'Why don't you start one?' said Diane's father, the Labour councillor, keeping up the pressure. They sat around Frank, polite but firm.

'I leave that kind of thing to people that're interested.'

'More celery?' Diane asked Frank.

'That's what the Germans said about Hitler in the 1930s,' said Diane's restless fourteen-year-old brother. He was crouched low over his plate. Frank noticed that he hadn't put his serviette on.

Tentatively Frank asked 'Wasn't Hitler a socialist?' He knew that was a mistake when the whole family leaned back on their chairs and looked at him very closely.

'He was a *National* Socialist, stupid –'

'Stop it, Paul,' Diane's mother interrupted.

'Sorry, Frank,' Diane said.

'That's all right, no, really, I was out of order on that one.'

'Of course, we think it would be advantageous if the level of political awareness were a little higher within the borough,' her father went on.

'Diane's always been very knowledgeable and I know you get on so well,' said her mother.

'I should say,' he said, and leaned across to put his arm round Diane in what he hoped was a serious but loving sort of way. The celery he was holding left wet marks on the shoulder of her yellow blouse. 'And don't you worry – I'll start a union on Monday.'

Frank could still remember the wedding. His side of the church was withered and pale. Diane's half was crowded with suits, bright hats and softly coughing relatives. Frank's mother let him down badly by not crying during the service. Diane's parents both wept like babies. Her family and friends, mainly atheists and free-thinkers, fidgeted through the sermon, while Frank's scattering sat in a torpor and only woke up when some of Diane's party applauded the vicar politely when he left the pulpit, as though he was part of a tired cabaret (Diane's brother Paul said he was).

Frank thought his young wife looked a dream, her little face tremulous under the thin veil pinned into her beehive. In later years she wished, she said, that she had opted for something more classical than the short white nylon dress and orange tights, but at the time even the photographer said he had not seen a more attractive couple in eleven years behind the shutter. 'Mind you,' he added, 'I normally just do police forensic.'

The reception afterwards was held in the George and Muriel Savage Memorial Hall, a high-ceilinged room that swallowed up Frank's nervous speech, which he prepared

during the Black Forest gâteau. Though only four sentences
long – and one of those was 'I *am* speaking up' – it was
longer than his best man Doug's by two clear sentences.
Perhaps it didn't matter (or maybe it mattered *more*), because
Diane's father was on his feet for fifteen long minutes,
reading out a hagiography of his daughter, supplemented by
a tentative fifteen seconds about the bridegroom.

'Let me end with this,' he ended. 'The way I see it we're
not losing a daughter,' the room wound itself up, 'we're
gaining the possibility of a grandchild.'

Frank did the rounds afterwards with his bride.

'Petra, meet the wife.'

'I like your hair, s'nice,' his sixteen-year-old sister said
gormlessly, and looked away.

Meet the wife, how good that felt. He had never said it
before. As he grew older he was entitled to more and more sentences.

'Grant, what do you think of your new sister-in-law?'

'She looks like a model,' he said.

'Here, I like your brother.' Diane put her shoulder affectionately against Frank and kissed him.

Frank had spent a couple of hours teaching his brother
that simple line. Except he was supposed to have said *top*
model, for heaven's sake. Frank hadn't slept with Diane yet
and he wanted her to feel confident in herself that night. He
did not want her thinking: well, I've got to take my clothes
off now and I look *nothing* like a top model.

'Mrs Stubbs, say hallo to the new Mrs Stubbs.'

What was it his mother had said? Wasn't it something
rancorous like 'I hope you have better luck with your husband
than I did with mine, luvvy'?

He missed out some of Diane's side of the family in his

rush to get her into a taxi, out of it again at the hotel and up the stairs, saying didn't you think it went well, and so on and so on.

The rumours about Diane fizzing like an epileptic had been fabricated, but they were more right than they were wrong. She didn't need any diagrams. When Frank had asked her whether she wanted the light on, she said 'We want to see what we're doing, don't we? It would be like eating in the dark.'

Frank pieced together Diane's personality out of scraps of behaviour and threads of talk. Although she didn't seem to be too sure about others, including Frank, she had confidence in herself. Even before she knew him well, the next morning, she asked him to stroke her neck. When he didn't do it the way she liked she said so and when he stopped too quickly she told him so again.

She was eighteen and Frank nineteen when they married. Most of the time they were both guessing as to what was proper procedure for married couples. Diane asked questions, whereas Frank more usually just sat there in their rented flat, breathing into her ear. He spent a large number of their hours together asking her to sit on his lap in their one armchair.

'Come on, leave that.'

'Don't you like the bed to be made?'

'Leave it. Come and sit in the armchair.'

She lay sprawled across him, her feet and arms dangling over the arms of the chair.

'Is my bottom hurting you?'

'What a question.'

'What do you fancy for tea, Frank?'

'Don't get up.'

'The kitchen's over there.'

'Oh, come on. Stay in the armchair.'

They didn't win the Nobel Prize for Conversation that year.

Diane started working in the Post Office but she didn't want a job, she wanted a baby. Anybody cashing their family allowance received a liquid smile from her on the other side of the counter. Out of love and jealousy Frank sometimes joined the queue and watched her tearing off stamps and explaining things to pensioners, having to shout.

'This isn't your pension book,' he once heard her enunciate. 'You've given me – I say, you've given me a copy of the Highway Code. Yes, they do look similar.'

When he reached her window he would usually say 'It's all right, I've left someone looking after the stall.'

'What do you want?' she would ask. 'I wish you wouldn't come here so often.' They had a different way of loving. Frank's style was instinctive and demonstrative, Diane's private.

'Di, we're married. We can do this.'

'There's a queue of people.'

'I queued up fair and square. OK, have it your own way, give me an application form.'

'What kind?'

'Give me a form for a wheelbarrow permit.' He turned and winked at a little boy behind him. 'My wife,' he explained to the kid.

Frank wondered what Diane saw in him. She told him once that she liked him because he was close to the surface.

'That's good, is it?' he asked her.

Maybe she liked the loose way he moved. Her own movements veered towards the robotic. When Diane knew she had to go across the room it seemed she just wanted to get it over with, and quick, tidy walking was the most efficient way. Frank, on the other hand, often liked to take his time. 'What's the hurry?' he used to say to her. 'Finish that, you'll only have to start something else.'

Diane had difficulty conceiving Jason. Previously, Frank had had the impression that making a baby was like boiling an egg. You just had to remember to put the egg in the water. He had been doing that regularly, and the water had been good and boiling.

After two and a half years of marriage Diane lay on her side in bed and asked 'What are we doing wrong, Frank?'

'I shouldn't have kept taking it out that first year.'

'We couldn't afford a baby.'

'You know how difficult it is, remembering to pull it out?'

'No.' That was another quality he admired in Diane – she didn't make up stories about knowing what she didn't know about.

'Plus, what's worse, it's like, it's like driving into a garage and saying "Ten gallons, please, mate," and then "Oh, and can you pour it over the bonnet please, ta."'

She sighed softly, winding a finger into his chest hair.

At first Frank didn't mind about there being no baby. It gave him a good excuse to persuade Diane into fertile-looking positions that were also a lot of fun to be in.

'Honestly, Di, I reckon we could be on to a winner with this one,' he would say as he folded her limbs.

But soon Frank's wife began to fret and say she felt that she was less than a whole woman. 'Are you crazy?' Frank would answer. 'You're more of a woman than I'll ever be.' These soothing words and others like it didn't help. Diane left the post office, as if conceiving a baby would come more easily if she sat at home all day and thought about pregnancy full-time.

One day Frank came home from a tiring day at the market. Norman had been trying to convert Frank to Jehovah all day. Frank had been parrying his thrusts with theological conundrums such as 'If you're one of the chosen, how come you've got such a huge wart on the side of your nose?' There was a bottle of sparkling wine on the table when he came in and Frank knew straight away why it was there.

'It's true, then?' he said to Diane.

'What?' she answered, beaming, knowing.

'Arsenal have got Charlton at home in the cup.'

'FRANK –' she started.

'I'm joking, honey. Come and give me a squeeze.'

He took her in his arms and rubbed her back with long, loving strokes. There were three of them there in the room.

'Show me,' he said, and sat her down on his lap in the armchair. He peeled up her blouse and put his ear to the soft, gently shifting skin.

Look at Yourself

'Grant Stubbs speaking.'

'Big brother here. How's it going your end?'

'Frank? Mustn't grumble.'

'Why's that?'

'Eh?'

Grant was another person Frank liked to make work extra hard, even on the telephone.

'What's the big whisper in the world of pet food?'

'Well, this month's figures look better than last month's. The new gerbil mix is going down a st– '

'Magic, Grant, that's enough small print.'

Frank had made more than twenty telephone calls. He had had about enough. As he explained about his party again he watched Janice dozing and listened to her thickening breathing.

'Do us a turn, pick up the old dear on the way,' Frank told his brother.

'It's ten miles off my route.'

'Hey, how often do I ask you for a favour?'

'Every time you ring me.'

'Yeah, but I don't ring you often.'

Frank heard Grant scratch the side of his face as he considered. 'I hadn't thought of it that way.'

There were some similarities between the two brothers. Petra, their sister, had once described Grant as 'like Frank, only less so', and there was a needle of intelligence within this apparent haystack of meaninglessness. Grant resembled Frank in his speech patterns and looks, but he was milder. After the last Christmas they spent together at their mother's home – 1972, the television had broken down, Diane had a cold-sore – they were asked how it went. Frank said 'I've had more fun dead.' Grant said 'It's been a little quiet, actually.'

Grant had a more temperate face, too, flatter features and fuller lips. He would have been more handsome than Frank, that was even Frank's view, but he had lost most of his hair down the years. When the two of them stood side by side, many people wanted to put a toupee on Grant.

Grant continued. 'Do you think it'll be Mum's kind of party?'

'What kind of party's that?'

'You know, polite.'

'There'll be no riff-raff, if that's what you mean. Anyone comes without their teeth in, they get turned away.'

'Oh, right.'

'You bringing a girlfriend?'

Grant had little luck with women. His peaceable manner and lack of anything vibrant to say would not have done him any harm if he had chosen the right kind of partner, but Grant targeted women who liked nightclubbing and deep suntans. Frank was partly to blame, because he had referred Grant to a few spare single women he knew. Babs, blonde with inch-long fingernails, was the least suitable of all, but Grant hung on for six months, coached in the background by Frank. She encouraged him to buy an Italian sports car with calf upholstery and to drive her to Cannes, where she abandoned him in a bar. When Grant got back to England, bewildered and alone, Frank said to him 'That's more or less the way it always is with Babs.'

Frank liked his brother, especially since Diane had stopped being around. He needed to know Grant was there, in the background, sifting rabbit food in a warehouse in Wanstead.

'I was just hoping I might meet someone at your, you know, occasion,' Grant replied, after thinking over Frank's question.

'I could make a phone call or two – '

'No, no, it's probably best if I just play it by ear.'

'Do that, Grant. It's about time you found a wife to go home to.'

'You don't need to worry about me, Frank. I've just bought myself a video player.'

'Handsome!' Frank said and rang off.

Janice had begun to snore cavernously, face cheek-down on the desk. Frank enjoyed her rhythm. When she breathed in, the air threaded quietly through her slack mouth, but at the top of each breath something collapsed and the air came out as a ragged blast. One of her arms dangled towards the carpet, the fingers twitching slightly.

Frank started to feel a bulging at his temples again. A wave of hangover broke across his forehead. 'Feels like I've got my arse on my head,' he said to himself, momentarily shutting his eyes. They felt better when they kept out the light. Having made his telephone calls, Frank decided he ought to allow himself a few minutes' sleep to prevent him being tired later. He rearranged himself in the chair opposite his secretary, straightened out his legs and rested.

Layla had kicked her bare legs out of the window and was talking to Grant, who was saying that he wanted to give her children. 'I can give you as many as five,' he said in a nasal voice, 'but we'll have to clear it with Frank.' On another chair Janice was sitting naked, talking to Frank about the importance of shorthand. Her legs were tightly crossed, plaited around each other, but Janice was unfolding them patiently, one after the other –

'I want a word with you, Stubbs.'

'Arch – '

'Right now,' Archie shouted, standing right in Frank's face.

'I was having a – '

'I've been thinking about you and me – '

Frank grabbed Archie with unnatural force, though still half asleep. There was a sound of stitches tearing in Archie's shirt.

'I was having a dream, you fucking pillock,' he said, shaking Archie so that his jawline kept squashing into his double chin. Frank wanted to settle back into the dream quickly before the storyline was lost for ever. It was rare for him to have dreams of such quality. The few he remembered were not worth having, about *football* and sometimes *shopping*.

Archie looked even angrier from being pulled about, when it was supposed to be he who was mad. He made round-arm swings at Frank's own outstretched arms and then tried to prise Frank's fingers away from his collar.

'You got something to say,' Frank said between his teeth, 'you do it calmly.' He released Archie, who stepped back.

'Calmly? Fuck calmly!'

'Yeah? And what's your difficulty?'

'Do something for me, Frank,' Archie said with more control, massaging his Adam's apple. 'Look at yourself.'

'Don't tell me to look at myself, Archie.'

'Go on, look at yourself.'

'Don't fucking tell me to look at myself.'

'Do it, try it.'

'All right, all right.' Frank opened his arms slightly and stared down at himself. He looked up again. 'All right?'

'You're not doing it.'

'I fucking *did* it, I looked at myself.'

'Yeah, like dick you did.'

They stopped for a moment. Archie had a look of disgust on his face. Frank was upset inside. He only enjoyed confrontation if it was his idea, and today he wanted smoothness and a good atmosphere.

'Shall I pop out for three doughnuts and some cups of tea?' Janice suddenly said, from behind Frank. He turned his head.

'That's it, get out,' Archie said quietly to a point on the floor just in front of him.

'Don't talk to her like that, what is she, a dog?' Frank threw back.

'Don't listen to me, love,' he said over Frank's shoulder, 'it's big-shot here who's pissing me off.' He walked towards Janice. 'Let me tell you about Frankie here.'

'Watch him, Janice,' Frank said, following him with his eyes. 'He's going to ask you to look at yourself.'

Archie had an expression of wound-up menace on his face. He didn't seem content to have a normal conversation, he wanted an odd, dangerous one.

'When I met Frank,' he started at Janice, explaining with his hands, 'he knew sod-all about bugger-all but at least he gave you the time of day.'

'Oh, Jacka-bleeding-nory,' Frank said.

'The first time I took him out selling – *Evita*, three months into the run, tickets are rare as big tits in a Japanese brothel. I'm well-stocked, see, I've got fifty best and I can sell them a hundred times over. So I pass half of them to Frank to sell so he can show me he can do it, also to keep the filth off my back. I've *schooled* him, I've *trained* him –'

'Get on with it,' Frank barracked, 'I've heard this one before.'

'Twenty-five minutes after curtain up we're in the boozer having a couple of liveners, Frank gets his rag out to blow his nose and a dozen, fourteen tickets come out with it.'

Archie had his mouth open, so did Janice.

'I don't get it,' she said after a moment.

'He's only *forgotten* to sell a grand's worth, hasn't he, today's money. You know what I do?'

'You're cross at this point, right?' Janice said tentatively, her hand playing nervously around her mouth.

'I do nothing,' he said, still looking amazed about it after all these years. 'I say, don't you worry Frank, you just pay me the nominal and we'll put it down to experience.' He drew closer to Janice. 'You think he'd do the same for me now, for anyone? Of course he fucking wouldn't! I borrowed a stamp from him the other day and he wrote it down in a little book! A little blue book!'

'It's a business expense,' Frank said simply. 'I have to write them down now, in a book.' He planned to explain his angle to Janice later on when he had slapped Archie down well and hard.

Frank stood up and said to Archie 'So, what was it you wanted to tell me?'

'From now on we work together like in the old days, or stuff you.'

Frank decided to humour Archie and sort him out later. 'We'll talk about it.'

'Too right. And don't you worry – if you can keep a little book with writing in it, I can run *two* fucking books.'

'Just bottle it, will you, we're having a party. Not that you've contributed a duck's fart to the arrangements.' Archie was about to speak up but Frank had done enough listening and cut him short with an eyebrows-raised glance. The street outside had the look of late afternoon about it. 'Get some food in while Janice and I buy some furniture. We've got sixty coming and the place looks about as festive as a Turkish karsy.'

'You're giving me orders again. And I caught Jason at the bus stop. He says you've given him over two grand for *Bitch*.'

Frank felt uneasy. 'It's just a try-out. He'll never get them.'

'Jason filled me in that you got some kind of tip-off.'

'Archie, the day you start believing what my son says, that's a sad day.'

Archie was not going to be put off. 'So you set me up to handle the tickets here, you rush me for three thousand quid to set up this shack of an office, with its chicken-shit little blue books, and then you keep back the class business for yourself.'

'And?' Frank said. 'So? And? Go and make some openings of your own.'

'I'm getting out. I'll have my lend back.'

'It's a bit late for that, or how stupid are you?'

'Just give it back.'

Frank had no intention of giving Archie his stake back. He had worked on him, painted him the picture of an office full of pert secretaries, and won Archie's assent. He was a persuader, and Archie had said yes.

Frank merely sighed heavily and said: 'Pick up your gear, Janice, we're going spending.'

◼ Ambition

Jason was born and the baby dominated Frank and Diane's lives. He was pretty, with brown eyes and whorls of fine black hair. When they took him out in the push-chair, people would look at Jason and his parents and allocate body-parts in the traditional way.

'He's got his mother's lovely eyes.'

'Hasn't he,' Frank might say at first.

'And there's a touch of his mum about the nose and his ears.'

'His ears come from my dad,' Diane said on two or three occasions. Jason was already beginning to sound like he had been assembled, rather than born.

One day Frank had to listen to a similar story from his mother-in-law as she crouched down in front of the boy, holding her pearls away from his grasp. '. . . and that's Uncle Jack's mouth, isn't it, Di, don't you think?' she shouted to her daughter, who was opening baby-food in their little kitchen.

Frustration made Frank say 'Do you know what he's got from me?'

'Ooh, let me see – maybe the chin, just a hint?'

'The push-chair.'

'Don't be silly, Frank,' his wife shouted through. 'He's got your personality.'

'No you haven't, have you, my little fellow,' her mother cooed, shaking Jason's hand to reassure him.

In most ways Frank was happy living modestly in their council flat in Hoxton. 'Who needs a big house? You can only be in one room at once,' he explained to Diane. ('Unless you've got, like, one foot in one room and one foot in the other,' he added.) But he had to think about Diane and the child. He knew she would not want to be married all her life to a stallholder, not that she ever told him so straight out.

After Diane was told she could not have any more children – Frank had asked the doctor 'What, not even a little one?' – it became even more important that he start earning enough money to give her a good time, cheer her up. It was time they could afford to buy Jason a bicycle instead of making up stories about cycling being bad for the bottom. Jason wanted one of those big orange balls you sat and bounced up and down on, and he had not taken to the one Frank made for him out of an old pillow and a plastic bag. Jason had been equally unimpressed with an Action Man carved out of a piece of wood by Frank and dressed by Diane, lovingly but ineptly, in a hand-sewn yellow duster. 'He's in desert camouflage,' Frank explained, but Jason cried nevertheless and hid it under his bed.

Frank's ambitions, awakened by the desire to please his family, never really went back to sleep. As he sold tools on frosty days at the market he worked on his better future.

'Arthur, what do you reckon's going to be the thing this year?'

'*Rock 'ard tomatoes, clear 'em up!* Friend of mine reckons there's a killing in coconuts. He says people don't realize you can make the shells into bowls and stuff. Cheapest bowls in the world, coconut halves.'

'Plus you get, you know, coconut thrown in.' Frank was trying to be enthusiastic. 'Hang about, hang about, wouldn't they roll about all over the table?'

Arthur Douglas thought about it and then said 'Yes.'

1972 started with a wave of disruption during the miners' strike. There were arguments in the Stubbs' household as Diane put the miners' case patiently in the candle-lit interior. Frank said 'I don't give a screw about working class solidarity – those power cuts are killing my mum's tropical fish.' The fish were her only pleasure in life, now that Grant and Petra had left home and her neighbour Nora had moved out to Hornchurch.

Soon a commercial angle emerged out of those dark and miserable evenings: candles were running out. Frank watched as a few sharp traders found supplies – some of the candles fat and creamy, looking suspiciously as though they had been lifted from churches – and sold them for tidy money. Frank made a few inquiries among his contacts but got nowhere. His last contact told him 'You think I'd let *you* have them if *I* had them? I should bollocks. Still, a word in your what have you, Frank: France.'

Frank had never been to France and he thought it was about time, but first he had to come by some money to buy the candles with.

'How much have we got in the post office, Di?'

'Forty-seven pounds. And it's staying there.'

'D'you think your dad would fancy a little investment?'

'Don't even think about it.'

Frank only turned to Diane's father because he knew he couldn't lose on this deal. He picked a good moment, phoning up the good councillor three hours into a power cut when candles were on everyone's mind. Frank tried to calm Diane down by saying this would bring him closer to his parents-in-law. Diane said 'How *could* you?' Two days later Frank set off in his van with cash in the dashboard, a map of Boulogne and a borrowed French dictionary, printed (he saw) in 1904. He only knew three French words: *Jeux sans frontières*, and he had no idea what they meant.

On the ferry he looked up the word *candle* and found that there were pages missing between *bothersome* ('*ennuyeux*' – Jesus, Frank thought, how do you say that?) and *she is in the chorus* ('*elle chante dans les choeurs*'). He didn't panic or turn back.

'What's French for candles?' he asked the woman in the empty duty-free shop.

'We don't have any,' she replied in Dover English.

'Watch my mouth. I don't want any,' he said. 'Well, I *do* actually.'

'We haven't got any. This is a duty-free.'

'Listen up, darling, what's the French, the *French* for candle?'

'I should think it's –' she thought visibly – 'can*delle*.'

'What, like the English only with a bit of wallop at the back end?'

'I'm only guessing. I've never got off the ship at the other side.'

He went into his first hardware store and after a few minutes of hard explaining he came away with nothing except a dislike of the French. He walked about, not enjoying himself, and then darkness fell and he saw a cheap-looking hotel. He went in, slept between cold sheets next to a noisy bathroom, and then got up. He felt guilty about not spending the night in the van.

'Have you got any *flat* bread?' he asked in the café when they offered him baguette.

'You are in Frrarnce now,' the man said kindly. 'We like our bread crisp on the outside and soft in the inside.'

'That's how we like our tortoises,' Frank said, trying to be funny. 'Tortoises. You know. Never mind.'

Towards the end of the day, a long Saturday of increasingly desperate wandering, he found a shop where they spoke good English and told him that Boulogne had been emptied of candles some time ago by British day-trippers. They also pointed out that candles were *bougies*.

'Boodgies,' he repeated, standing there in his wet raincoat under a ceiling of hanging ironmongery.

'No, *non*, the g is not so hard. It should pass softly in the mouth, like an oyster.'

'Well, fuck me.'

Frank did not manage to leave Boulogne before the shops shut, so now he had to wait until Monday morning when they reopened. He thought about driving home but his investments had already piled up: ferry, hotel, two days' lost earnings, blistered feet. The only way he could go home now was with candles in his van or a shame-bag over his head.

On Sunday Frank tried to ring home but couldn't understand how the telephone worked. He had slept the night in the van, leaving his clothes feeling damply horrible. These were the first nights he had spent away from Diane in eight years and he was missing her. He drove inland for an hour, located a large supermarket, parked his van in the car park and saw through the rest of the afternoon by drinking a litre and a quarter of red wine. By six in the evening he could be heard singing at the top of his voice inside the van in the middle of the deserted tarmac. By half-past he was asleep.

Frank successfully filled five trolley-loads of candles, his eyelids heavy in his bad head. A small crowd gathered as he stacked. Comments were passed, meaningless to Frank.

One aspect of the buying operation he could cope with was the sums – he watched the long-haired student at the check-out for sharp practice. 'I see you've got the decimal here too,' Frank said when he started to trust him. 'We've got the decimal, now.'

The trip back felt good to Frank. He always enjoyed going home, from wherever he was. He sat on the ferry and took pleasure in his tea. Naturally, he knew that as a commercial enterprise this trip had been flawed: he had bought retail when he should have bought wholesale, the scale of the operation was too small to get excited about, and he didn't have enough French to put behind his ear. But even Marco Polo had probably started out quietly, Frank thought, with just a string bag of merchandise.

Frank had not been anticipating problems from the customs authorities.

'What do we have in the back of our vehicle, sir?'

'I don't know about you, but I've got a few domestic items here.'

The uniformed officer was tall and had to bend down low to get his head under the level of the roof. Frank had only opened the window a few inches so the man's head came at him as a horizontal band. 'Perhaps you could wind down your window a little more, sir,' he was forced to say. Frank did so. 'Are these items for your personal use?' the man went on, as if he were reading the words from a card.

'Yes, me and my wife Diane.'

'Could you open her up for me please?'

'Yup, I've got the keys right here.'

It looked worse than it was because when the van door

was opened a number of plastic-wrapped packets of candles fell out onto the customs man's feet. The packets went on slithering out for a few seconds, then stopped, and then a few more slid out. For a while the load looked as though it had settled, and then another few packets slithered out.

'I should have asked for a box to put them in,' Frank said.

'May I ask if you have an import licence, sir?'

'I told you, they're for the wife and I, what with all the black-outs.' Frank started to throw the packets back into the van. 'The wife's afraid of the dark, comes over all clammy.'

'I don't much like it myself.'

'Want to buy a few?' It was an entrepreneurial reflex, which Frank immediately regretted. Fortunately, he seemed to have got away with it.

'I wouldn't like to deprive you and your wife,' he said, as Frank scrambled around at his feet. 'Besides, haven't you heard? The strike's ended. No more power cuts.'

Frank sank to his knees on the oily concrete and experienced a moment of pure humiliation. He felt the whole burden of his smallness and failure, glimpsed Diane and Jason waiting for him at home. Oh, this was bad news.

But only a fool worries, Frank suddenly thought. He straightened up and said into the tall man's face 'Still, they'll do great for dinner parties.'

Frank Sinatra

Frank was still over the limit and knew he was, but he drove his car to the furniture shop. He could feel the lager sitting with him in the driver's seat. Janice was quiet, staring ahead of her at the corridor of road. She had furniture brochures on her knees but did not look as though she wanted to read them.

'Happy?' he asked, a question he had put to Diane a thousand times.

'Yes,' Janice smiled and said.

Diane's way of putting the same question had been 'Not too unhappy?' Frank was too tired to spend long wondering whether that was significant or merely interesting.

Over the dry clicking of the indicator, he asked quietly 'Would you mind staying around this evening, see me through all this?'

'Mm-hmm,' she nodded, her top teeth sunk into her lower lip.

'That's . . . kind.'

She looked sideways at him. 'Don't go all sensitive on me now, Frank, just when I've got you down as a hard case.'

He looked levelly at Janice and then turned his eyes back to the brake lights of the car in front.

Cuffleys Furniture ('Try Us – We Might Have It!') was not

as well-stocked as Frank had hoped from their handouts. It looked like they were waiting for a big delivery. Frank showed them the smoked-glass table, the leather settee and armchairs he had picked out. They said they would have to order them from Sweden. When Frank said he needed it within the hour the three assistants' heads all began to shake, two of them in quick, waggly negatives and the third with slow sweeps of his head. Frank began to panic.

'What am I supposed to say to my people – you'll have to stand up for a bit, the sofa's in Sweden?'

'Frank, stop it,' Janice said, tugging his sleeve, urging him. 'Buy something else, these are nice.'

'You don't understand, it's in the catalogue. I've permutated all the options.' The whole point for Frank was that he had intended from now on to be in charge of his own destiny, and now he was compromising again.

Frank was too disenchanted to give Janice all his attention as she steered him around the showroom, followed at various distances by the three dead-faced men in overalls. He said 'Yes, I suppose those will have to do,' to an expensive suite of low-slung leather and chrome. He took Janice's advice and gave his approval to a glass table. 'Sure, let's put them in a big bag and have them sent over. I don't want to spend so long chewing this over that it loses its flavour.' They added a hatstand, four swivel chairs and a cupboard.

'I'm paying cash so I'll be wanting the usual ten per cent minusing,' he said to the senior of the three men. Frank always asked. He believed passionately that you were going nowhere if you didn't try it on.

'What ten per cent is that?'

'Please, come on boys, I'm standing here – we all want to go home.'

'We don't do discounts.'

'What are you – Harrods? Course you do discounts. You probably haven't sold anything full price since Shakespeare.'

They settled on five per cent off but the price still knocked the breath out of Frank.

'I could have bought my flat off the council for half as much,' Frank said as he counted out the money.

They still had to haggle over delivery, and now the men had the money in their hands they took more wearing down. Frank had to pay most of the five per cent back to persuade them to bring it round before eight o'clock.

The shops were beginning to close. Across the street an awning was being wound back with a squeaky metal lever by a greengrocer. The roads were filling up with even more cars, some throbbing with music.

'We've got about half a second to get the rest,' Frank said as he pulled Janice's hand towards his car. Maybe you weren't supposed to hold your secretary's hand, he didn't know.

They found a general store that was just closing. Frank parked the car half on the pavement and they went in. Two of the staff had their coats on. Frank stood with his back to the door, barring the way. He said: 'Nobody leaves.' Everybody froze, eyes flickering. 'I'm having a party so I'll be wanting ashtrays, balloons, maybe some party hats, paper serviettes, paper plates, three or four pictures of, er, hunting scenes – '

'Are we invited?' the plain girl in the coat asked.

'Sorry love, Frank *Sinatra* only gets to come because he's agreed to go round with the gherkins.' One of the assistants had started to help Janice fill a wire basket. 'Hey, yeah, I'd like some of those paper mats with the little holes in, and plastic flowers – have you got any of those?'

'We've got dried flowers.'

'Are they as realistic as plastic flowers?' Nobody could think of an answer. He waved his arm in little circles to hurry the reply. 'No worries, sort me out a bunch anyway. What am I saying, *five* bunches.'

Back in the car, Janice was looking amused. When Frank had driven the offside wheels down off the pavement and they were heading back to the office he said 'Did someone tell a funny?'

'You're an odd bloke, aren't you?'

'If you let that novelty salad set fall off your knees I'll give you such a telling off.'

'Well not so much odd. You live in a world of your own.'

'You've got it,' Frank agreed. 'Whose do you live in?'

'I mean, this evening hasn't exactly been planned, has it? Do you always do things at the last moment?'

Frank leaned over, avoiding the salad set, and kissed her on the lips, insistently and full-bloodedly but without violating her mouth too much. With Frank's eyes off the road, a kink entered the car's trajectory. Janice did not react visibly.

'See that? I'd never have enjoyed that as much as I did if I'd had to plan it, know what I mean?'

Frank was watching her. She was considering, but considering what – suing, putting her cap in? Neither, Frank hoped, not yet. He wanted her to say nothing until after the party, because he, too, was considering Janice.

'Frank?' she said.

'Here.'

'Do you often act like that?'

'No,' he said as he drove.

Frank wondered how much he should tell Janice about his past, about his wife. His marriage had unbalanced his relationship with other women.

'Not at all,' Frank added. Soon he found himself saying 'Technically, I'm still married,' and then regretting it.

'In that case you're very naughty,' Janice said.

They climbed the steps to the office. Frank was carrying the doilies, plastic basket-effect bowls for the crisps and four pictures of sunsets on black velvet. Janice struggled behind him with strings of tinsel and a safari-motif umbrella holder. Frank opened the door to find Archie with Nobby Spicer. Archie had a brown ale in his hand and was talking expansively. Nobby was sitting alongside a bottle of whisky, its neck already empty. Archie stopped speaking when Frank came in.

'I got here early,' Nobby said. 'In case I could do anything to assist, wipe a glass or two.'

'You'll do nothing, Nobby. Just sit there, have yourself your own happy hour.'

Nobby was not looking good. His face was tired, bloated and red, with little veins starting to show as purple threads on the wings of his nose. He was only a few years older than Frank but he looked as though he had spent his whole life tethered outside in a howling gale. For Frank, this winded Nobby in the shirt with one side of his collar sticking up could never be anything but an after-image of the man with a light tan and ballet-dancer's legs in the sixties and early seventies, who for ten years made defenders look as though they were playing football in skis.

'Where's the food, Archie?'

'Here it is,' he said, smiling and wearing a new slyness on his face. With his hand he indicated a small ginger cake, a Cornish pasty and an apple with a bite out of it. Archie went on 'Leastways, that's what I'll be eating.'

Frank, tense and hot in the head, said 'Can you come into the other room for a moment?'

'Say it to me in here,' Archie answered as he reached across for his apple. Frank knocked it out of his hand and it scudded across the room, smashing into the skirting board. Behind him, Frank heard Janice's knees click as she bent to pick it up. Diplomatically, she went back out to the car.

'Archie,' Frank said, almost gagging on the strength of his anger, but not wanting to do anything in front of Nobby, 'as I have said, we can level this one in the morning. What say you just disappear now, then tomorrow we can straighten out one or two details, starting with your face.'

Archie was not listening. 'I was standing there in the supermarket about to load up,' he said, 'and then I got to thinking: *Nah, Nah.* So I came back to pick up one or two things –'

'Can it, Archie. If I want you to make any noise I'll come and put my foot in your balls, how's that?' Frank said and started to look around for nails to hang his pictures on, maintaining a pretence of normality. Nobby had managed to keep his party smile on but it was looking more and more taut and thin. He raised the bottle to his lips. Archie stayed sitting, occasionally drinking from his own bottle. Janice reappeared with the final load from the car, looking nervous. Frank caught her just outside the door and said quietly 'Janice, Archie's just resigned from the firm. Can you do me a big one – go to the off-licence and get me this much's worth of jungle juice, various.' He gave her some twenties. 'Go easy on the fizzy water, J., remember this is supposed to be a knees-up, not a coffee morning. And don't go spoiling yourself carrying more boxes, get hold of a delivery boy.' She nodded and disappeared.

When Frank returned Archie was telling Nobby 'Of course, you was never as good as Bestie. He could turn on the sharp end of a fucking pin. I tell you, if he'd have shaved off some of his hair he'd have made you look like a total dead-arse *every* Saturday instead of just most of the time.'

Nobby was looking miserable, putting the whisky to his lips regularly as if doing it kept out what Archie was saying. By now his bottle was clear glass half way down the label.

'You insult my guest once more,' Frank shouted, a fleck of foam jumping from his mouth, 'I mean it, I'll total your nose, Archie, I'll make you pay in teeth.'

'Not only that,' Archie went on. For a moment Frank could not accept that this painful scene was happening – how could anyone harm the feelings of a legend? It was like kicking a racehorse, scarring a baby. 'Now, as I hear it, you need a bottle of strong just to turn your alarm clock off in the morning.'

Frank came storming across the room, picked Archie up with both hands and threw him across the carpet. It seemed to be what Archie had been working towards. Nobby had turned his sclerotic eyes to the ground. Archie got up like a giraffe, first straightening his legs then pushing off with his hands. He came back at Frank, swaying and struggling. Frank realized that the bottle in Archie's hand had been the last of a six-pack. What am I going to do, Frank thought, just show him the door or put his head through it, glass and all? Instead he decided to restrain Archie, which he did by catching his hands and bending them so that Archie had to sink to his knees, groaning thickly but becoming less disabled by drink all the time. Still holding his old partner's hands, Frank moved behind him, crossing Archie's chubby arms in front of his throat and putting his knee into his back. Frank hadn't performed this sort of move for years.

'Now then,' Frank said, holding the pose, 'I want you to

say you're sorry to my friend Nobby Spicer here, who is a living *legend*.'

'Leg*less* is what he fucking is,' Archie said, his face passing from pink to red on the way to purple.

Nobby, one hand on his head as a mark of confusion, started to say 'It's very kind of you Frank, but –'

'No buts, Nobby, absolutely no buts. This one's on me.' Frank pushed further in with his knee, but already his anger was tinged with pity. Archie squealed. Frank said 'Say after me: I apologize Nobby, you are a legend.'

'I, I –' Archie was having trouble breathing.

Frank wanted to get it over with. He prompted: 'A-pol-o – come on, you can remember.'

'A-pol-o –'

'Gize – keep going.' Nobby now had both hands on his head and his eyes clenched.

'Gi –'

There was a knock and suddenly Frank's sister was a yard inside the door, a glittery handbag swinging at her elbow. She stepped further into the room and looked at the two panting men and the drunk.

'I can't say I'm surprised,' Petra drawled, taking off her red leather gloves one finger at a time. 'I just *knew* I'd arrive before Princess Margaret.'

Easy Ride Chauffeur Hire

Frank took a while to recover from the candles. His business horizons closed in around him again. He moved out of hand tools, into pets (not a success, not a success at all), back into tools and then into clothing. A gross of shirts brought many of Frank's customers out in a rash. They complained in numbers.

'Look, purple spots.'

'Actually,' Frank said, 'they suit you. Straight up, it makes your skin more interesting.'

'I want my money back.'

'Not a smell, mate.'

'I'll take you to the Office of Fair Trading.'

'I don't care if you take me ten-pin bowling, John, you're not getting your money back. That's all I get nowadays, threats, talk about the law. OK, so once in a while you buy yourself a bit of duff — so do I, so does everyone. You supposed I *asked* for a bum lot of shirts? Exactly how wet do you think I am?'

When the tenth complainer came along, Frank decided he had had more than enough. 'Watch this,' he said to the man with the little dog and clipped moustache. 'You don't like my shirts, see what you think of my blazers.' He made a pile of the remaining shirts and put a match to them in the middle of the market. People stopped to warm their hands on the fire. Frank stood by, feeling extravagant.

He was disciplined by the Market Traders' Association and stayed at home for a couple of weeks to think about his future.

'Di, what am I going to do?' he asked on the third day.

'What do you *want* to do?' she said again. She was washing up after breakfast, standing at the sink on one leg, the other foot resting on the inside of her knee. Frank watched her.

'Let's go to bed, sex is different during the day.'

Diane left her hands in the water and looked over her shoulder, smiling. Frank was charmed.

'My brother's started mini-cabbing,' she said.

'He's given up waiting for the revolution, then. Or weren't there any vacancies?'

'Don't be unnecessary, Frank. He's got responsibilities now. Wife, kid.'

'OK, don't rub it in. Have I ever kept you short?'

'Yes, you have,' Diane said, suddenly quiet and serious. She went on staring into the sink. For a minute the only sound was a melancholy sloshing.

'Short*ish*, on occasions, never exactly *long*.'

'It would be nice to go on holidays like other people do. You know, holidays, on an aeroplane, with suitcases.'

Frank was aggrieved again. 'Honest, Di, I spend all day thinking of ways out of this. I just want to do it my way, on my own.'

'You're not on your own, though, you've got me and Jason.' She dried her hands on a tea-towel and walked towards Frank, who was sitting at the table, wearing the free sun visor he had just cut out from the back of the cornflake packet. 'And you don't want me to work.'

'Don't start on that,' he said. 'Down the street I grew up in, a wife and mother only worked if her old man was away doing a stretch.'

Diane sat down on Frank's knee. He rubbed her thigh all the way up from her knee. Soon he was lowering his mouth to the precise place where he knew, without looking, under the pale polyester, he would find her right nipple.

She put her hand over her breast just in time.

'Phone Andy Theofanopoulou first, then I'm yours all day.'

Frank ruminated. 'Including lunchtime?' he asked. She removed her hand and pulled his face to her breast. Through the fabric he mumbled 'But if I catch you faking it I'm going to stop your housekeeping money.'

Andy Theofanopoulou was a friend of Frank's who had abandoned his household-linens stall in the market (and his catchphrase 'Hey, Mrs!') to become a chauffeur. He had since sprouted thick gold around his neck and on his broad Greek fingers. On the phone he told Frank again 'Oil money. These Arabs are *drowning*. They go on a shopping bender all week and by Friday they've still got more than they started out with. I tell you Frank, these guys don't have wallets, they go around with their dosh in *carrier-bags*.'

The chauffeur-hire company Andy worked for said they would fix Frank up with a car and a peaked cap and told him to buy a grey uniform.

He arrived at the office looking like an usher at a wedding. They took him around the back. 'What's this, a fucking Lada Basic?' he said when he was shown his car.

'It's a Datsun. You're down to take Mrs Steinglitz and her kids to school, St John's Wood. If you're late we kick you off the forecourt.'

'No shit,' he said.

Later that day he met Andy Theofanopoulou in the drivers' room, talking in Greek to his brother Theo Theofanopoulou. Together they were wearing enough heavy jewellery to open up their own heavy jewellery shop.

'Sure,' he said, 'we all start off with Mrs Steinglitz and the little Steinglitzes. Who do you expect for starters – Sheik Ali Ben Mussafa?' A few of the other drivers sniggered without looking up from their cards. Frank didn't like not knowing what was going on.

'I heard Tommy managed to park himself on Mrs S. one morning, the way he told it,' one of them said.

'She's not easy on the eyes though, is she, couple of chins, face as ugly as a turkey's gubbins.'

'Don't know about you, I never look at the dashboard when I'm revving the engine.' It felt like they were used to waiting around playing cards.

'How long before I'm working with a decent motor?' Frank interjected. He had promised Diane and Jason trips to the countryside playing with the electric windows, picnics from the back of a Rolls Royce. It was bad enough having to work for somebody without having to do it in a Datsun.

'Month or two in the Dat, then on to Mercs if Skuse thinks you're clean. He might start to talk Roller six months after that, but you'll probably have to let him kip with your wife first.'

Larry Skuse, the owner, was a showy businessman. He was flamboyant enough to wear a white linen suit regularly, and to wear it with a tulip in the lapel. He had a complex relationship with his drivers – he wanted them to stand up to him but also to know when to obey. Frank took the trouble to learn how to handle Larry, because he wanted the keys to the pink Rolls then being driven by Nelson Tunks. He had heard anyway that Nelson had more problems with drugs and drink than a man can live with and still drive such an expensive car.

. After six weeks Frank was moved off the Datsun. He was sad to see Doris, Reuben and Rebecca Steinglitz go but they couldn't afford the blue Mercedes he graduated to. They bought him a battery-lit St Christopher and he said 'Take care, kids.'

Frank learnt to hang around in the drivers' room waiting for the next job. He normally just listened in.

'Harry had a bloke did a runner on him yesterday. The guy's been chalking up the hours over six, seven days. He's been dragging Harry's nuts all over town –'

'Also, Tuesday last he only goes to a restaurant, doesn't he, keeps Harry waiting five hours, doesn't he, and then throws a sickie.'

'He doesn't! Drops a big spit on the, what, on the back seat?'

'Yeah, Indian. Harry had to sluice out a quart of chicken marsala.'

'I can tell you from personal, that stuff would leave a stain on a, on a fucking –'

'On fucking *water*.'

'Right. So yesterday the punter, smart Lebanese or some-such, Libyan, just as Harry's starting to insist on a few quid up front, loses him in Selfridges. He's out the side door before you can say Gaddafi, and pinned to the back of the driver's seat you know what Harry finds? Piece of paper with the words *Thanks for the ride, Mr Peanut*. Now, is he a cunt or is he a cunt?'

Frank's rides in the Mercedes were usually foreign men in suits. He generally had them for a day or two and they treated him like an adjunct to the upholstery of the driver's seat. Sometimes this suited Frank but at other times he grew lonely up front in his cap, so he talked.

'Where are you from then – Norway is it? Germany?'

'Denmark.' The blond businessman stopped looking out of the window and turned decisively to his paper.

'Hell of a thing,' Frank persisted. 'Home of the old, er, doings.'

'Bacon, probably,' he said from behind his pages.

'There's a coincidence. I had a top egg man where you're sitting yesterday, giving a speech to the Egg Board or what have you. I said to him "I expect you get them free, don't you?" He says "What?" I say "Eggs." He says "I can't eat them – too much cholesterol." "That's a bit of a pisser," I say. "Between you and me," he says, "nothing good ever came out of the back end of a chicken!" And this chap's like *Mr Egg* in the country, he's the Big Omelette in the whole of the UK. How'd you like that, you being in bacon?'

'I'm not connected with bacon,' he answered.

Frank could feel it coming, what he'd often wanted to say: 'Yeah, I've had all sorts in the back of my motor.'

'You can drop me here,' the Dane said. That was how it usually ended.

Frank was good at his job. He drove like an old hand, protecting his car as though it were his own and washing it with a deft chamois, as gently as he would a baby. He learnt the West End by heart, helped by Diane who sat at the kitchen table with a map.

'Royal Garden Hotel to the Playboy Club, taking in the Science Museum,' she said.

'That's not a very likely itinerary, is it?'

'Come on.'

'Really, Diane, I could do this with my face on backwards: left into Kensington High Street, past the Albert Hall, straight, straight, straight – no, hang about I've forgotten the frigging Science Museum. Right into Queen's Gate, drop off the ride, sit in the car, sit, sit, pick up the punter again, "How was it, nice was it? Yeah I love all that science myself –" '

'Get on with it.'

'Back into Exhibition Road, through the gates, wind her up down South Carriage Drive, point out Rotten Row – maybe tell my crack about how many nobs you can get in a pair of jodhpurs – then whip her across Park Lane, back down the one-way, hang a left and Have a Nice Day.'

'Good. What's the quickest way from the Post Office Tower to our flat?'

'Don't be simple, Di. Nobody wants to come to our flat.'

Frank was earning well but to do so he had to work long hours. It hurt, putting money into someone else's pocket, and he hated spending evenings away from Diane. He often had to hang around in the hotel district, where he would wait for the call from control. Sometimes it came from the dismembered radio voice of Larry Skuse himself, who liked to be known as a doer as well as a signer of cheques. He used to say he was prepared to help out his workers in any way, although he stopped saying that the day the soil pipe in the staff toilet exploded.

'Mercedes Fifteen. Where are you Frank? Over.'

'Fifteen. I'm in Hamilton Place, Lal. Been here so long I've got ivy growing up my radials.'

'Say again? Over.'

'Hamilton Place, as it goes.'

'Frank, if you don't start saying "over" like it says in your manual I'll rip your bloody radio out. Over.'

'Over, OVER – *Jee*sus.' There was a pause. 'Over.'

'Thank you. I've got something special for you here. Witney Gudgeon, the American tennis champion, supposed to be a cow as you may know but you'd better treat her well. Twelve forty-five at the Inn on the Park, going to Wimbledon. Got it? Over.'

'Trust me, Larry. Over and out. Over.'

She kept Frank waiting twenty minutes. The journey started off smoothly. His young blonde passenger sat quietly chewing gum, attractive in a hard-boned way.

'My guys told me I'd be getting a stretch limo,' she drawled, two hundred yards down the road.

Frank looked in his rear-view mirror, asked 'You short of room in the back?'

'Sure I'm short of room. If I want a Mickey Mouse machine, I'll ask for one. Fucking first-round losers' car.'

Frank said 'Do you want me to get out and lengthen it for you?'

She grunted, swung her legs up on to the seat and went quiet. They were good legs but Frank was an idealist – good legs were not enough.

'Shit country,' she said.

Frank had had happy experiences with Americans. He liked the way they spoke (closer, in many ways, to the way he spoke than most City businessmen in London) and how they usually treated him, more like they shared the same planet. Maybe it was because he was used to better that he decided he had to put the woman on the right track.

'You what?' he asked.

'Shit country,' she repeated. 'I'd rather be sitting in a dustbowl in fucking Mexico than here.'

'*I'd* rather you were.'

'Don't crap around with me, just drive the car. I'm paying for a bit of peace – not that I need it to beat the fat Brit they've lined me up with today. Boy is she a sight. I've seen better footwork on a donkey-farm.'

'I guess it puts people off, having to play a sad old bitch like you.'

She looked severe and cold in Frank's rear-view mirror.

'Somehow I don't believe you'll be in the same job tomorrow,' she said and sat back in the seat with a bitter look.

'If it happens it'll have been worth it,' he said. But Frank suddenly realized she was probably right. Ms Gudgeon's handlers were big clients who would complain hard, so Larry would kick him out.

The way Frank saw it, if you've got to go, go loudly. He started driving the wrong way, heading out west towards Putney. His passenger had closed her eyes, so she missed Barnes, Richmond and Isleworth.

'We should be here by now,' she opened her eyes to say. She sounded more mellow now but it was too late, they were parked in a slip road to the West Middlesex Drainage Works.

'Would you believe it,' Frank said, 'it looks like my electrics have packed up. I'm afraid you'll have to walk.'

For a minute or two the young tennis player shouted a lot, demanding to know where they were, hitting Frank on the shoulder. He sat impassively for a while then fetched her big tennis bag out of the boot and repeated that she had better get out and walk. Eventually she did, her language dark with American swear-words that captivated Frank, who was always on the look-out for colourful abuse. 'If I miss my match, you're *dead*,' she shouted back.

'See if you can organize it,' he said as he watched her drag her bag off down the dusty track.

For twenty minutes Frank sat looking at the birds circling against the clear blue horizon, before starting up the car and driving back into town.

The whole business took a few days to die down. As the tabloids told the country the next day, Witney Gudgeon flagged down a sewerage maintenance van and demanded to be taken to Wimbledon, but arrived too late and was disqualified. Her British opponent moved apologetically into the next round, where she lost to a player from Cameroon. The press tracked Frank down and he was quoted as saying 'I did it because she called Britain a shit country. I like Americans. Yes, the manager of Easy Ride Chauffeur Hire is behind me all the way on this. We will be contesting any case that is brought against me or Easy Ride Chauffeur Hire.'

The publicity worked out well for Larry Skuse so he didn't sack Frank. 'What can I say, Frank,' he said, 'except that if you do it again I'm going to use the heavy spanner on you, nothing personal.' Public sentiment was squarely against Witney Gudgeon and Frank enjoyed a day's minor celebrity as the man who took a stand against arrogance. The threatened court case for loss of earnings was dropped when even the player's father, her manager, said it would teach her 'and teach her good. She's always had a mouth like a goddam loudspeaker at a demolition derby.'

Frank took over the pink Rolls that autumn when Nelson Tunks was arrested for driving with an excess of alcohol in his blood and a lump of marijuana the size of a bar of soap strapped under the steering column.

Leaning against his blue Bentley, Andy Theofanopoulou spoke to Frank as he sat in his new car. 'How does it feel? Like a good woman?'

'It's a bleeding car, Andy.'

'Yeah, but they're just like women, you know? I always say you've got to make love to a woman like you're driving a car.'

'I think you've got that backwards, my son.'

'You do it your way, Frank.'

'The only reason I want the Roller is so I can take Di and the kid out for a picnic. I've bought a little Kodak to take some snaps of us.'

'You're one soft git, Frank.'

His commission and status upped, Frank started to drive the very rich around, a family of whooping, royal Bahrainis, two troubled and frowning Saudi sisters, a Nigerian with four oil rigs in his back garden. The VIP suite at Heathrow, the parking arrangements outside the Carlton Club, a Muslim's dietary requirements – this was the world Frank entered.

It was the silent world of service. Sitting in his peaked cap, surrounded by glass, Frank stared out at the road.

Irritation and Disappointment

'Good man, Petra. You're looking sharp.'

'Thank you, Frank.'

Archie was panting as he raised himself from his knees, tapping his pockets to check nothing had fallen out. He said 'Don't bother to introduce me, I'm fucking off.' He walked uncertainly to the door. Frank followed him. Standing by the door, Archie started 'There's one thing I want to say before I go –' but Frank bustled him outside and shut the door.

'So that's that,' Frank said.

'What?' his sister asked. She had removed her gloves.

Archie opened the door and managed to say 'Gobshite' before Frank swung round and kicked the door shut.

'I'll be able to offer you a full range of gargle in a moment or two, Pet – what'll it be: G and T?'

'What is this, an overcoat party?' she said, looking at Frank and Nobby.

Frank also looked around. 'Yeh, let's take our coats off,' he said. The three of them did so. 'Tell you the truth, Petra, you've caught me on the hop here. I'm running well late.'

Bending at the knees to look at Nobby, who had lit a

cigarette and was resting his forearms on his thighs, she said 'Don't I know your face? Wait a sec – don't you play the old man in the ad for expectorant?'

Frank jumped in irritably. 'You've got all the social graces, haven't you, you lot down in the scampi-belt. This is Nobby Spicer, the famous footballer.'

'Oh, pardon me for existing. Who do you play for, then, Gillingham?'

Frank groaned and took their coats. Nobby said 'I haven't kicked a ball in nine years.'

'What team did you used to play for?' she asked without much interest.

'I moved around towards the end, fact I changed clubs so often they used to call me –'

'I used to like Chelsea, they had all the nice-looking men, you know, with the perms.'

Petra had become more nasal since she moved to Essex. It sounded to Frank like she needed tuning. In his part of East London you only spoke through your nose if your mouth was broken. She was tall and stately, her dark hair pulled up tight. To Frank she resembled a Spanish flamenco dancer who had carried on just past her prime.

'Mind you,' she said, walking around idly, 'I don't know one end of a football from the other.' Frank carried on draping some tinsel along a curtain rail. 'Drinks are in the other room, is it?'

'I told you, the booze is on the way. Anyway, where's my sexy niece Dawn – at home looking after your hubby, Mastermind?'

'I would have thought you'd had enough of teenage girls to last you a lifetime,' Frank's sister said with a dry jeer in her voice.

Frank looked at her coldly. 'Some things I don't find funny.'

'I suppose not,' Petra said, more circumspectly. 'Anyway, I left her in McDonald's. Dawn doesn't enjoy her food now unless she gets it in a polystyrene carton.'

'Food,' Frank realized, and winced. 'I'd better get some in.' There was a rap on the door pane and Frank shouted out 'If that's you, Archie, I am going to come and open up some of your veins.'

'Anybody at home?' It was Ron Rumsby. Frank would have preferred someone else, or nobody, rather than Ron Rumsby. He was useful in business, but so were paperclips.

'I'm running behind time, Ron.'

'Ticketty-boo, Frank.'

'Eh?'

'You know what they say.'

'Yeah.'

'The early bird catches the worm.'

'That's fascinating Ron, really major. Perhaps you'd like to gab along to my sister about that while I order up the catering.'

Frank watched Ron sidle secretively over to Petra, who was sharing an awkward silence with Nobby. Ron's trousers stopped four or five inches from his shoes, that was the sad thing.

Over on his chair Nobby was slipping further and further between his own knees. Frank watched Ron looking over each shoulder twice, checking, before he spoke to Petra.

They were taking a long while to answer Frank's telephone call.

'Jack's Fish, what is it?' Frank heard.

'Jack, this is Frank.'

'I can't talk, mate, my fat's jumping.'

'I'm in for some fish, Jack, if you can do me.'

'Fish, what is this – a fish and chip shop?'

'So you're not too busy to be sarky,' Frank said. Grant had just come in with their mother. Frank waved hallo and, pointing at the telephone, mimed the word 'telephone' with big movements of his mouth.

Jack was coming to the end of his sentence, saying: '. . . bleeding all over the saveloys.'

'Can you do me an order of fifty fish and chips for nine-ish?'

'What, fifty? That's, like, a *shoal* of fish –'

'And could you send your Bridget round with them, you'd be doing me a blinder.'

'She's only just come back from casualty, Frank –'

'Magic. She's a fucking trooper, that's what she is.' As Frank put the phone back he thought: Didn't I plan to have *nibbles*? What happened to the idea of little squares of toast with prawns on?

'Any chance of a beer, Frank?' Grant asked. Frank's brother had done his best to smarten up. He had a silky cravat on, threaded into some kind of silver ring and dangling in an open-necked shirt.

'In your own time, Frank,' Ron said. 'When you're ready.'

'Anybody else want to tell me how to run my party?' Frank said with a frenzied smile. He rushed around with ashtrays, trying to find some furniture to put them on. 'There,' he said. 'Get smoking. You all right there, Nobby? You're looking a shade, I don't know.'

'I'm well stonkered, Frank.'

'Frankly, Nobby, if God meant us to stay off the bevvy he'd have shut down the off-licence in Dalston Lane, know what I mean?'

There were a few items left in boxes but Frank decided there was no time to put them out. He had to talk to his family before the showbusiness element arrived. (Where was the drink? Where was the furniture? Where was Jason?)

'Glad you could make it, Mum. When did you get the hat?'

'I've always had it,' she said listlessly.

'It's the tops, that hat, isn't it, Grant?'

'It's a good hat,' Grant said.

'New dress?'

'I bought it in 1962.'

'There's nothing dowdy about that dress,' Grant said. Grace Stubbs looked at him closely for a moment.

'Are you still getting noise from the neighbours?' Frank asked. To his left he heard Petra saying to Ron 'Have you got a light?' Ron answering 'There's a funny story attached to this lighter,' Petra replying 'What's that over there, is it a picture?'

'The walls in our block are like paper,' his mother answered.

'They should shoot those architects,' Frank said. 'I wouldn't put walls like that in a, in a, I don't know. It's like, you don't need to get to know your neighbours, because you know them already, you've been listening to them all day through the fucking wall.'

Grant said: 'That's true, actually.'

'Language, Frank.'

Frank remembered the hat now. His mother wore it at Jason's christening. She was fuller in those days, although still thin. It was as though her skin was pumped up then but now a little air was coming out all the time, more each year. When she died they would be able to roll her up tight and bury her in her hatbox. Looking around at old people, which Frank did sometimes, he noticed that they were mainly very fat or very thin. They either wore their flesh like seven overcoats and a couple of scarves, or their bones went all but naked. Frank himself was going down the fat road.

'Do you like the office, Mum?' he asked.

'It's modest,' she said.

'Nah, well, the thing of it is, this is phase one,' Frank told her roughly. He wished he hadn't bothered to praise her hat so much. 'There'll be more people along soon, more of everything.'

Janice appeared at the door with two plastic bags of clinking bottles. She looked hot but had the bloom of the cool evening air on her cheeks. Frank felt proud of her prettiness, as though it made him prettier.

'The rest is coming up,' she gasped. 'Sorry I've been so long.'

'People, this is my personal assistant Janice. Ain't she a dreamboat?' Frank put an arm around her shoulder.

'She's got a lovely pair of carrier-bags on her, Frank, if you get my meaning,' Ron said out of the side of his mouth. Janice smiled wanly.

'Ron, you're a waste.' Frank apologized quietly to Janice: 'Ron here's a business contact. Some people like to have him around because he makes them look sharp, matter of comparison.'

'I heard that, Frank.'

'Seeing as you can't take a joke, Ron, I'll just have to shut my noise, won't I,' he said as he rummaged in one of the boxes for the paper cups. Janice looked in the other, leaning forward slightly in profile, her hips dense inside her skirt. Frank wanted to find a quiet corner of her body and bury his face in it. Stop the party. A quiet corner. Bury his face.

Four boxes were being brought in by the limping Irishman from the off-licence. Frank gave him a five-pound note. He had picked up heavy tipping when he was a driver. Then, if he was given coins instead of paper, he would say 'Thanks. I'll put that just here next to these notes,' or something similarly political. If you tip small – he realized then – it may well be because you are small.

'Right,' Frank said, turning round. His guests were looking stiff and bored. His mother had her back to him but he could predict that her expression was one of sagging melancholy. 'What'll it be?'

'I don't suppose you've got a real glass, have you, Frank? Paper cups give me the creeps,' Petra said.

'No, Petra,' Frank said very clearly and irritably. 'You'll drink it out of paper like everybody else, I'm sorry.'

'I see old Sureshot over there's not too fussed.' Everyone looked at Nobby, who was getting to the bottom of his bottle without the use of a cup of any kind.

Nobby peered upwards and, with a new look of bitterness, said 'What's it to you?'

Petra came towards Frank, saying 'Now this is typical of you, Frank, inviting somebody here to abuse me.' She had moved out of her drawling sarcasm into something stronger and more instinctive. Her index finger had shot out straight at waist level and was pointed at Frank, quivering at him.

'Hold up, hold up.' Frank stepped in. 'I thought I just asked what you all wanted to drink.' He looked round at them all. 'I didn't say anything about who wants a ruddy good row.'

'I'll have a lager, please, Frank,' Grant said.

'I'm doing the ladies first, Grant, all right? Mum, d'you want your usual? Where's she gone?'

She had wandered off into the other room. 'I'm looking for a chair,' he heard her say from the other room.

He went in and brought her back gently, explaining: 'The furniture's on the way.'

'Oh. It's on the way, is it?' she said. She had a way of making him sound like a liar.

There were just three chairs, only two had arms and Nobby was sitting in the only safe one. 'Nobby, let my mum have your chair, would you, she likes a chair with an arm.' Nobby had a go at getting out of the chair, but he was having trouble with his legs. 'No, stay there, I like you where you are. Janice, sorry love, I know you're out of breath.'

'The leg's not completely safe,' she said, getting up.

'Grant' – Frank was determined to see this through – 'come and hold the chair while Mum sits on it.'

'I think I'll stand,' she said. Grant hesitated.

'Mother, come and sit in the chair.'

'It's not safe.'

'*Sit in the fucking chair!*' he shouted. She moved slowly towards it.

'Language,' she and Frank said together. He knew her timing.

Behind him Frank heard the door open. It was Jason with a smile on his face. A few scratchy little hallos came from Frank's dispirited cluster of guests.

'Why so miserable, Granny die or something?' Jason said. Petra looked away with distaste. 'Oh no, there you are.'

Frank said 'Look, help yourself to what you want, people, you're not crippled.' He took two cans of lager and went over to Jason, drinking from one. 'Warm,' he said, looking at the can. He gave the other to his son. 'How was it, Jase? I like the look of that smile.'

'Easy as that,' he said. He ripped off the ring-pull and threw it on to the floor.

'So easy?' Frank relaxed. The money they made on these tickets would pay for the furniture. He could probably afford to let Layla go now – she dragged Frank's outfit down.

'I reckon I'm a natural.'

'Is that what you reckon? So when did that make any difference?' Frank took Jason's cheek in his fingers and squeezed, affectionately. 'Did you get them all?'

'I got more than you asked for.'

'Eh?'

'Top price wasn't twenty-five, it was thirteen and a half.'

'Eh?'

'Yeah.'

'Jason, top whack for *Bitch* is twenty-five.'

'Maybe the guy was doing discounts.'

'Now don't, Jason, don't – Show me the tickets, show me them.'

Jason lifted a fat envelope out of his breast pocket. Now they were in Frank's hands. Tickets for *Bantu Banana*, enough to wallpaper a couple of big rooms.

'Are you joking me here?' Frank said quietly.

Jason was still grinning, but the corners of his mouth were beginning to come down. 'Something not right?'

'You've bought the wrong tickets.'

By not thinking, Frank was managing to stay calm. If he could hold that level of otherworldliness he could be through the next ten seconds. Then he could begin to tackle the ten seconds after that. Unfortunately he already sensed the scum of a bad feeling gathering in his head.

'No way,' Jason said, snatching back the envelope and looking at a ticket. 'Look, this is spot on. I remembered the show because it's got two Bs in it and the theatre's called after a royal geezer.'

'Jason, what's royal about the Lordship Theatre?'

'Oh,' he said, looking at the ticket again, 'have I got that wrong?' Frank took the tickets back gently. Jason was saying 'Yeah, I seem to have been a couple of inches out on that one.'

Frank felt frozen and heavy. He tried to remember – still calm – why he had entrusted Jason with £2,500. Had he been . . . testing himself (oh Lord, what a foolish test)? Or had he been a victim of his feeling, contrary to all the evidence, that today was the start of something, a time when even the gambles looked like certainties?

'Go and grab yourself another drink if you want one,' he told Jason in the blank voice his mother used.

'It's OK then?'

'Yes, you're all right.'

Frank went quietly into the other room and shut the door.

Frank knew *Bantu Banana*. It was the type of play you couldn't give tickets away for even if you promised to wrap them in five-pound notes. Frank remembered a press quote on a billboard outside the theatre: 'This tragic satire deserves to be seen.' As an encouragement, those words ranked alongside a high barbed-wire fence. From what Frank had heard, the play ('Quite rewarding' – *The Arts Council Review*, that was another) had only stayed on this long because it had a cast of just three, and probably no lighting and scenery. Frank's one chance of getting his money back was if the play closed, but that wouldn't happen now that he had sunk that amount of money into it. Trying to persuade a refund out of a box office was, as Archie had put it, 'Like getting a rabbit out of a bicycle'. He might strong-arm a few sales out of one or two dazed tourists, he could advertise discounted tickets, but he would still be left about £2,000 short.

Why was Jason the way he was? When he wasn't being vacant he was being actively stupid. The only time he stopped acting the fool was to *be* a fool.

Everyone Can be Queen

Frank drove on in his pink car. It was not everyone's favourite colour, and effectively barred him from driving serious-minded businessmen or government ministers, but the Arabs thought it was classy and the Roller went down well at weddings. The drivers didn't like doing weddings. The profit margins were low and you got confetti in your guttering.

'I had this wedding on Saturday, right?' Frank said. Three or four drivers were sitting around. The stuffing was out of the sofa and the ashtrays were full. On the wall the Nut and Bolt Company's topless April model stood uneasily on a beach, holding a large fibreglass bolt.

Somebody said 'Right.'

'I've got me white ribbons on, heating's set cool so she doesn't arrive with sweat in her togs, you know.'

'Uh huh.'

'So the dad gets in, knocks his hat off on the door, like they all do. Girl appears out of this Tudor semi in Wembley, comes down the garden path carrying her wedding dress out in front like she's got a trolley under there or something, and I'm thinking: she looks like a difficult one.'

'Yer, naa,' Frank heard.

'The old dad's saying how nice she looks –'

'So what happens?'

'We're poking along, and halfway to the church she puts her glasses on and says "I'm not doing it." "The fuck you're not doing it," he says. She starts giving it the "I don't want to get married," plus a bit of the "I don't love him," and the dad's practically begging her.'

'So he asks you to try and persuade –'

'Any chance of me telling this?'

'Right.'

'Yes, as it happens, I have to sit there a couple of minutes and tell her I've been happily married for years and years, since I was, like, *young*, and it's Sunday every day and the sun's always shining –'

'She believe that stuff, the kid in the bins?'

'Sure she did, goes in through the big doors like a dream. Funny thing is – they come out, get photoed all over the shop, get back in the back – and she's totally all over the husband now. On the way to the reception she zips him open, swear to God, and he jams his hand up between her knickers, when he can find them under all the chiffoney stuff she's got on. By the time we reach the place it's all moaning back there and I've got to have the vents on super-max to keep the steam off of the windscreen.'

'I had some newlyweds one time –'

'Well, how about it?' Frank interrupted.

'So tell us the punchline.'

'Well I'm saying, it's a mad world, isn't it?'

'You think *that's* mad, listen to this . . .' And so it went.

Life was good while the oil money held up. Frank had a regular sheik. When Khalid came to town Frank dropped everything to be there, practically bundling his current customer out of the car at the next lights. 'My prince has come,' he said to Diane when he got the call once in the middle of the night. 'Let's go steal ourselves some kingdom.'

Frank knew that Khalid could afford it. The kitchen in his house in South Kensington was the size of Frank and Diane's whole flat, plus most of their next-door neighbours the Lamberts' living room – 'about as far as the cocktail cabinet', he explained to Diane.

Frank was on a cut or lump-sum from a number of establishments if he brought the young and eager Khalid there – a straight £50 from most casinos, five per cent from a selection of escort agencies. 'I get more cuts than that barber with Parkinson's off the Clapton Road,' Frank said once, and then again a week later.

He did more than drive Khalid. He got him home at night when he couldn't see his feet at the end of his legs. If anyone else tried to cheat Khalid, Frank was there to help, in his own way.

As he drove, Frank told Khalid candidly: 'I'm more by way of a social worker to you. You see, you're *exposed*, like I would be out and about down the Jeddah cash-and-carry. There's people trying to separate you from your ackers the whole time.'

'What is ackers?'

'That's your crackle, money.'

'Social worker?'

'They come and visit you if you kick your littl'uns about. If you're lucky they give you money to –'

'Ackers. They give you ackers?'

'Yeah, they give you ackers.'

'What is cashencarry?'

'Cash-and-carry? It's a big shop where you get your nosh, your bog rolls –'

'Wh – '

'Food and toilet paper.' These conversations made Frank very tired.

'You're good for my English, Frank. I'm learning many words.'

'That's all right then.' Frank's eyes went back to the road, its tattoos of white and yellow lines.

'What is littl 'uns?'

Frank drove the Rolls Royce for three hard, lucrative years before the gravy train slowed down, kicked out a lot of its passengers and then came to a halt.

Khalid's father stopped him coming to Europe after there was a difficulty over a paternity suit brought by an ambitious part-timer from Lovely Ladies. 'What am I supposed to have done,' Frank protested to Larry Skuse, 'made sure he was only knobbing nice girls? He didn't get to meet any nice girls, poor kid. He's not going to go out with the girl next door, is he, he's not going to get Nanette Newman if he phones round a bunch of baggages.'

It was sad how everything fell apart. Larry Skuse's suits frayed at the cuffs and he began to sleep under his office desk in a sleeping bag so that he would be there if any business came in during the night. The Arabs were going to the United States, to Switzerland. They were withdrawing their wives from the Edgware Road and moving their families on.

Andy and Theo Theofanopoulou had gambling debts. Frank saw how it happened. After a while the drivers started to want some of what their customers had. He admitted to Diane: 'You start to think it would be nice to have the option yourself. Sometimes the punters invite you up into the clubs, or into their suite, and they're up there sniffing I don't know what, and there's paid women running around. You're out in your motor, and you've got the heating off because otherwise it'll do the battery in. So you're tempted to say yes, with them being so friendly.' Diane trusted Frank enough not to ask whether he joined them in their snorting, womanizing and gambling. Nor did she have any need, because Frank knew where he did not belong.

One day Frank went in to work and found the cars all gone. He went to see Larry in his office.

'It's all over, Frank. The bank's taken back the cars.'

'They can't do that,' he said. 'I had a packet of digestives in the side pocket.'

Frank thought about looking for another chauffeur company but he felt he had been in service long enough. He had caught himself calling the man in the butcher's *sir* by mistake. Servility was entering his bones. And he didn't want to leave Diane on her own so much in the evenings. She was watching too much television – he had been getting in from work at two in the morning and she would want to talk him through from that evening's *Nationwide* to the first Open University programme.

And at the time Frank thought he ought to spend more time watching Jason grow up. That was supposed to be why you had children, although Frank had established an early preference for watching Jason growing up as Jason was sleeping. The boy was well into junior school and was finding it easier now that Diane could afford to buy him a proper black uniform instead of dyeing other clothes, which left grey marks on his skin that showed up when he did PE. Now that Frank had earned a decent wage for a few years he could pay for them all to go inside London Zoo.

Previously they had had to walk round the outside, staring through the perimeter bars at the distant shapes of animals.

It was early 1977. Frank had money in the bank. A man in his situation had little choice but to try to make some profit out of the Silver Jubilee.

'Do you get the feeling people would go for a Silver Jubilee musical butter dish?' he asked his wife. It was that pleasant time at the end of the day. They had just gone to bed and were sitting up drinking cocoa in subdued lighting. Outside they heard some drunks singing themselves home from the pub on the corner and kicking empty cans across the windswept concrete.

'Please, Frank,' Diane said, 'sell something useful.'

'What's useful got to do with it? We're celebrating twenty-five years of glorious, you know, reign. Listen, you just buy these transfers with the Queen on from this bloke down the warehouse for about two quid a hundred, and you can stick them on anything. Les Bone's been trying to flog these butter dishes for years.'

'What tune do they play?'

'The theme from *Match of the Day*. I'm surprised he can't shift them, to be honest.'

'I don't remember us celebrating twenty-five years of the National Health Service.'

'Di, give it a holiday, will you?'

Diane's family were members of the East End's dissenting republican minority. Years before, her father had made it on to page four of the *Hackney Gazette* by not standing up for a council toast to the birth of Prince Andrew ('Labour councillor says "Do we honestly need another royal?"'). Frank had never thought much of Prince Philip – 'Makes himself out to be a Greek. Did *you* ever see a bubble, looked like that?' –

but he thought the rest of the family were worth a street party. And Frank was worried about Charles and his wife problem. He knew how tough it must be, trying to chat up someone new while you were opening a biscuit factory.

Diane removed her bed-jacket and smeared some white cream on her face from a big jar under the bed. It was her way of telling Frank not to start making all those little moves that meant he wanted to make love. After she had turned off her light, Frank did some thinking. By the time the cream had turned translucent and entered his wife's lovely skin he had roughed out some ideas in ballpoint pen on the back cover of her Harold Robbins.

Initial response to Frank's advertisement in the local press was lively. You could be Queen for a Day for 65 guineas (guineas – that was marketing), or Queen for an Evening for 35, couples a little dearer. The first few calls to Frank's flat suggested that the public was more interested in being a Queen for the whole day, if they were going to be a Queen at all.

Frank's first clients were a quiet couple, Thelma and her husband Brian. Thelma had recently fallen off her moped, as Brian explained it, and he wanted to 'take herself out of herself' for a day.

Just before lunch Frank picked them up from their home in the ageing brown Bentley hired on extended loan through his chauffeuring contacts. The Union Jack he had rigged up on the front grille blew off on the Euston Road. He had stuck pictures of the Queen inside the car, on the ceiling, and Diane had carefully Letraset-ted *25 Splendid Years* and – even more contentiously – *Everyone Can be Queen* on two strips of cardboard, stuck on to the doors.

Frank turned down his tape of Twenty Golden Patriotic

Greats. 'First stop is local,' he said, turning his head and talking to the more benign-looking Thelma. 'Because let's not forget' – he had prepared this – 'the royal family love the honest simplicity and warmth of the East End.' Frank slowed the car and parked it outside a café. He went on, 'During the war, the Queen often drove past this café on her famous lorry-driving expeditions. She almost certainly stopped to eat here at one time or another. So let's take a look inside, shall we?'

Their plastic Union Jack tablecloth looked out of place on the reserved table and their smart clothes clashed with the overalls at the other tables. Frank sat outside in the car while his friend Len, the owner, served them their roast lamb and bottles of English cider. The drink seemed to take the sparkle out of Thelma and Brian's eyes and they both came over tired after Frank had parked in the sun outside Buckingham Palace for half an hour.

Frank's tour took them past Kensington Palace. 'This, of course, is the home of the Princess Margaret, but there's no time to stop today!' he told his passengers. His delivery was modelled on the old newsreels he occasionally saw as a child, the heavy voice-over, the rallentando as he wound into one of his jokes.

As they arrived in Windsor he said 'Now, in the pocket in front of you behind my seat you will find two tumblers and a flask containing orange squash, the Queen's favourite beverage. Please serve yourselves.' Frank bought two tickets to Windsor Castle as they sat and sipped their squash, and then he watched them walk off up the hill to do the tour.

'We'd already been to the Castle, in actual fact,' they confessed when they returned three hours later.

'Terrific, isn't it?' Frank said.

As part of the package, Frank photographed them standing next to a sentry and then drove them down to Ascot, where they sat outside the racecourse in the penumbra and ate the cold meal that Diane had prepared for them that morning.

'How you doing in the back there?' Frank called out.

'Fine, thank you,' Thelma said. Brian just looked out of the window.

Frank went on to have a few dissatisfied customers but he always made sure he had the money upfront. If his passengers looked as though they were going to complain he threw in an after-picnic Tia Maria, which normally calmed them down, or he said 'Well, what did you expect for that kind of outlay – Concorde to Balmoral?'

He gave the money back only once, to a sixty-five-year-old woman who had just opted to be the Queen for an Evening (a ride in the Bentley, free orange squash, meal at Windsor Pizzaland with half a carafe of wine). The car had broken down on the way back and Frank had to borrow her cardigan to wipe down his leads. 'In fact,' Frank told her, inventing freely, 'exactly the same thing happened to the Queen once on the A40, except she used her headscarf.'

'She's a credit to the nation,' the woman agreed automatically, but still insisted on having her money back.

■ Party

　　　　　Frank was ready to return to the party now. Alone in the back room he had given the wall some hard, jabbing kicks – a trickle of sand came out of the cracked plasterboard – and driven his fist into the frame of the door. Jason, the money – could anything good come out of this? The only sense of gain Frank could feel was that he had held back from shouting at his son. Frank had had enough of pushing people around. It felt like maturity might be starting to crowd into the big space where crudity and bullying had been.

It was too bad that this lesson in philosophy had cost a couple of thousand pounds and his respect in the ticket-touting community. When word of this got out, Frank realized, his name wouldn't be worth spit on a manhole cover.

'You've been caught bending here, Frank,' he said to himself, trying to cheer himself up with the sound of his own voice.

In the other room voices and a few thuds were softly colouring the silence. The dividing door rattled, probably with the front door opening and guests coming in. Frank had picked a bad moment to come over depressed.

'You all right, Francis?' a new voice said on the other side of the door.

'Got some last-minute paperwork,' Frank shouted out.

'You got any ice in there?' said a woman. 'In there with that paper?'

Frank rose to his feet, lined up the twin points of his shirt collar and threw back the door.

'Surprise!' he said, smiling and imagining a sea of faces.

There were only three new guests, and one person seemed to have left. The room was full of furniture still in its packaging. So it had come. The Stubbs family trio were sitting on the paper-wrapped sofa, which was facing away from the rest of the room and almost against the wall. Frank could see Petra absently tugging on the makings of a double chin. He wanted to go over and tell her she was going to make her chin worse that way, and undo all the good work she put in at her Jazznastics class over in Ilford. Grant had let the hairs grow back on the mole that studded the nape of his neck like a rivet, appearing to keep his head on. His mother was sitting between them, sipping from a paper cup.

Jason had disappeared, perhaps sensing that he had had a bad day, even by the low standards of achievement he set himself. Frank remembered once watching the satisfaction and pride on Jason's face when he finished ironing his first shirt at the age of twenty, and he hadn't even switched the iron on.

Facing Frank stood Ted Nuttall, his wife Brenda and their twenty-year-old son, Darren. Ted had taken his flat cap off and had it screwed up in one hand.

'What's all this doodah, Frank, pass the parcel?' Ted asked, nodding at the furniture. 'What is it, pass the parcel, is it?' he repeated.

'I'll give you a clue, Ted,' Frank said. 'If you help me get all this stuff off I'll let you sit on it.'

'Funny, exactly my first words to the wife here,' Ted said, and laughed. His wife, still short of her ice, looked away out of the window.

Janice left Nobby, whom she had been nursing on one side of the room, and helped Frank and Darren to tear off the packaging. Darren was the sort of son Frank would have liked to have for himself. Fair, quiet, his hair short but not too short, Darren hadn't argued the toss about removing the packaging from the furniture, he had simply taken off his jacket and helped to do it (Jason would have said 'What, *now*?' or 'Can't we get a guy in to do that?' in a belligerent way).

'Looks a treat, all this gear,' Ted said. 'Wouldn't you say, Bren?'

'Our Audrey thought about getting a sofa like that, once,' his wife said. Frank picked up the way she said *once*, leaving that pause. She was a large woman and the scooped neck of her dress left a broad tongue of white skin open to about her fifth rib. Frank knew Ted's taste in women from a long way back. He thought that slim women were feasible, but only as an interim stage until you found yourself a fatter woman. 'Say what you like about those Germans,' he used to say, even when Germans were very far from everyone's mind, 'you don't get much change out of a hundredweight with their women.'

Frank's office looked like a playroom on Christmas morning, with all the paper over the floor and the bauble-like chromium of the table and chairs. Darren was becoming friskier now, tearing about and placing the table here and there to see how it looked. Janice steered Nobby into a safe corner, where he sat in groggy tranquillity. Ron Rumsby had gone quiet and was cupping his drink seedily with his back to the wall. Darren had shooed Petra, Grant and their mother off the leather sofa and they were now standing over by the far window with a hemmed-in look on their faces.

Everyone stood around, watching the room taking shape. By the time it was over Darren was breathing heavily, his hands on his hips. Frank took the hatstand and placed it carefully by the entrance as though adding the last piece of a ten-thousand-piece jigsaw.

'Thanks for the assistance, Darren,' Frank said. 'Double ta.'

'Anybody else coming?' Ted said, after a stretch of silence.

'Don't you worry on that score, Ted. Like I said earlier, it'll be a circus in here in half an hour.' He clapped his hands together and rubbed his palms. 'Janice, let's freshen up these cups, shall we?'

As Janice moved towards the drinks table Darren said, 'I've got to slip off and meet some –'

'No,' Frank said, louder than he wanted to. 'I mean,' he added more softly, 'I tell you, this place'll be on fire in a mo.' Janice pushed a can of lager into Darren's hand.

'Oh, cheers,' he said with a tiny smile.

'You should have arranged some music,' Petra said.

'Tell you what,' Janice said with sudden animation, 'I'll get my little radio out of my handbag.' Everybody watched her tap across the floor on her heels and rummage in her shiny white handbag. 'Here it is,' she said, producing something that hid itself easily under her fingers. She fiddled with a switch and set it down on the table.

'Is it on?' Grant asked after several seconds.

'It's probably warming up,' Janice reassured them.

Frank had lapsed into an uncharacteristic lethargy. He stared at the little black casing of the transistor radio as if it controlled his existence.

'It's built-in obsolescence, of course,' Grant said. 'It doesn't make economic sense to manufacture anything that lasts more than five or so years.' They were all staring at the radio now except Frank's mother, who was looking over the rim of her paper cup as though something had fallen into her drink. 'We've got this bagging machine at work that broke down last week and nobody will come and repair it,' Grant went on. He looked around him, surprised that nobody had tried to interrupt him. 'It's a Megson HD42, actually, do any of you know it?'

Frank felt a surge of solidarity and love for his artless brother. Frank, who had spent a lifetime trying to create an illusion of sharpness, took his hat off to anyone who could still say *It's a Megson HD42, actually* with that much simplicity.

Walking across to the radio, Frank said 'No, I don't know that particular unit, as it happens.' He shook Janice's radio against his ear and a faint scratching sound started to come out. Carefully, Frank put it back on the table and walked away.

'Ooh-oh, I can feel a conga coming on,' Petra said with sullen irony, looking down at the floor with her arms folded.

'Have you got any Pet Shop Boys?' Darren suddenly asked Frank, breaking out of his silence.

His father intervened to say 'Don't talk wank, Darren, it's a radio,' and walked across to the drinks table. Frank was relieved as well as saddened to see that his own relationship with Jason was not so unlike Ted's with Darren.

Ted poured himself a vodka that went on and on. He turned his back on Frank as he squeezed in a squirt of tonic on top. Brenda joined him by the drinks and added a splash of gin to her gently softening cup. The two of them returned ceremoniously to where they were standing with their backs to the door. There was a moment of silence and then Grant took his turn to walk quietly to the drinks table, making a small polite ducking movement as he entered the circle across which everyone was staring. He picked up a bottle of wine and said quietly to himself 'I think I'll move on to wine.' After spending a while looking at the label, Grant put the bottle down and murmured 'No, I'll stick to lager.' As he poured the lager into his cup he said 'lager, lager, lager' in a playful, sing-song voice. He repeated the polite ducking gesture when he returned to his place by the window, between his sister and his mother.

Frank was wondering if this was the worst case of group paralysis he had ever seen. There had been that bad evening in the Pig and Pig the evening after Les Bone's wife was diagnosed with leukaemia. As he remembered it, the circle in the lounge bar had widened as the evening went on until there were as many as ten people standing around in the sad pub not saying anything. Everybody wanted to leave but it would have seemed as though anyone who did was giving in to cancer.

'What's happened to your Dawn then, Petra?' Grant asked. Nobby abruptly belched and apologized, then belched and apologized again.

'She's probably sitting in the back of some boy's car by now, knowing my Dawn.'

Grant looked aggrieved. 'That's terrible, Petra, the back of cars.'

'Don't worry, she always keeps her tights on up to the waist. We have an arrangement.'

'No, he's right,' Frank said, sensing some invigorating controversy. 'When a boy gets a girl in the back of a car he's not going to ask about her mum's arrangements, is he.'

'Too right,' Ted cut in. 'The boy's going to go the whole way, normally, once he's got his todger on red alert.'

Darren said 'I've really got to get off now, you know, my mates –'

'In two minutes our Darren'll be combing the car parks for your Dawn,' his father said.

Darren took his jacket and left. The conversation died again. The procession to the drinks table resumed. Ron Rumsby started up a quiet conversation with Ted Nuttall over on one side, which left Brenda looking dull and desperate. Janice's radio was still on, but the sound it generated was like a small piece of metal being scraped along a wall several streets away.

Frank was suffering. On a philosophical level, Frank had squared up to his character some time ago: he was coarse-grained and realistic and was happy with that. He was often surprised by how emotional and obscure others were. People on the television, particularly, were always crying and flying off the handle whenever something small went wrong with their lives. What do you expect, Frank thought – big fun all the time? Even so, it was gone nine o'clock and Frank was suffering from a sense of abandonment.

He was making a mental list of everyone who hadn't bothered to show up.

Wally Burtenshaw was on it. He was not everyone's idea of the perfect person to be stuck in a lift with, but he had party-craft and could shift a conversation. Wally was a loan shark who pioneered the use of the tiny printed disclaimer in newspaper adverts. You needed an electron microscope and a jar of paracetamol to sort out most of his ads, until they brought in legislation. He used to tell friends that he did two kinds of loan, the one where you ended up losing your

furniture, and the one where you ended up losing your
furniture and your house. So why had a convivial person like
Wally failed to appear? If you gave Frank *any sort* of invitation he would be glad to go, let alone a party with
drinks promised.

And Stu Sheekey, who told jokes. 'Name any subject and
I'll tell you a gag about it,' he would offer. Frank once said
'Lawnmowers'. 'What make?' he replied. That was how
good Stu's memory for jokes was. Now Frank came to think
about it, on the phone Stu had mentioned some problem
about not coming because his wife was laid up with de-
pression.

Ada Dodds, also missing. He had recently given Ada some
assistance after she had gone through her divorce from
Frank's friend Russ, who had bought a bar in Portugal and
only one plane ticket. Frank offered to help Ada out with his
power sander when her bedroom door started sticking, but
they both knew what he meant. They hadn't lasted long
together as lovers, mainly because Frank's heart wasn't in it
but also because she so frequently said 'Sorry, I prefer the
way Russ and I did it,' and 'No, no, that's not the way Russ
did it at all.' Still, it would have been nice to see her.

Where were the O'Brien brothers, Nick Diskin, Lee Shar-
man? And Laurie Eakes, the used-car dealer who boasted
that he had even wound back his mother's birth certificate,
so she could get her pension a few years earlier? Frank could
not even rely on the people he didn't like to turn up.

'Frank,' Janice was saying, 'the fish has arrived.' She
looked concerned for Frank, her face still pretty but tired. He
realized he ought to send her home, but her presence reassured him.

'That's all we need,' he said.

Bridget came in carrying a cardboard box, panting from the stairs. Her hand was heavily bandaged but she made it to the middle of the room and put the box down on the new chrome-and-glass coffee table.

Bridget looked around wearily at everyone and said 'There's more downstairs, Frank.'

'Cheers, toots. Why not grab yourself a cup of wine on the way out.'

'No, ta, brings my ankles up.'

Frank went downstairs to the fish van to pick up the other box. The fresh air, laced with vinegar, felt good on his face. An elderly couple walked slowly past arm in arm, he leaning slightly on her.

'What's that then, some kind of do?' Bridget asked as she counted out Frank's money with her greasy fingers. It was she who had served Sandy, Frank's second girlfriend, when she went into Jack's Fish all those years ago, with Frank in his raincoat a couple of places behind in the queue. Bridget's waist had been willowy then but now it looked more like an old redwood under the checked apron. Frank liked that – when a tree thickened into a fat tree, nobody accused it of *letting go* the way they did when women put on a few pounds.

'Yeah, it's supposed to be some kind of big do,' he said, 'but I overcounted.'

'Still, you're thinking big, all that food. You've got to do that nowadays.' She looked up at him. 'Jack and I should have bought the shop next door way back, years ago, knocked it through.'

'No, you didn't need that.'

'We could have opened another place. Jack wanted to get into baked potatoes, because we already had the contacts in potatoes.'

'You've got to be happy with what you've got. Twice as many potatoes, twice as many problems.'

'Well, let's hope so,' she said. Shutting the back of the van with her big fists, she added 'I've put some of them little wooden forks in, in case you've got anyone posh up there.'

'Don't worry, Bridget, there's nobody like that in tonight.'

Upstairs, they were staring at the packets of fish and chips packed inside a cardboard box with *Trill Birdseed* x *12 packets*. It had aroused the professional interest of Grant, who had crouched down to read the lettering.

Frank put the other box down beside it and said 'Righty-ho, anybody *not* like fish?'

Tory Party Rules

Frank gave up his tours at the end of the summer. The pictures of the Queen were stripped out of the Bentley and the car was returned. He was glad it was over but worried about his future. His life had come to another fork.

'Shit, Di, another fucking career decision.'

'Frank,' she said, looking up from polishing the table, 'do you *need* to swear?'

'Look, love, it's communication, it's the power of language.'

'The Lamberts next door don't do it, or the Howards on the other side. I bet Sue Lawley doesn't.'

'I think if you run a tape over Bert Lambert you'll find he swears like a bleeding football special. You polished that table yesterday.'

'There's a lot of things I did yesterday that I'll do today.'

Frank took a bite out of his piece of toast. 'What's it like being a housewife?' he asked. He had hardly ever thought about it before.

She continued polishing. 'Pretty disappointing.'

'Oh.'

'Pretty *fucking* disappointing,' she added.

Frank looked at her acutely but she didn't glance up. His sharp, inquiring gaze lingered for a moment and then faded away for lack of an audience.

The winter passed by quietly. Frank did some shopping. Once or twice a week he bounced Jason on his knee, although he was nine by then. He thought about going back to work in the market but, as he said to Diane, 'You should never go down the same road twice.' He realized later that the advice didn't stand up too well, so he added 'I'm not talking about real roads, mind.'

It was in the spring that he met Archie and made a new career for himself. After Archie had overcome his suspicions about Frank, that night they met in the West End, they talked in a Soho café.

'Socialism, eh,' Archie said.

'Yes,' Frank said carefully, trying to guess which way Archie was jumping, and jump with him. 'It's a, it's a –'

'We want a backlash, is what we want. More emphasis on supply and demand.'

'That's it, that is it.'

'I should be allowed to buy what I like and sell it for what I can get.'

'We need that backlash,' Frank said, shaking his head wistfully.

'Imagine, you've got a house you've bought, all on the legal, like I do these tickets, and the filth turns up in its boots and says to you, "Here, move along, matey, you can't sell that house for the going rate," in spite of all parties being well happy.'

'It's a choker,' Frank agreed.

'Let's face it, it's envy. They don't want the likes of me to have the drop on the cosy operators with the shops and the overheads. I call myself a ticket broker actually, a leisure trader.' Archie was enjoying explaining the way of the world to Frank. His mouth was moving confidently from one word to the next. 'You know what my overheads are?'

'Seventy pence?' Frank guessed.

Archie looked at him as though he were simple. 'Shoe leather. That's all.'

'I get it,' Frank said softly, nodding and making his eyes look perceptive.

'And I'd need shoes anyway, wouldn't I?' Archie smiled, so Frank assumed it was all right for him to smile too.

'How do you know what you should buy?' Frank asked after he had bought Archie another tea from the Italian behind the counter with the dead cigarette between his lips.

'Talent,' Archie said, massaging his chubby cheek below the bristle line.

'Just talent?'

'Flair, talent. What do you think you need, a fucking diploma?'

Frank and Archie handled anything, from *Carmen* at Covent Garden – Archie would stand outside with a fan of tickets in his hand and say 'Come along now, this is the one with the bull-fighting in it' – to boxing. Frank started studying *The Stage* every week, fascinated by the doomed-looking magicians and veteran comedians on the back pages.

Nevertheless, he made a few errors early on.

He bought into Shirley Bassey and turned up a day late to sell the tickets, by which time she had been replaced on the bill by the Reverend Lionel Hucker and his Evangelical Roadshow. After the problem with Archie over *Evita*, Frank started to tighten up. He preferred not to commit funds into shows in advance but to just turn up, buying and selling hand to hand outside the venue. That way he didn't tie up capital, and the buzz in the air and the density of the crowd told him whether to buy short or long or go straight home. Sometimes with Archie, sometimes without him, Frank wound among the crowd, muttering at a controlled level: 'Anybody want a two, a two? I've got a spare three, clear these up now. You want those taken off you, darling? I'm paying ten, I'm paying a straight ten. Fifteen? Not even if you blow on it. Can I help you or are you just looking, yes, step over here.'

Frank's technique had to be modified from his style at the market, where he had tried to lob his voice into the Thames three miles away. It was important, Archie said, to create something approaching mystery: suggest the fringes of illegality, bring out the bandit in your punter, coax out the yes. Judge your event and your buyer, double the price if she's wearing a fur coat, knock a few per cent off for anyone carrying a shopping bag – they're probably up to their spending limit. Don't bandy with Mediterraneans – they haggle for fifteen minutes and shout around. Never overplay the intelligence of the public; you can sell most people an old shopping list, call it two dress circle enough times, and it *becomes* two dress circle. Divert people's attention with information, whether true or creative:

'Don't broadcast it, but this pair's on an aisle. You can stretch your legs out, while other folk'll be wedged there like frigging boat people.'

'Stalls R23, I can clue you in here – that's where the *producer* always sits when he sees the show.'

'Funny, its *better* in the top balcony, what with the special sight lines.'

When buying from the public, say 'Well I can *try* to sell them,' or 'Did you *pay money* for these?'

Archie: 'Then, of course, there's always the chance the force will do a moody, start jerking us around, infiltrating. But don't worry, you can tell the plainclothes from the bulge of their radio. Or, if it's a Status Quo gig, they'll be the ones with the clean fingernails.'

Frank was arrested and charged with obstruction a few times but the stigma – of climbing into the police van and sitting inside over the wheel arch, of the official letters falling on his welcome mat – wore off. Archie's view was that 'They need the fines to pay for the police cars.' Frank came to see it as the authorities' way of taxing the section of the population which, like Frank, thought a national insurance number was an unnecessary encumbrance, like a ball and chain on a long walk.

Diane was not always happy about what Frank was doing. As the years went by she told him so.

'If it wasn't for little Jase's needs,' she said, 'I wouldn't let you go off like that, ripping people off.'

'Love, love, I let you choose the wallpaper and the telly programmes. Leave the nine-to-five to me, will you? And stop smearing on that bloody cream, please.'

'I often wonder whether you have any feelings.'

'Di, the thing is this. We're talking about people having a good time, right?'

'Do you want some face cream?' she said, waving a blob at him on the end of her finger. He smiled and nodded.

'Where was I? Yes,' Frank resumed, 'the more you pay, the more you enjoy it. You shell forty quid, you get a forty-quid show. If you spend two quid, you get a two-quid show. I mean,' he said as his wife smoothed the cream in little circles on his forehead, 'there's *nothing there*, is there. A good time, it's all in the air.'

'Hold still or I'll get it in your eye.'

'Lay off now, Di, it's all cold and greasy.' As Diane screwed the top back on the jar and put it back under the bed, Frank wondered which was more fundamental in shaping a marriage – the little games and shared toyings, or the serious discussions and arguments. He went on, 'I'm not taking bread out of kids' mouths, you know. I'm just scraping off rich folk's jam.'

'Robin Hood, as I live and breathe,' she said, and clicked off her lamp.

Frank turned his own bedside lamp off and they settled down in the dark.

'Any way up,' he continued, his voice strangely resonant without the distraction of sight, 'it's Tory party rules now, or haven't you heard? Anyone who doesn't hustle gets his social security stopped.'

Frank made the friends he needed in the touting business, hall porters in big hotels who had clients just flown in 'from Stuttgart, especially', box-office managers who agreed with Frank that a crate of spirits or a plump, hurriedly passed envelope were more than legitimate commercial tools – they were the cement between the bricks of business. He linked up with ticket agents working from West End offices containing a telephone, a chair and an ashtray. Wimbledon line judges, chorus girls in hard-to-get musicals, they were all in Frank's little brown book, which he consulted again and again over the years, folding open the pages in a thousand different telephone boxes. He developed a shifting list of soccer bosses who could squeeze out a cup run occasionally and who knew the statistics on managerial longevity and the size of Frank's sweeteners. From the stale, steamed-up phone box Frank might say 'Any chance of you magicking me up an allocation, while you're still in the job? How are the kids, all right are they?'

Among the small operators Frank and Archie were doing

nicely. The industry had its big players, men who operated through other men, but Frank and Archie had their own ideas about success.

'In every field of activity you have your Wellington, your Alexander the Great, your Alf Ramsay,' Frank said to Archie late one night.

'And our guys – your Mickey Suttons, your Joe Wagstaffs, Lou Chittock,' Archie said, hunched over his lager. 'Mind you, who's Mickey Sutton?'

Their conversation had been furring over for some time. Perched off-centre on bar stools, they were rounding off a good evening's buying and selling. More money from nothing.

They didn't often drink together. Archie preferred his local near Hackney Marshes, where he had status and his own dented pewter tankard, and Frank liked to be at home with Diane with his feet up on the coffee table and Jason safely down at the youth club or out breaking windows.

'But who needs that responsibility?' Frank went on. 'Do *you* need it?'

Archie thought for a moment and said 'Eh?' then shook his head and said 'Nah.'

'And do you know why?' Frank said seriously. 'Because the thing is this: our home life is more important.'

Confidence

Frank and Janice had already been drunk once that day so they were taking it easy. Nobby Spicer had also cut down on his drinking in the last half hour, by falling asleep. The others were taking long pulls on their paper cups, but much of the alcohol had been absorbed by all the fish and chips Frank had been pressing on them. Grant had managed three cod and now stood stiffly with one hand resting on his stomach. Brenda Nuttall had grease round her mouth but nobody could find a polite way of telling her, now that a couple of minutes had passed since they had stopped eating. The fact remained that nine people could not eat fifty cod and chips in a single sitting. 'Unless,' as Frank put it, 'they're specialists.'

Frank had been cheered up in the last few minutes by his mother who, after a slow start, had been lured out of her shell by the magical chemistry of fish plus two cupfuls of Portuguese wine. She seemed to be working towards something.

'Yes, Frank's big ambition when he was growing up was to be in charge of a circus,' she told the group, looking down at her feet and smiling slightly. 'We never actually took him to a circus but he saw an old poster of a ringmaster in a red coat, stuck on the side of the bus garage, and then sort of followed it up by going down to the library and asking for some books on the subject.'

Janice was picking the mascara out of her eyelashes again, as she had that morning. Her personality had filled out in Frank's mind since then, when Frank had watched her like a tourist in front of a landmark.

Mrs Stubbs was still speaking. 'And, surprisingly enough, they found two books about circuses. So Frank brought them back in the old cardboard satchel he had at the time. Well.' Frank's mother paused for effect but the effect was overshadowed by the sound of Nobby falling forwards in his seat and hitting his head on his knee. 'Well, Frank somehow forgot to take the books back to the library. I don't know what happened to one of the two books, but I was looking through an old box of possessions this morning and what do you think I came across?' She paused again.

'Some old photographs?' Ron Rumsby said.

Janice sighed and put her head on one side. Petra looked at the ceiling.

'Old school report, was it, some old caper?' Ron tried again.

'Jesus, Ron,' Ted Nuttall complained.

'I found one of the books,' she went on, in triumph. 'And I would like to present it to my son now, all these years later.'

Grant cut in, 'Because, as I understand it – you can put me straight on this one, Frank – what Frank is planning to do now with his life is not so different from being the ringmaster in a circus, handling acts, and more in that line.'

'Lou Grade with a foreskin, eh, Frank?' Ted said. His wife looked away, as she regularly did whenever he said something.

There was polite interest – an *mmm*, a couple of forward tilts of heads – as Frank's mother rummaged in her large handbag.

'Well, this is a bit of a turn-up. I'm, no, I'm touched,' Frank said, and he was. 'I'm no good at speeches myself, as anyone who came to my wedding will, erm – Anyway, ha, ha. A lot of people haven't been able to make it tonight but . . . this makes up for . . .' He trailed off. Just when things seem shot to pieces, a symbol arrives. The book was heavy and compact in Frank's hand.

He tore off the wrapping paper and there it was – *Conquer Your Nerves* by J. D. Fott. Hesitantly, he held it up for the others to see.

'Oh,' his mother said, as she peered across. 'Have I wrapped up the wrong one?'

'That was one of mine, actually,' Grant said, and ran the flat of his hand uneasily over the few glistening threads on the top of his head.

'I must be getting old,' she said.

The single naked lightbulb cast a circle of limp human shadows against the scuffed walls. Janice stepped back and leaned gently against the wall, where her head met and eclipsed its shadow.

Petra raised her hands slightly, took a step forward and said, 'Well I ought to be making –' when the door handle rattled and the door opened.

Dave Giddings didn't say anything as he stood in the doorway. He just smiled. His tan made his teeth and shirt look like they had white lights inside them. His nose curved slightly to one side, but it didn't matter; in fact, a curved nose suddenly seemed the smartest kind of nose to have. His dark double-breasted suit was modelled, not worn.

Frank thought: first thing I must do tomorrow, throw out my old fawn anorak.

'Frank,' Dave said evenly, 'Ted, Ron.'

'Dave,' Frank said.

'And you must introduce me to these other lovely people, mustn't you,' he told Frank in the same measured way.

Petra was already wiping her right hand lingeringly on her hip so it would be just right, dry and warm, when the time came to link up with the hand of Dave, this interesting friend of Frank's.

Frank saw it all and introduced Petra as 'My sister Petra. Unfortunately she says she has to run along now and look for her seventeen-year-old daughter.'

Petra gave her hand to the new guest, saying 'She's fifteen, as I think you know, Frank.'

'I'll bet you look like sisters,' Dave said, but it sounded to Frank like a bad case of words.

'Actually, you don't really, do you Petra?' said Grant earnestly.

Nobby Spicer, sitting slumped in the background, was missed out of the introductions. Frank had intended to take Nobby on one side that evening and outline his plans to relaunch the old footballer's career. He didn't mind the fact that Nobby had left a sleazy, washed-out impression, and even perhaps lowered the tone of the evening a notch or two with his semi-conscious gruntings and minor bodily collapses as he sat in his chair. Frank didn't mind, not only because Nobby had an old hero's entitlement to special forgiveness, but because his alcoholism was part of Frank's plans. Step one was to get Nobby off the drink. Step two, Frank would ring up a tabloid editor and map out a story about Nobby's *booze hell*, his *maestro misery*. He had noted down a few lines for his man to memorize and repeat when they came to interview him:

I hit the bar – every night of the week.

I drank like a sponge, but now I'm drier than the Gobi desert.

They used to say I had a lot of bottle. Before long I had a lot of bottles.

That was the kind of thing you had to say, and the way you had to say it.

Then Frank planned to move Nobby into mainstream celebrity. His movements would be orchestrated and plotted by Frank and Janice from their office, maybe with coloured pins stuck in a map. 'Where's Nobby, as we speak?' Frank imagined he would say, to Janice, who would have a phone under each ear. She would be power-dressed in black silk and would answer 'He's just finished the after-shave ad in W1 and he's on his way to the Pro-celebrity Crazy Golf. Be with you in a tick, Frank, I've got David Vine holding on line seven.'

Grant interrupted Frank's reverie.

'I'd better drive Mum home, Frank, you know how it is.'

'Thanks for coming, kid.' Frank looked around. Dave Giddings was talking to Brenda Nuttall and Petra, his face alternating between a charming smile and a charming gravity. Their expressions were entirely regulated by his. Frank wanted to know how he got his shirts that white. Apart from the first time he wore them, Frank's own white shirts usually looked like they had been rinsed out in a bucket of cold coffee.

'I keep meaning to have a do round my place,' Grant was saying. 'Start with a few cocktails and then microwave up a few set meals.'

'Look forward to it, G. Help yourself to a few fishes on

the way out, make the place look a bit less like Billingsgate first thing on a Friday morning.'

'Great cod, Frank. Lovely batter.'

'If you drive Nobby home I'll give you the recipe,' Frank said. Grant wavered. 'Tell you what,' Frank went on, using his old techniques, 'I can see you're undecided – I'll throw in a bottle of sherry and an ashtray.'

They woke Nobby up and led him away.

'I'll be in touch, Nobby,' Frank said.

'Was I snoring?'

'Just look after yourself. You want to watch your liver.'

'I only drink to pass the time, Frank.'

'It's a good way to pass the time.'

'Don't shit me, Frank. It's a bad way.'

'Nobby –'

Nobby buried his head in his reddened hands and said hoarsely 'I'm losing everything.'

Oh no, Frank thought, he's going to cry. Don't cry, for your sake. I love you, Nobby, but go and cry at home, in front of the television or crawling on the kitchen floor, like everyone else.

Nobby lifted his head and sniffed generously, shifting his fluids around his sodden body. 'It could be worse,' he said.

'Yes,' Frank agreed.

'I mean, I could have played for Everton.'

Frank was pleased to hear Nobby joking. With a couple of stiff coffees inside him and a little work on his timing Nobby would do just fine for *This is Your Life*.

Frank's party was over. He heard Grant outside in the street, saying to Nobby 'You'll have to shift some of that rabbit mix off of the back seat.' Two, three car doors slammed shut. Lights. Engine.

Inside, leave-taking mechanisms had been engaged, handbags were being felt for under chairs.

'Ta-da then, Petra. Smack your Dawn's bum for me, won't you?' He leaned towards her. 'And try and get to see Mum, now and again.'

'I ring her up every Thursday, I think you'll find,' she said curtly. Softening, she added 'We don't seem to know what to talk about.'

'Brenda,' Frank called out, 'you're not off too?'

Ted took Frank's arm as he went to find Brenda's coat. 'You in for a session, Frank?'

Frank considered. 'Is Dave in?'

'Face it, Frank – that's why he's here. Ron's in.'

'Ron's in, is he?'

'He's in, I told you.'

'What're you doing about your wife?' Frank asked.

'Putting her on a bus.'

'She mind that?'

'I didn't ask.' Ted lowered his voice. He jerked his eyebrows up into his forehead, and then back down. 'So what's happening with you and the girl, you been the distance with her yet?'

Frank's anger bloomed in his throat again, as it had at lunchtime when Janice, sitting with the O'Briens, had been talked about as though she didn't understand English.

'Keep it in your face, Ted, will you? She works for me.'

'She works for me as well, know what I mean? Oh yes, she certainly does the trick.' Ted still had his flat cap in his hand. His face, folded into a wide grin, looked old and flaky. Frank saw again what he most hated about Ted: his lips were an unnaturally bright red, as though he licked them too much.

'Ted, you're a sad case.'

'Why's that then?'

'You, talking about women like you've got something useful to say.'

Ted looked at Frank as though he suddenly found his face interesting.

'Let's just play cards, shall we?' he said.

Frank positioned himself to help Brenda on with her coat. She stood in front of Frank with her arms out behind her, as though she was about to dive into a swimming pool.

'Couple of fish to go?' Frank asked her as she flexed inside the coat. 'You can probably put it in the freezer. I bet it'll freeze down really nice.

'No, thank you.'

Scratching his head casually, Frank pursued the subject. 'I heard on the box that they found some of that explorer's fish rations, Scott of the Antarctic. It had been there, lying under a bloody, I don't know, under a bloody piece of ice, for sixty years and they fried it up and it was really tasty all that time later.'

'What kind of fish was it?' Brenda asked. Frank wished he had just said goodbye without mentioning any of this. It was an early evening kind of story.

'They didn't say,' he said.

Janice was going for her coat. She had it in one hand and was thinking of putting it on. Frank watched her. He liked her hesitancy: she was looking around self-consciously, as though she were waiting for someone she admired to ask her to dance, or waiting for her boyfriend to come out of the toilet at a party, so she could leave. Maybe, on the other hand, she was thinking about how the hours would look on her time sheet by Friday, wondering if she should ask for double time for staying so late with these four dubious men.

Frank knew how cruel the young could be. There wasn't much that girls like Janice, in their early twenties, did not find funny about most men in their forties. Frank started talking to two at the bar one evening. 'Old guys like you,' one said to Frank while the other giggled, 'you wear those underpants that pull up really high on the waist.' They started to giggle in relays. Frank thought at the time: yep, that's us. We *do* wear that kind of underwear. And we don't even notice we're doing it until it's pointed out.

But Janice had something understanding in her character. He could see it in the seriousness around her eyes, which Frank had noticed settling on him as he sleeved Brenda's arms. Of course, she had to look somewhere. The only dissonance was her voice – like an expensive car running on an engine taken out of a moped. It was nasal like Petra's, but Janice made her vowels last, as though she wanted to hang on to each word as long as possible. Frank thought about his own voice – deep and jagged – and how they would make a fine duet if she was noisy in bed. Frank was vocal, too (a growled threnody, some indeterminate gurgling), but only if his partner started it; otherwise he restricted himself to a long groan when he –

'Frank, I think I ought to leave,' Janice said. She had her coat on, a short imitation wild animal, possibly cheetah.

Frank took her aside slightly. 'Why don't you stay, eh? What say I play a couple of games to keep the boys happy, then I can drive you home.' Frank smiled benignly, then interrupted himself abruptly. 'Your home – not my home.'

'Umm.'

'I'll drive you in *my* car to *your* home,' Frank said.

'Yeah, yeah, don't go on, Frank.' She started taking off her coat. 'If you want me to help, you only have to say the word.'

She went to make herself up in the small toilet with the cracked sink at the end of the corridor. After introducing herself to Frank the day before, Janice's first words had been: 'You want to get that sink changed. Cracks harbour all kinds of germs.' Frank had said 'Here's a fifty – what say you go out and buy yourself a new sink.' She had bought it, and it was now sitting under the old sink in the toilet.

The men arranged the table, except Dave Giddings.

'Sorry lads, this suit's design parameters don't include stretching and bending,' he said, standing by the window.

'I'd take issue with that if I knew what you were going on about,' Frank said as he brought a chair over.

Ron said 'Yeah, what's that in old money?'

If Dave didn't like a question he didn't answer it. Frank had tried the approach out himself, but with him it didn't give an impression of high-minded selectivity, it merely looked like deafness. Dave just scanned the room, once peering up at the ceiling and raising his head to expose an evenly tanned underjaw. Eventually he said 'Have you got plans to decorate this place, Frank?'

'Oh I've got more than plans. I've got fucking ideas jotted down.'

'The walls are –'

'Are you in to play, Dave,' Frank cut in, irritated, 'or do you want to do some wallpapering before we start?'

'Sure, let's play,' he answered smoothly. As he came over from the window, Dave removed his suit jacket. He put it over the back of a chair like a boxer taking off his spangled robe. He sat down opposite Frank.

Dave Giddings was nothing when Frank met him, as Frank often told people. 'He wasn't even a nobody,' he exaggerated. 'Dave Giddings worked behind the desk at Lou

Chittock's ticket agency, quiet as a mouse, but you could see he was thinking about something – I used to think he was thinking about, you know, *lunch* or something, but the sly bastard was already working on his own stuff, speculating in Lou's time. Then one day, suddenly, he's left Lou and got his own headed letter-paper and the full poop on this and that from Lou's bottom drawer. You've got to watch him, but you've got to admire him.'

Frank and Archie saw men like Dave come and go. Young and over-confident, most of them lacked what Frank and Archie had: enough humility to take the bus home. Many of them bought expensive coats, became taxi people and lost their business edge. It happened to Harvey Townhouse and Dean Antrobus – Frank and Archie had *watched* it happen. 'See that?' Archie said to Frank one night as they touted in the rain. 'Harvey Townhouse, getting into a cab when he should be out working,' Frank answered. They both shook their heads sadly.

As Frank understood it, Dave had diversified into boxing promotion and other areas: a launderette, a majority share in Disco Princess, a successful racehorse, and Tracie, a no less successful greyhound with unusual markings, time-share connections in Sardinia.

Frank was scared of Dave. Nevertheless, Frank had tried to stay in touch with him because he had what Frank wanted: a portfolio of interests, *presence*, sophistication, but not too much sophistication. By way of contrast there was Archie, who treated the world as though it stood still and who thought financial planning meant keeping some change back for the cigarette machine. At a certain point in your life, Frank realized, you had to choose whether you wanted to be Archie or Dave.

'Where shall I sit?' Frank heard Janice ask. She was standing behind him. Now it smelt as though she had been soaking in a barrel of perfume for a couple of hours.

'Sit right here beside me,' Frank said. 'What's that smell you're wearing?'

'I can't remember. The name's rubbed off the bottle.'

'It smells . . . expensive,' Frank said. The other men were looking at him. Frank's eyes flickered between them.

Janice pulled up a chair. 'Well, if you can't smell nice, what *can* you do?' Nobody tried to answer her question.

'You're staying then, are you, love?' Ron asked suspiciously as he ripped the cellophane off a pack of cards. Positioned to Frank's left and opposite Ted, Ron sat very tall in his chair, his upper body straight and taut like a long plank.

'Good sleuthing, Ron,' Frank said. 'The coat off, the "where shall I sit?" You put all that together and made a conclusion out of it.'

'I was just checking.'

'Anybody got any objections to Janice staying?' Frank asked. His confidence was returning. Dave, sitting opposite, was beginning to seem laughably *low* in his chair. His shirt still blazed whitely but there was a button missing half way down the front.

'Maybe Janice would like to play,' Ted said. 'We can phone down for a deck of pink cards.'

Frank turned and saw Janice smiling at Ted with her lips while her irises seemed to twirl facetiously.

'Pink cards for the lady,' Ted went on, and cut the cards. Frank felt confident about Ted Nuttall too. What could Ted teach him? Was there *one* thing?

They started to play. Frank's method was aggressive and talkative. He hated the silence.

'I'll raise you that much,' he said in the first game, pushing out his cash. 'Are you following this, Janice? You see, I'm raising and telling these guys I've got good cards. They can take my word for it or they can –'

'Hush up, Frank. Less bunny, will you?' Dave studied his cards without looking up.

Frank carried on addressing Janice. 'And if you manage to give Dave the hump, that's psychology. Some players reckon you're a bit of a dick if you don't do your poker in dead silence but that's just their point of view.'

'Uh-huh,' Janice said, taking it seriously.

When he won the first game Frank said to Janice 'OK, Jan, Dave asked to *see* me, but unfortunately he only had jacks in trips whereas I had a full house eights on fours. It looks like Ron was shooting for a straight but he didn't get near, and Ted folded early, didn't you Ted?'

As Ted gathered up the cards he said 'Can we have a bit less of the Harry Carpenter, Frank?'

'I'd rather keep it social, Ted, you know me. I'm telling Janice how it goes.'

'You sound like a bloody kid tonight, what's got into you?'

Frank couldn't concentrate. Janice's perfume hung in a cloud around him and his cards seemed to be playing themselves. In the first half hour he won steadily. Ron and Ted were playing cautiously and slowly, as if the cards would change in their hands if they waited long enough. Dave was stroking his chin a lot with his fingers.

'Confidence,' Frank said to Janice, 'it's all down to confidence.'

The room was so gloomy Janice had to lean forward to see the cards on the table. Twice she touched Ron's leg by mistake. They each said quiet, darting *sorries*.

Frank didn't enjoy poker and knew he should not be playing, especially at the end of this heavy day. The long grinding sessions bored him, the solemnities and ceremonial irritated him.

'Jesus, Ron,' he said, 'you can soften up on the poker face between hands, you know. You're making me ill with that expression of yours.'

He could only ever concentrate for a few minutes at a time. It was not long enough to win consistently, so he glamorized his shortcomings, persuading himself that he didn't just play cards, he *raided*, whereas the others merely sat there calculating pot odds. When he was winning, Frank's lack of orthodoxy often produced pinched faces among the more mathematical players, but they were also glad to have such a loose thinker at the table.

Not that Frank was guileless – years of trying to sell merchandise that didn't do entirely what it was supposed to had taught him how to straight-face money out of anybody. Frank had sold three hundred ratchet screwdrivers knowing they didn't have a working ratchet between them. It had taken six years and a terrible amount of bluffing. 'You probably jolted it in the bag on the way home,' he usually told his customers when they came back. 'I reckon that's what happened.'

Frank had brought a thousand pounds in cash to the table that evening, four times as much as he allowed himself the last time he played poker with Ted, in the back room of Wayne Depp's drinking club. Tonight he had to win back what Jason had lost, and there was Janice to think of. He felt like he was playing for her.

'You all right there Janice?'

'Fine, thanks.'

'That's terrific,' he assured her, spreading out his fan of cards with his right-hand fingers.

'You know the key to this game?' he continued.

'Con –'

'Confidence, that is more or less the complete thing.'

'Is it?' She sounded cheerful but tired.

'What else is there – just pieces of cardboard with a few symbols and numbers.'

'Maybe,' she said.

Patting the soft pile of notes he had amassed, Frank said to Janice 'Seems to me I'm in the chair tonight. Much more of this and I'll need an extension on my safe.'

Dave then said gently 'I heard you're trying to represent the O'Briens, Frank.'

Frank was casual. 'They're on my books.'

'Who else have you got lined up, anyone interesting?'

'They're all interesting.'

'I used to like that song of theirs. What was it, didn't it have a whip in it?'

Frank thought. 'I don't know any song with a whip in it. They had one with castanets.'

Frank didn't like the interest Dave was showing. Dave didn't appreciate pleasantries – every comment was there for a reason. Friendships had become contacts, compliments were business investments. A conversation with Dave was little more than a round of negotiations.

Frank smiled at Janice and she gave a sort of smile back, although in truth it was little more than a twitching of her cheeks.

'You see,' Dave said as he dealt the next hand with slow circling movements, 'the O'Briens happen to be represented by a friend of mine, Max Angermeier.'

'Friend of yours, is he?' Frank said.

'And he wonders where you got the idea they needed new management, seeing as they're already contracted in over their ears.'

'That's not the way I got it from the horse's mouth. You want to have a word with Gerry O'Brien.'

Ron and Ted had been silent for a while now, saying only the minimum to keep the games going.

'In fact, I was talking to Max about it before I came here tonight,' Dave went on.

'Interesting. Janice and I were putting our position to the boys over a working lunch,' Frank said, pressing forward. 'We see pretty much eye to eye. Seems your friend Max works about as well as that car-phone of yours. Listen, the O'Briens almost got the nod for Eurovision one year, when it *meant* something, and now their manager thinks he's doing favours if he finds them a first-on in a deaf school.'

Dave was carefully neutral. He was slowly rebuttoning the shirt button that Frank had thought was missing. 'Who paid for the lunch, Frank? More likely we're talking about a few pints anyway.'

'Who do you think? They were my guests.'

'No, Frank, you were their free lunch. They're the oldest juveniles in the business, but they know how to tank up when it's not their tab.'

Ted cut in. 'Frank, don't piss about, any chance of a bit of progress?'

'Raise, RAISE,' he shouted. 'Jesus, God, I mean, is there a fire or something?' He only had a pair of jacks, but he wanted to push ahead while he had his confidence. If he folded now he would be seen to be accepting the rebuke from his younger opponent.

'The funny thing is –' Dave started.

'What's the funny thing, Dave, tell us what's funny.' There was no mistaking Frank's annoyance. That was what Frank hated about Dave – he didn't *mean* funny, that was just the most strategically irritating word available.

Janice was suddenly absorbed in smoothing her skirt down towards her knees. Ron Rumsby threw his cards in and made his stiff-legged way to the table to pour himself a drink.

Dave called Frank's bet and resumed what he was saying, at a drawl. 'Max tells me he has to issue them pocket-money. He says if he gives them their fee straight out, less his slice, they've cashed his cheque before he can get the top back on his pen.'

'Good of you to take an interest, Dave.' Frank squeezed it out between his lips.

'They're lucky to be working at all, now that you've got to be under twenty-one to get a sniff at a record deal. They're on the wrong side of forty for this business, and so are you, Frank.'

'That's enough, fatmouth,' Frank said. Dave Giddings carried on scrutinizing his cards and touching his chin with the tips of his fingers. Most of the enmity was still below the surface, but it was drifting towards the light.

Frank couldn't clearly explain why he was getting so heated. Dave was not saying much that he could not have thought out for himself. So the band didn't refuse a few free drinks, they didn't always have their building society books handy – what were they, Irish pop singers or librarians?

Sitting on Frank's right, Ted pushed some more notes into the middle of the table. Frank didn't know what to do with his hand. He wanted to ask Janice for advice, but her only experience of cards, she had said, was the little ones taxi companies push through the letter box. She seemed apprehensive.

'Let's take it up a bit higher,' Frank said, easing some notes out of his own pile and doubling the amount in the centre of the table. Dave still preferred to look at his cards rather than Frank. He called Frank's bet. Ted took a last look at his cards, tossed them face down and rose to his feet. He joined Ron over at the drinks table.

'Just the two of us left, eh, Frank?'

'And I'm not sure you really count,' Frank said.

'I have cards here that say I do.'

'Talking cards, Dave? Fuck me, but that's impressive. You sure they're not saying *bullshit*?'

Frank was confused about the game and wanted to go for a quiet drink with Janice. He was coming round to the idea that she must want him, and as the idea sparked it lit fires in Frank – a cheerful, spitting bonfire in his head and an oily smoulder in his groin. It was hard to believe, but why else would she still be there by his side? He, Janice, her cushiony blouse, the night, a new beginning. He hadn't wanted anyone else this much since Diane. The pubs would be near to closing by now, people would be talking in happy groups. He and Janice could be a happy group too, if Frank could just remember how to relax with a woman.

He tried to concentrate. By now there was a large pile of money on the table. Frank blew some air out of his mouth and asked for two cards to go with his two jacks and a nine. Two twos. A pair of mean little clubs and spades, drowning in expanses of glossy white card.

Frank decided to bluff his hand out. He was not encouraged when Dave took only one card. Why wasn't Dave looking up at him, didn't he know you were supposed to read your opponent's face? Frank was keeping a medium grin on his face on purpose, and it was beginning to ache. Frank couldn't imagine Dave would give anything away, but he looked for indications anyway. (Ron was an outstanding example. He used to give himself away, until someone took pity and told him – whenever he had a strong hand he used to gently stroke his left nipple. Ron was devastated when he heard.) The three middle fingers of Dave's right hand were pressing down on the table while the two others were angled upwards. Maybe that meant he had a three, or maybe not. Perhaps he just liked to hold his fingers that way. It didn't matter anyway – he would have better than two pairs. He probably had something fancy, a fistful of pictures or a solid flush. Frank would have to burn him off.

A minute's rest was what Frank needed. He called out, 'Let's make this the last shot, can we? I think Janice is too polite to say she wants to get off home.'

'Don't worry about me, I'm allowed out after ten,' she said, with a little more bounce than she had shown recently.

'You really have dished the evening, haven't you, love?' Ted said as he poured some more vodka into a new paper cup.

'Shut it, Ted,' Frank snapped.

'What time do you call this, Frank?' Ron joined in. 'You got to be up in the morning?'

'What is it with you two, haven't you got anything better to do than push cards across a table all night?'

Ron was morose. 'I've put people off to come here.'

'You've put people off when you've *been* here,' Frank said.

'No smoke without fire, yeah?' Ron added mystifyingly.

'You *what*?' Frank said.

Janice joined in. 'Who's winning the match?' she suddenly asked.

'Bloody hell,' Ted said, turning his back to the game. 'Honest, Frank, you take a woman out of the kitchen, you're looking at a permanent headache.'

'Ask your boyfriend who's winning,' Ron said. 'He wouldn't be so keen to call it a day if he was on a hiding.'

'Oh, he's not my boyfriend, are you, Frank,' Janice pointed out, an expression on her face somewhere between amazement and scorn. 'No, my flatmate's cooking her new bloke a lasagne at home and I said I'd give her, you know, time to let him try to get her bra off.'

Just for a moment, Frank wanted Janice dead. He looked across at her with his mouth half open.

'No?' she said, looking at Frank wide-eyed, one hand clasped to the side of her neck in a gesture of confusion.

Dave also had his eyes on Frank. 'Let's get on, shall we?'

Janice leaned closer to Frank and started urgently 'I mean, you're not –'

'Leave it, Janice,' Frank retaliated tersely. 'I'm in the middle of a big game here.'

There had been a misunderstanding. The fires Janice had lit in Frank went out quietly. The single lightbulb hanging pitifully under the mottled ceiling seemed to lose some watts, and then some more.

Frank urged himself to put Janice's accidental cruelty into perspective, but every perspective he drew had Janice dominating the foreground, her young face curling its lip. Behind her stood the image of an impassive Dave alongside Jason, waving tickets for the wrong theatre. Further in the distance, fanning out behind Jason, was Diane, with her head in the air, and an obscenely gesturing Archie.

Frank stared at his five cards and decided that, if there was one thing he would do today, it would be to send Dave Giddings home with less money than he came in with.

'Bet, all of this,' Frank said. He picked up the substantial pile of notes that remained and put them alongside the smaller pile in the middle of the table. His chest seemed pumped full of air.

'What happened to stake limits?' Ron asked. He was standing next to Ted with a drink in his hand and a crescent of beer-froth on his moustache.

'Didn't you go out of the game?' Frank shouted. The sudden push of air through his throat released some of his tension.

Dave reached across a tanned hand, picked up Frank's new bundle of notes and looked at it, counting. He added all his own money and said 'Call, Frank. The rest is in my jacket pocket.'

'If it's not on the table, it's not on the table,' Frank said slowly, suppressing his panic. He had been expecting Dave to respect him enough to back down. Frank wrestled with his face, trying to keep its lines taut and confident. He had to give the impression that he welcomed as much money on the table as possible, that it was only a matter of time before he would be gathering it up and stuffing the notes into the safe like leaves in October.

Dave leaned over for his jacket and took a flat, dense bundle of new notes out of a leather case. He peeled off the difference and laid it on his heap of money. 'It's on the table.'

Frank said 'Are we going to allow that, seeing as you didn't have it with you on the table?' The conservative side of Frank's character was making its last pitch.

'If the money's too much for you, Frank, we can always play for paper cups.'

'I don't know about you, but for me that would be a waste of a good hand.'

'Maybe you should be saving up. Between you and me, you've got as much chance of making money out of your business plans as you have of walking on the moon. Nobby Spicer – fat old pros like him are queueing up in tens down at the Job Centre. I don't think we want another Jimmy Greaves, do we? Can't we all agree that one is more than enough?'

'You know what you know?' Frank said, quietly seething. 'You know fuck.'

'Who else have you got signed up, your Mum tearing up phone books?'

Everyone was silent. Frank should have been flattered that Dave was taking the trouble to goad him, but he had lost his ability to analyse the content of what he was hearing. He merely heard the words.

'I'll raise you five grand,' Frank said. The moon above his cuticle was white against the pressured red of his thumbnail as his hand gripped the cards tightly.

'Um, Frank?' Janice asked nervously.

'Where is it?' Dave asked.

'There, in the safe.'

He paused only for a moment. 'I'll call you, Frank. You're deep in the shit here.' He reached into his jacket, took out a pen and leather-wrapped cheque book, turned to the first blank cheque and wrote. As he did so, Frank was staring impassively with a small smile still on his face, looking at his opponent's face and wondering what he should go for first, should he push in Dave's eyes with his thumbs or flatten his gleaming teeth against his gums like a broken down picket fence. All Dave's arrogance had to be answered, all the

smooth faces of Dave's generation of jumped-up entre-
preneurs had to be nailed bleeding to the card table, now.

'When you've finished writing,' Frank growled, 'I'm raising
you the other twenty thousand in the safe.'

'Don't be a stupid cunt, Frank,' Ted said.

Frank was thinking: *Oh, oh, oh, here we go.*

Dave looked evenly at Frank for a long moment and then
said 'Fine.' He tore off one cheque and wrote another to go
with it.

Frank's mouth started to open and close. 'You're what,
you're –'

'Let's see you, Frankie.'

They stared at each other for a moment. Frank started to
blink uncontrollably.

He tossed his cards face-up on the table, in shame. The
two pairs accused him of incompetence. Dave gently laid
down his three kings. He spaced them out slowly with his
fingers.

'Oh dear, Frank,' Dave said suavely. 'You seem to have a
problem.'

Stella

Frank noticed the first grey hair on Diane's head on the day before her thirty-ninth birthday. She screamed when he told her.

Alarmed at the strength of her reaction, Frank added 'No you're all right, Di – come to look at it, it must have been a reflection.' She was already out of the bed and running to her dressing-table mirror.

'My mum didn't start going grey until she was fifty-three,' his wife said as she studied filaments minutely in the hinged oval mirror.

'Yeah, but be fair, Di. She only uses her head at weekends.'

'Nnn,' she said, more interested in her hair.

'My old dear went white around the time my dad did his bunk. I reckon he slipped off with her dye in his case. Did I ever tell you he took the plunger from under the sink? We could never work that one out.'

'You told me.'

'Leave it alone, sugar,' Frank went on, scratching his shoulder through his striped pyjamas. 'What's wrong with grey anyway? If it's good enough for the bloody HMS *Belfast* it'll do for you.'

Diane tutted and sighed softly. 'There's another two on

this side.' Putting her hand to her forehead, she said 'What am I going to do?'

'Soon as the shops open tomorrow I'll buy you a couple of hats,' Frank told her.

There were other signs of physical alteration in Frank and Diane. Some of the changes had happened so slowly that they only noticed them when they brought the family photo album out at Christmas, and they weren't so keen to do that any more. Diane was still trim, but her high bottom had settled at a lower level. *Contents may settle*, Frank often read on the side of his cereal packet, and thought of Diane. Her facial features had sharpened and there were a couple of new scars on her hands from cooking mishaps (a sardine can gash in 1978, a bouillabaisse scald in 1985 – her injuries a reflection of increasing internationalism in the Stubbs' little kitchen, although Frank still preferred food he could pronounce).

Diane walked slowly back to her side of the bed. 'At least I can still touch my toes,' she said.

'Why would you want to do that?' Frank asked. 'If you need your toes touching you just give me a shout and I'll do it.'

'And look at you, slumped like that. You always used to sit up so straight in bed.'

'Well, I hadn't discovered this position, had I?'

'Maybe you should start going to the gym,' Diane said, settling back in bed and putting on her reading glasses.

'You can't fight nature, love. Anyway, if I want to get a sweat up, I'll sit in on one of Jason's driving lessons.'

Frank's stomach had gone the usual way of stomachs. The flat band of muscle had lost itself under the silt of several thousand heavy lunches. His underjaw was still taut but nowadays it seemed to join his neck further down, so Frank could see more of it in the mirror. He was also gaining more hair every year, as it claimed a wider and wider plot across his chest and sowed itself in the tops of his arms. He had been to the local swimming baths with Jason just recently, like old times, and his son had said afterwards 'Dad, at your age you want to think about keeping yourself covered up.'

'That's solid muscle, that is,' Frank said, slapping his belly.

'Give it a rest, Dad. That gut'll still be wobbling this time tomorrow.'

'That's true, actually.'

Frank didn't worry. His legs were as slim as the day he got married and he was still fit enough to sit in his car in traffic-jams and touch his nose with the tip of his tongue. He thought he had come to terms fairly well with the passing of the years.

'You only get old in the body and die once, so you might as well enjoy it,' Frank had said.

Frank and Diane's thirties were much more prosperous than their twenties, now that Frank had left the market for richer pickings in chauffeuring and touting (or as Archie described it: shifted out of goods into services). They took family beach holidays in the Mediterranean which gave them diminishing tans from August to October. After Jason turned eleven they started sending him away on activity holidays, the more active the better, in the hope that it would tire him out for the rest of the year. They went off on their own, to sit on foreign balconies with duty-free spirits in their hands and wonder what was happening back in London.

Frank had to smile when he compared the places they visited now to Ethel's guesthouse in Kent. The new hotels had paper belts round the toilet when you arrived, whereas

in Ethel's place you had to put in a special request for use of
the toilet brush. If any of her guests had asked for the little
sachets of shower gel that Frank and Diane had been given at
the Albergo Buon' Aspetto in Jesolo she would have looked
right through them or said 'I can borrow you a bit of pumice
stone, if you're in need.'

Relative affluence changed little otherwise. They stayed in
their small flat, but now they had a proper decorator in, who
managed to put the wallpaper up without leaving the surface
wrinkled like elephant hide. They discussed moving out to
one of the new towns in the east, trying to buy a house in
Billericay or maybe something small but sweet in Chigwell,
but the suburbs made Frank think of his sister and brother-in-
law in their fenced-off houses where everyone drove to the
shops and the only living sound you heard was dogs barking
to be let in. They decided to stay and buy a new carpet instead.

Frank came to realize that in the 1980s a husband no
longer had the right to stand in the way of his wife if she
wanted to get a job. He never claimed to be an usher of
change but he was usually happy to move with a trend.
Besides, he loved his wife and she wanted to work.

Diane took an afternoon job in a building society, but as
far as Frank could see the core of her life beyond her family
remained the female friends she had made in the flats in their
1930s block. She related some of their discussions to Frank in
the evenings and he found himself becoming drawn, at a safe
distance, into their problematic lives.

'So did Leslie let her bloke back then, after he thumped her
about?' he would ask.

'She's giving him his last chance, she says.'

'That chap, he gets more last chances than most people get
chances.'

'We've told her. Anyway, she thinks she might be having his baby and her ex has stopped sending the maintenance on her two. Anne-Marie's –'

'Anne-Marie's which, the one with the kid with the syndrome and the blue Granada?'

'Yes, little Neil. And I don't know why you have to say what kind of car it is all the time. The only car I recognize is the old Morris Traveller with the wood on the side.'

'No, with a Granada you've got this squared-off tailgate –' Frank started to reassure her, recreating the rear end of the Granada with hand movements.

'– So she's told Leslie that she and Frances aren't minding her kids any more unless she keeps this druggy guy Nick out of her flat, with Frances only having the temporary door since the break-in.'

''Streuth, it's all problems, isn't it. How come we don't get trouble this bad in our lives?'

'Maybe we will one day.'

The polarity of the questioning was reversed when Frank told Diane his stories.

'We're having real bother trying to get hold of stuff for that concert pianist who's coming to town, Russian pianist, looks about as old as, like, an old person's grandad.'

'You're always having a go at the elderly, Frank.'

'No, I'm just saying. Anyway, people're trying to catch him, you know, while he can still make it up on to the stool.'

'*Frank.*'

'They're only doing postal bookings and strictly four tickets maximum. So Archie's tried to do a bit of a sly one without telling me, he's applied for seats by postal order, using made-up names, and given the addresses of a few mates of his –'

'Why didn't he use their real names?'

'Well, he's made several bookings for each address, see. Archie hasn't got all that many friends, know what I mean? Seems he got the names by going down the card of jockeys at Haydock Park. Anyway, they've smelt a rat at the box office – chances are Archie spelt the pianist bloke's name wrong the same way in each letter or something.'

'We ought to have Archie over. How is he?'

'Listen, listen. So, they've banked his postal orders, written back saying the place is all sold out and refunded him in cheques made out to these invented names.'

'Oh, that's a clever idea,' Diane said simply.

'So now Archie's got all these cheques payable to a load of jockeys, and he can't touch the money. Unless he opens about forty bank accounts in all those names.'

'He who lives by the sword, dies by the sword.'

Frank looked at his wife. 'What are you talking about, swords?'

Jason was Frank and Diane's only consistent worry.

'Jason,' Frank once told him, 'you are the nail in me and Di's tyre, you know that?'

Frank had been a rebellious boy, but the scale of dis-obedience had grown since his childhood. Frank and his short-trousered friends knocked on doors and ran away. Jason's generation knocked down the doors and went in. Nevertheless, Jason's misdemeanours – bending car aerials, setting fire to the dry innards of a skip, leaving squirts of superglue on lift buttons – were minor enough for him to be brought home by a policeman rather than held for collection at the station. Frank and Diane shouted at him or talked to him but generally they just hoped for an improvement.

Diane worried, in particular, when it became clear that

Jason was struggling at school. She wrote down numbers of private tutors from the local newspaper and sent Jason for two one-hour maths lessons a week with a Mr Millet. Mrs Millet prepared Jason hot Ribena in the middle of the lesson, but it wasn't enough. Jason stopped turning up after a couple of months and they sent the advance lesson money back with a note wishing Jason luck for the future. Their kindness made everything seem even sadder and more hopeless.

Diane had wanted Jason to go to college; Frank saw a lot of himself in his son and was more realistic.

'Di, the only way Jason's likely to get into a college is if he breaks in. He's not interested. You've got to be interested in something to make it happen.'

'Further education's for everyone, Frank. It's not like when we were at school and almost everyone ended up serving in shops or working on the buses.'

'What's wrong with serving in shops?' Frank said indignantly. 'There's too many people nowadays that think a job's not worth doing unless you do it in a suit with a tie slung round your neck.'

'Why are you shouting, Frank? I'm just talking about giving Jason a few choices, that's all.'

Frank continued more reasonably. 'It was bad enough when I finished school and they packed me off to the insurance company like my premium bonds had come up. I'd only just got hair on my top lip and they were giving me the spec on the company pension I'd be getting in fifty years' time.'

'Frank, it's not boring putting money by for your old age, you know. Some people live for thirty years after they retire.'

'Not us, Di. We're going to keep going till we're too senile to give a toss, like those Russian presidents.'

Jason passed through the education system like a large piece of sharp plastic going through the digestive tract – painfully and to no obvious purpose. By the time he turned fifteen Frank and Diane had worked out what Jason's problem was: he could not sit down for long. After ten minutes in class he had to create diversions to take his mind off sitting down. He didn't stay at home much in the evenings, but while he was there he roamed about.

'Jason, will you stop fucking roaming around please?'

Jason walked around, perching on furniture, opening the refrigerator door, never sitting longer than it took to smoke a cigarette.

His restlessness eased when he left school and took a job in a timber yard. There, unlike at school, sitting down was equated with idleness. For a few months he was happy, and as a result Frank and Diane were happy. Frank felt that at last they had reached a level of poise and rude family companionship that could hardly be bettered. They ate together in the early evening, each contributing to the conversation. Even Jason made reasonable sense as he picked splinters out of his hands and talked.

It was then that Jason met Stella and brought her home.

They had started working at the timber yard on the same day. Stella had only just turned sixteen. Jason tried to describe her to Frank.

'There's a girl that works at the yard,' he said.

'That's nice,' Frank said absently as he watched the early evening news. 'A girl, eh? That's nice.' He suddenly shouted over his shoulder, 'Here, Di, they've changed the background in the bloody newsroom again.'

'She works, you know, in the office.'

Frank was still not paying full attention. 'Works in the

office, huh, doing the old, the old er . . .' He trailed off completely.

'Accounts,' Jason said. 'She doesn't cart wood around or anything.' Dispirited at this lack of questioning, Jason climbed off the arm of the chair and went to his room.

Frank only remembered the conversation two weeks later, when Jason came home with Stella. Frank could not recall them ever having a sixteen-year-old girl in the flat before and she filled his home with something new. It seemed to him that her small body was not carrying an ounce of anything that shouldn't have been there. Her face was small too, and pale and open.

'Dad, Mum, this is Stella,' Jason said vigorously, as though issuing a challenge.

'Hallo, Stella,' Diane said, drying her hands as she came through from the kitchen.

There was a moment's silence. 'It means *star*,' she said confidently.

Frank looked at her carefully. 'Hallo there, Stella. You sure you know what you're doing, letting Jason bring you home?'

'How d'you mean?' she asked.

Frank was watching Stella alongside Diane and comparing them. For the first time he looked at his wife with complete dispassion. Diane's face was cool, dark and matter-of-fact, carrying its weight of years, while Stella's eyes were bright and her skin looked as though it had just been unwrapped. Stella wore pale blue jeans that were tight enough for Frank to see the line of her tucked-in shirt fringing her hips. Diane wore a plasticized apron with information on it about how to gut fish. Their hands were very different: Stella's were creamy with translucent nails, Diane's were the same size but redder, with slightly raised veins that trailed over the backs of her hands and up into her wrists. Frank thought: so that is what has happened.

'We're just going out,' Jason said. He unballed his fists and took Stella's hand awkwardly. She followed Jason in the direction of his bedroom.

Frank called after them, 'Hey, out is this way. You've gone the in way.' They heard Jason's bedroom door close.

Frank and Diane exchanged ominous, confused glances. Frank said 'Well don't ask me to go in after them.'

A cassette player was turned on inside Jason's bedroom. Diane shook her head and said 'I don't know, they're still very young to be alone in a room with a bed. Did you talk to Jason about . . . what we agreed you should talk to him about?'

'What, about taking the rubbish down?'

'Oh Frank, you promised –'

'He *knows*, give him a bit of credit. Jason's known his way in and out of a packet of three since before he knew how to tie his shoelaces.'

'That's all Jason needs – a pregnant girlfriend before he's even opened a bank account.' Diane sighed and looked at Frank pityingly.

'Don't worry,' Frank reassured her. 'He'll probably get the brush-off and settle for showing her his hubcap collection or his West Ham programmes.'

Diane let herself be reassured. 'She seems older somehow. Pretty girl, don't you think?'

Frank pretended to give it some thought. Eventually he said 'Yes, but I think she's a bit on the young side.'

'She's Jason's age. It's better than him picking up habits from an older woman.'

'Oh yes,' Frank said. 'I suppose she's not too young for Jason.'

Jason brought Stella back to the Stubbs' flat regularly over the next few weeks. He started to relax more with her and even to leave her with Diane and Frank when he had to go off for any reason. As Jason relaxed, Frank became more nervous. He found he was not going out touting if there was a chance Stella would be visiting. Stella's body and her various clothes became familiar to Frank. He loved her in her pale blue jeans.

'So you're not too keen on living with your dad then, Stella?' Frank asked her one day. Jason was out doing a late delivery of piranha pine. Diane was listening in the kitchen.

'He's pretty horrible, really,' she said. 'That's why Mum went to live abroad.'

'Abroad, eh? That's a bit of a trip.'

'He expects me to run around after him all the time, but I don't see why I should after I've been working all day,' Stella said. She spoke politely but Frank sensed her determination.

Diane called through cheerfully, 'Hear that, Frank?' and went on peeling the potatoes. Frank was relieved that, after all their years of marriage, Diane seemed unable to imagine that Frank could be infatuated with another woman. Jealousy had fallen into disuse after a few years, left like an unnecessary wedding present mouldering in a box under the sink.

'You don't work all day,' Frank called out to Diane.

'Nor do you,' she replied.

Stella looked intently at Frank. He wanted to drive her away somewhere in his car.

'So,' he said instead, 'how's the timber business?'

'Well, I'm having a bit of trouble with the figure-work,' she said, and a temporary furrow appeared in her forehead.

The following week Stella was sacked from her job.

Jason was upset. 'She made a few little mistakes, right?' he told his parents. 'Dead, like, *weeny*, right? And they've booted her arse off the yard.'

Frank couldn't help himself: he pictured her bottom being kicked off the timber yard. He realized immediately that this would enable him to see Stella on his own, now that she no longer worked with his son all day. Frank wasn't thinking about any consequences – he was in free fall. Stella had unbuckled the straps that had bound him to Diane for more than half of his life. Frank had not discussed Stella with anybody. There was nobody to take him aside and whisper Diane's name in his ear.

Inside the chemist's, Frank said 'Hallo, Stella.'

She looked up from behind her counter.

'Mr Stubbs, what're you doing here?' she said. She sounded friendly but knowing. Frank felt transparent.

'I was just passing so I thought, you know. I was just passing. Call me Frank.'

'Oh, lovely,' she said.

'How's the new job?'

She leaned a little closer towards Frank, across the plastic display of cosmetics, and lowered her voice. 'I really wanted something clerical, but they didn't have anything in.'

'No,' Frank said. 'Sometimes there aren't always the jobs that you want. In.'

'No,' Stella said.

'There are jobs that'll do –'

'Yes.'

'But they're not the ones that you want,' Frank went on. He smiled quickly at her, making Stella intensify her own smile. There was a silence.

'I just sold some eye-liner,' she said, casting around for something to say.

'Eye-liner. Does that come in different colours?' he asked. Stella nodded assurance that it did.

Frank felt he ought to move the conversation on before he said something downright banal.

'I've been thinking about what you were saying about wanting to move out of your dad's place,' Frank said, drumming his fingers on Stella's counter.

In Stella's lunch-break Frank took her to see a small flat in Shoreditch. It was being rented out by Todd Billinge, another of Frank's friends, like Ted Nuttall, who were rich but hid it well. Todd Billinge owned property on a dozen different streets but looked as though he personally had been living and sleeping in a car for a number of years. The phenomenon of hidden wealth taught Frank to be suspicious of visible prosperity. He shared this tendency with his mother, who considered it flashy to wear jewellery more than once a week.

At first Frank had persuaded himself – effortlessly – that he was helping Stella out of common decency, that he was reaching down a fatherly hand. Standing in the sparsely furnished flat, he told her: 'I'm just trying to help you out here, Stella. You're not far short of being one of the family, true? Hey look, you've got a nice view of the car wash from here.' But the next moment he was saying to her: 'You'd better not mention me in this when you speak to Jason. He'll put two and two together and come up with –'

'Four?' Stella said brightly.

Frank thought, so you know what this is all about then.

He said 'I was going to say five, as it happens. Except, knowing Jason, he probably wouldn't get that close.'

'Yes, it's nice,' Stella said quickly. 'I'll take it.'

Frank gave her money to help her out. During the week that followed, Stella put up some new curtains in the flat and cleaned. Frank talked to her on the phone twice and helped her, chastely, to stick back some carpet tiles. She talked excitedly about how glad she was to have a place of her own.

'She's fucking ditched me, Dad,' Jason told Frank two days later, throwing himself into the armchair.

'Why's that?' Frank said as lightly as possible. He carried on pretending to read *The Stage*, but the headline Comedian Dies in Dressing Room only swam abstractly in front of his eyes.

'She's fucking bloody fucking fucking ditched me –'

'Yeah, OK, less of the –'

'I really liked her, Dad,' Jason said.

'There'll be others,' Frank said. 'Your age, you should be spreading yourself around town as thin as rice paper.' Frank was thinking, *Oh God, what am I doing?* Though happy with his life, he was thinking all the time that he could allow himself this little thing. He had begun to worry that he was something of a pervert not to have slept with anyone but his wife for over twenty years. It was embarrassing. Frank knew Diane and knew that she would not see it the modern way, but he needed to have Stella. He had to see again what it was like to be with another woman.

During that week, Frank's mental scrapbook was full of pictures of Stella sprawled in various imagined ways, often dressed only in a white vest.

'You're miles away,' Diane said to him, looking up from her book in bed. 'What are you thinking about?'

'Oh, you know, the usual,' he said. 'How's the book?' he asked, trying to lull her.

'I've read it before,' Diane replied, looking back at her novel. 'Bill Sikes is about to murder Nancy.'

'Oh,' Frank said, and thought about Stella some more. 'Thriller, is it?'

Frank turned up at Stella's on a grey afternoon, half hoping she would make life easy for him by serving him a cup of tea reluctantly and then telling him to leave, but she seemed so grateful to be living there quietly on her own, away from her tyrannical father ('Honestly, Mr Stubbs,' she had said, 'he's so crude and old-fashioned') that Frank started to feel fine. They made love and Frank enjoyed it as it occurred, although it felt strange and distancing. Frank could see that it was not the first time for Stella, but she was ghostly and passive throughout.

When it was over Frank continued to feel fine for some minutes and then stretched out an arm to put round Stella, as he liked to do with Diane, and found instead that his hand had come to rest on the shiny plastic nose of a soft toy that had been wedged under one of the pillows. His hand jerked back.

'That's Teddy,' Stella said simply. 'Ted.'

Frank wanted just to crawl away. He sloped quickly back into his clothes.

'I've got to go,' he said quietly.

'Did I do something wrong?' Stella asked. 'Is it the bear?'

Frank went away promising himself he would never go back. The experience had been the opposite of liberating – instead of unlocking his marriage and letting in a little air, Stella and her flat had created a new, smaller cage inside the bigger cage of his marriage. And Frank wasn't even sure that his marriage *was* a cage – generally speaking it was a comfortable and airy space.

Frank went back to Stella the next day, and again after that.

'Do me a favour, Stella, put your fluffy toys in the bloody cupboard, will you?' he said as he unlaced his shoes.

'I don't see why,' she said, taking off her own shoes as she sat on the other side of the bed.

'Because it takes years off you, that's why, and you can't afford them.'

'Look, I know I'm not quite seventeen but that's only if you measure it in years,' she said.

'How else do you measure it, Fahrenheit?'

Stella was folding her clothes item by item as she took them off. 'I'm not a child, Frank. I've had to grow up quickly, if you really want to know. I lost my virginity when I was thirteen,' she said curtly.

Frank turned to her. 'Yeah, and I think that's too early if you want to know.' It was true that Stella appeared older than sixteen, and she had put on years since Frank first saw her in his living room.

The relationship was undermined by Frank's insistence that what she was doing was wrong, when he knew all along that it was he who was wrong doing it to her.

'You should be messing about with boys your own age,' Frank said as they entered their third week. 'Why don't you take yourself off to discos and find yourself a kid in a denim jacket?'

'I will just as soon as I'm settled in here. Don't you want me to be nice to you?'

'I'm just a bit confused about what we're doing here,' Frank said.

'Well, you're helping me out so I'm making you happy for a while.'

Soon the situation seemed to be winding down the way Frank wanted. Stella's youth was beginning to pall and she was showing signs of irritation with him, complaining that he always turned up just as she was about to go out.

The end came for Frank.

He had been out late with Archie, working a cinema in Leicester Square – Saturday night, last house of *Horror Hog Sex Swamp II*. 'Combination like that,' Frank said to Archie, 'the only way we lose money is if we decide to give it away.'

Frank came through his front door and called out to Diane conventionally enough, as he often did, 'Hallo, love, I'm back.' With an awful, doomed playfulness, on that evening he added 'Come on out, hotpants, Frankie's got a big bone for you to bury.'

A few lights were on but there was nobody at home. Frank approached the table, which was covered with pieces of white and multi-coloured paper. He picked one up and turned it over, finding an orange-coloured leg standing next to a pair of brown trousers.

Diane had cut up the wedding photographs. There – Frank's mother with the side of her head cut off, pieces of blue sky. There – the dismembered arm of a bridesmaid.

A pair of scissors also lay on the green tablecloth. Frank reached across and closed its jaws.

For a moment, Frank prayed he was the victim of a psychopathic housebreaker with a spoiled marriage, but there was no doubt that it was Diane and that she had found out about Stella. She must have been in a state of disarray, because she always bawled Jason out when he used her dressmaking scissors to cut paper.

Frank wept.

There was no note, no turmoil in the flat. The eloquently sliced paper was all there was. A message of hate scrawled in blood would have been less damning. Frank realized that everything was now twisted and broken and soiled.

'Oh, good Christ,' Frank said, his face smeared with fluids.

Diane had already taken away her few personal possessions that did not have the smell of Frank's money and taste on them. The jewellery he had bought her during their marriage was still in the drawer, the jewellery she had chosen herself was gone.

Frank walked through the flat feverishly. He imagined it felt like this after you ran a child down in your car.

It was important now to find Diane and explain to her. He rang her best friend Anita.

'No, Diane's not with me,' she said cheerfully. 'How are you, Frank?' A small wave of television studio laughter broke in the background.

'Not too good –'

'Maybe it's flu?' she said.

'No,' Frank said distractedly.

'Why don't you get Di to put some honey in a hot –'

Frank put the phone down.

He rang Diane's parents but her father would not let him talk to her.

'Look, what's all this about?' Frank said, just in case. 'I'm coming round.'

'If you so much as set a foot on these premises I'll have the police over in a flash.'

'They use Metros round our way,' Frank said. The joke, though only poor, helped Frank's equilibrium.

'If you think this is funny for my daughter –'

'I NEED TO SPEAK TO MY WIFE,' Frank shouted. He didn't recognize his own voice.

His father-in-law hung up.

Frank drove round to Stella's flat. He held his arms out rigid on the steering wheel to stop them from shaking. Stella met him in her dressing-gown with a frothy toothbrush in one hand and foam at each corner of her mouth.

'Oh, hallo,' she said, matter-of-factly. 'I had Jason and your wife round earlier this evening.'

Frank looked at her expectantly.

'They didn't stay long,' she added, resuming her brushing.

Frank spent the next two months trying to speak to Diane. Jason, who had sworn never to speak to Frank ever ever ever again, spoke to Frank two days later on the Monday. It quickly became clear that Diane would not treat what Frank had done as a misdemeanour. She was acting as though he had dissolved the marriage.

'She'll never have you back,' Jason said as he ate his breakfast cereal.

'Didn't you say something about not talking to me ever again?' Frank asked him. 'Well, how about it?'

'You've got responsibilities to me.'

'Don't go giving me words like responsibilities, Jason. Not till you know what they mean.'

'You know, do you?' Jason said into his cereal bowl, which he was scraping the glaze off with his spoon.

Frank's hand went out and clipped Jason round the head. 'Sorry,' he said immediately. 'I'm sorry.'

The doorbell sounded. It was Anita with a polythene bag in her hand, looking fierce about the face and neck.

'Good morning, Anita.'

'I don't know how you have the gall to call me Anita at a time like this.'

Dispiritedly, Frank asked what was in the bag.

'It's the part you helped get for my husband's car. I don't want anything to do with you and your car parts, and neither does Don.'

'Jesus, Anita, you need a carburettor to –'

'You're the scum of the earth, you are.'

'Yeah, I know.'

Frank's mum had called his dad slime. Now Frank was scum. A dynasty of mucilage.

It must have taken quite a while to remove the carburettor and the bag was heavy, with oil-smeared insides. Frank couldn't stand the idea that her husband had done this willingly – for his own sanity he had to believe that Anita had been standing over his good friend Don with a whip or a kitchen knife.

Frank went back inside, feeling like he was carrying his heart or Diane's in the bag. Jason explained how it had happened, how he had come across Stella by chance in the chemist's. She had been friendly, talked about the help Frank had given her, and written down her address for Jason. Jason had gone home, mentioned Stella – 'Like, really *vaguely*, Dad. Mum must have just seen you coming a mile off' – and Diane had forced him to take her round. It had not taken Diane long to seize the facts she needed from Stella.

'Mum didn't cry or anything. She was just mad, like that time I slit out her shoulder pads to use them to polish my hubcaps. No, she wasn't mad, she was just cold. She was really cold.'

Frank rang Diane every day but he was not allowed to speak to her. 'I'd sooner put through the devil and all his cohorts,' her mother told him.

'All his what?' Frank could only say.

He put his business interests aside and staked out Diane in her parents' house. Sitting in the anonymous hired car, he thought about how she must be suffering. He played over their best moments together, his mind always coming to rest on the image of them sitting quietly in bed at the end of the evening, with Diane maybe smearing on some cream. All those evenings.

Diane seldom left the house, but Frank felt happier being near her anyway. He followed her car to the shops three times. When he tried to speak to her in the supermarket she dropped her basket and walked out. The next time she asked the assistant to fetch the manager. In the street, the third time, she listened to Frank's moment of pleading and then spat in his face.

Two months later Frank was allowed to talk to Diane, briefly, in the sitting room of her parents' house. She was wearing a businesslike blouse buttoned up under her neck. Frank's voice caught in his throat when he saw the dullness in her eyes.

'Come on back, Di,' he said, putting his hands on her arms across the mahogany table. 'One little mistake. I'm sorry.'

Diane snatched back her arms and hid them under the table. Very slowly, she said: 'You took a sixteen-year-old child, you removed her from her father's home and protection. You set her up in a sordid flat where you used her for your own pleasure. You lied to me, you destroyed any feelings your family had for you, and you turned the memory of the last twenty years into a nightmare.'

The outline of the story was vaguely familiar but Frank couldn't recognize himself. Who was the man who stole the kid? How could anyone do that?

Frank had come with apologies, entreaties and explanations, but all he could find in himself to say was 'Please. Come on back, Di.'

Since then Frank had sent Diane two birthday presents, two Christmas presents, bunches of flowers on two Valentine's days, some clotted cream from an unsuccessful weekend in Devon with Jason, eight short but heartfelt letters and their joint invitation to Archie's fortieth birthday outing to Walthamstowe dogs. The last thing he had sent was a photograph of a fuchsia she had grown from seed. Four inches high when she put the scissors through the wedding pictures, it was now nineteen inches tall.

In return Diane had told him that she would wait a while, as she had been advised, and would then be seeking a divorce.

'You had yourself a lovely wife there and you bollocksed it up for a bit of front door you didn't even want,' Archie told him as they watched the mechanical hare. There were just the two of them there to celebrate Archie's fortieth birthday.

'Back of the net, Archie. There's nothing I can teach you about human nature,' Frank said. They had been drinking.

'Still, at least we've got the business.'

Frank thought and said 'Yes, that's all I've got.'

Safe

'Oh dear, Frank,' Dave said. 'You seem to have a problem.'

Frank had just lost about £27,000 – his earlier winnings plus the contents of his safe. It was virtually all he owned.

He felt everyone's eyes on him. Dave's hard blue rivets, Janice's gooey lozenges, Ted's veiny bulbs and Ron's slits.

'Have I got this right –' Ron started.

'Dave,' Ted cut in, 'what say you let this one ride. Frank didn't have his mind on the cards.'

'No, no,' Frank said in a dreamy voice. 'We're giving the man the money.' Looking at Dave, he said 'It's been burning a hole in my pocket. What it needs now is to be given away.'

'That's a good attitude,' Dave said.

They all watched as he quietly tore up his two cheques, put the pieces in the ashtray and began to gather up the money on the table. The room was silent for the minute it took.

Frank watched Dave's hands. He thought about Diane again, trying to mend her rubber gloves with the iron, back in the days when money meant something.

To his left, Frank could feel Janice trying to think of something to say. Twice she opened her mouth, took in some breath and then changed her mind.

'Fra-ank,' she eventually said. 'Isn't that rather a lot of money, really?'

'Oh yes, it's a lot of money,' he answered, still dreamy.

Terrible implications began to work their way, pushing and shouting, through Frank's crowd of thoughts. Janice would have to go back to the agency. The office would have to go. Money piled up over fifteen years had disappeared in less time than it took to gather it up from the table. By the standards of some of Frank's friends it was not a lot of cash – it was only a lot if it was all you had. Worse than the money, there was the failure. Frank didn't know if he could find the energy or interest to fill a safe again. He would have a small bank account like everyone else, with a plastic cheque-book cover and a ring-binder to keep the statements in.

Frank felt tired. He closed his eyes.

'I'd better have the rest out of the safe now,' Dave said. 'And I'll be very disappointed if it's not all there.'

'Leave him alone,' Janice lashed out.

'Dave, give it a breather,' Ted said.

Dave opened his palms and said gently, 'Who kicked the bidding through the roof? Was it me or Cincinnati here?'

Ron finished his drink and said 'Well, I'd best be getting home before they shut off the snooker.'

There was a sudden clunk at the window. Slumped in his chair, Frank glanced up to see a spider's web of cracked glass. Janice was the first to the window, opening it quickly and sending a shower of glass down on to the street below.

'Bloody vandals,' Ron said, managing to put on his coat and shake his head at the same time. 'That's what happens when you stop giving kids the cane in schools. What do they get now? Free bloody periods.'

Janice was leaning out of the window. Frank found himself

looking at her tight skirt again but he couldn't remember what the significance of it was.

'It's Archie standing next to a smashed-up car,' she said blandly.

Frank, Ron and Ted joined Janice at the window. Frank could already hear Archie shouting: '. . . power-assisted steering, tinted windows and loads of ashtrays.'

Janice called out into the cool air, 'Archie, is that blood on your hand?'

He was about ten feet away. Behind him, diagonal to the pavement – not so much parked as *stopped* – was a newish-looking car that had either been rolled or set about with something blunt and heavy.

'I've always wanted one of these,' Archie said thickly.

'Wouldn't you rather have had one without so many creases?' Janice asked naively.

Archie's jacket was ripped and dirty. He was drunk, swaying. There were four of them squeezed into the aperture of the window – four Juliets to one lurching Romeo – but Frank suddenly felt Archie's eyes targeted at him.

'Hey, boss, what d'you think of my car?'

Frank was confused by this new incident, coming on top of such an evening. Wearily, he called down 'You've got no money, Archie. Where did you get the car?'

'I bought it.'

'So why did you smash it up?'

'Feeling crazy,' Archie said. 'Took it out for a spin, leaned over to try –' Archie interrupted himself, raising his hand as though about to sneeze, and was hugely sick in the gutter.

'Euhh, revolting,' Janice said.

Archie didn't seem to mind. A little groggier, he went on,

'– leaned over to try out one of the buttons and flipped the motor over on a, on a fucking embankment.'

'What's it feel like to do that?' Frank asked. He felt disembodied.

'Good, felt good.'

Ted pulled back from the window and walked away, saying 'I don't know what's up with everyone tonight.'

Frank stared at Archie. The blood was congealing darkly on Archie's wrist and hand. What was the point of this peculiar dialogue from an upstairs window?

'But don't you worry about me and my car,' Archie said. 'Because it's not my car, it's your car.'

Frank was patient. Gently, into the night air, he said 'It's not my car.' Two men in leather jackets walked past, looking hard at the corpulent, spattered figure and the beleaguered car. It cannot have been easy to drive it like that, the distorted frame rattling and grinding, but Archie was in such a bad way he would not have noticed. Frank felt they should go and help him. 'What say you get home to bed before you get given a bag to blow into? Because I'm warning you Archie, you're off the dial.'

Archie smiled and answered, 'I bought it with your money, so I'd say that makes it your car. I'm delivering it.'

Frank rested his arms on the window sill and looked blankly down at Archie.

'You bought it with my money,' Frank repeated.

'Company motor, isn't that the sort of item you were keeping money in the safe for?' Archie gave a deranged laugh and then grimaced. Looking at his hand for the first time, he said 'What's happened here?'

Frank walked quickly to the safe, crouched down and opened it. He counted the bundles. Silently, Frank went back to the window, passing Dave, who was still sitting quietly at the table.

'Why did you do it, Archie?' Frank asked, still calm.

Archie was straightening up after making another contribution to the gutter. Frank wondered when the horror would end.

'Archie?' Frank coaxed.

Even in the dim street lamp, Frank could see that Archie's face now had a new greyness about it. Summoning up some last lucidity, Archie said 'You got greedy, Frank. So fuck you.'

Frank felt cold as well as tired. He just wanted to keep a grip on himself for as much of the rest of the evening as possible.

'Wait there, Archie,' Ted shouted down.

They shut the window and turned back to the room, which felt quiet and tense. Ted and Ron finished pulling on their coats and told Frank they would go down and take Archie home. Meanwhile, they waited. Janice sat in embarrassed silence on the side of the table, her jacket round her shoulders.

Frank placed the contents of the safe on the table in front of Dave.

'It's eight grand short,' Frank murmured. 'It will take me some time to get it.'

Dave looked into Frank's face. 'That won't do, Frank.'

'Oh really?' he said, barely audibly.

'You don't have the money, so where are you going to get it?'

'No, I don't have it.' Frank suddenly felt vulnerable. He swallowed. 'You can take the furniture.'

'I don't want it. Furniture wasn't on the table.'

Frank had to admit that Dave had authority in the way he spoke. He never said *er* or *you know*. His words seemed to count, whereas most of what Frank said was either negotiable or playful or he knew it was wrong.

'I'm including the hatstand,' Frank said.

'You don't see me smiling, Frank.'

'Maybe you should have a word with Archie. It's Archie you have your quarrel with.'

'No, Frank. Archie is of no interest to me. You bid the money.'

Frank said 'Yes.'

There was a moment of silence before Dave added 'You'd better come and work for me, hadn't you, Frank? Until you've paid it off.'

Frank had his mouth open. 'Me, come and work for you?'

'That's it,' Dave said, rising to his feet and slowly putting his jacket on. 'See you at my office at ten tomorrow.'

The three men made for the door together, leaving Frank standing by the table in the middle of the dim room. The smell of fish still hung in the air.

As Ted left he said sympathetically 'You'll have better days, Frank.'

Frank nodded mutely.

'Look at it this way,' Ron added. He paused for a long moment at the threshold as the others went on down the stairs. 'No, I've forgotten what I was going to say.' He backed out through the door.

Frank sensed Janice staring at him but he couldn't bear to look at her or imagine what she was thinking. He felt cold, tired and oppressed. Small and old. And stupid.

To ward off the panic Frank could feel fermenting, he said 'So, do you think the guests enjoyed themselves?'

'Oh yes,' Janice said. 'Very pleasant.' Frank could see her expression of sympathy now. 'I know what I said earlier,' she began to say slowly, 'but I find you really, really, really nice. Not at all, kind of, ooh I don't know, not *old*, you know?'

'Sorry, Janice, I've got some things to do,' Frank said. He was leaning heavily on the table, his hands ground into its surface.

'No, really, Frank. We can talk about it in the car. I feel terrible for you.' There was a hysterical pity in her voice now.

'No, Janice,' he said. They looked at each other for a moment. 'I'll make sure you get your wages.'

'Thanks.'

'I was a bit gobby back then, over the cards.'

'Bit carried away?'

'That's it,' Frank agreed. 'I tried to, you know.'

'Yes.'

'Shit all over Dave.'

Janice nodded determinedly. 'Are you going to work for him?'

'Why would I want to do a thing like that?'

'Because –'

'Oh yeah, course,' Frank said, remembering. 'I'm going to work for him. Back into service.'

Janice looked at him anxiously with her head on one side. Frank relaxed one hand from its grip on the table and put his thumbnail convulsively into his mouth. Staring distantly at the surface of the table, he gnawed. Janice started to eat in sympathy. She selected a strand of hair from the right side of her head, drew it across her cheek and put it in her mouth.

'Your family are very nice,' Janice said aimlessly.

Frank said abruptly 'I can't drive you home, Janice. Do you mind taking a cab?' He fished twenty pounds out of his pocket, shuffled over to her and put it gently in her hand.

'You can't afford it now, Frank,' she said, shaking her head.

Distractedly, Frank looked in his pocket again and brought out a brown note, taking the twenty back. He wasn't sure what he was doing.

'Frank, this is a Scottish one, have you got an English note? You know what taxi drivers are like.'

He gave her back the twenty and sat down heavily in a chair.

'Will you be all right?' she asked.

Frank had his back to her and had put his thumbnail back in his mouth. He swivelled slightly as though surprised she was still there and said 'I'll be terrific.'

At the door she said 'I'll probably see you around then. Locally.'

The door closed. It took a while before Frank felt able to look up at the room. The empty safe. The tinsel, the safari-motif umbrella stand. The cardboard box of cold fish stood in the corner and pieces of greasy paper littered the floor. Paper cups mushroomed on surfaces, many of them moist with unfinished drinks. For a small party they had used a lot of drinks, Frank was thinking. Then he realized: they had tried the wine Janice had bought but didn't like it. So they didn't even like his wine.

Frank couldn't stand it any more.

He jumped to his feet, turned round and kicked over the chair he had been sitting on. The card table still had the cards and two ashtrays on it. He swung himself up on to it, kicked the ashtrays at the wall, and leapt up and down on the fragile green baize table, once, twice, five times, until struts splintered and broke and Frank was tossed off on to the low glass table, which shattered under him.

Waves of energy were passing through Frank's body, even as he lay on broken glass, framed by the chrome skeleton of the low table.

He clambered back on to his feet and grabbed the hatstand. Taking hold of the curls of wood at the hat end, Frank swung the heavy base at the light bulb in the middle of the room. He felt a piece of hot glass land on his forehead and tried to adjust his eyes to the new darkness. The darkness felt right to Frank.

Not knowing which part of the room he was in any more, Frank felt his way around the walls. He found a picture and smashed it against the wall. His hip came to rest against Janice's old desk, the drinks table. Frank picked up bottle after bottle and threw them against the floor, walls and ceiling. He admired the clean, crashing noises and the spectacle. Soon the room glinted with glass, dripping and glugging discreetly.

Frank began to feel his energy and euphoria ebbing away as he started on the lager cans, opening them and throwing the thin steel pods. He stopped, went to the window and opened it. With some difficulty, but powered by misery he could not express any other way, Frank dragged over the leather sofa, manhandled it on to the window sill and levered it up and into the void. There was a ringing clunk. Frank looked out and saw the sofa straddling the scarred roof of Archie's car. A sofa leg was wedged into the windscreen aperture and a chrome bar was bent.

The light from the street lamp streamed through the open window, round Frank's back and shoulders as he sat on the window sill and gazed into his broken office. He had lager running up his arm. An intact wine bottle was still rolling on the thin carpet, but Frank didn't have the strength to get up and smash it. Instead, he watched it teeter around the floor until it gently, gently stopped.

Thoughts and faces turned over in Frank's mind. Dave, Archie, the spare sink in the toilet, the typed sheet of paper with the word Acrobats, Janice eating her cheek, Nobby, the shame of the money on the table, Janice opening manila envelopes that morning, Diane, Ted's wife with the grease round her mouth.

Suddenly one thought replaced all the others.

He walked on broken glass and damp carpet over to the telephone. The receiver had been knocked off its cradle but the line was still good. Frank dialled and the information came surprisingly easily.

He locked up the office, walked down the stairs and out. He took a while to find his car. At that time of night all cars looked the same.

Frank drove with what seemed to him to be blinding efficiency, a parody of sobriety and normality. Though he lost his way once, he felt collected and sure of arriving. Towards the end of the journey he wound down the window, looking carefully at the street names and then the house numbers.

Frank felt a small stone in his shoe as he made his approach after parking the car. He ignored it.

A small house with a neat garden. The light was on. He rang the bell and Diane appeared quite soon behind the first glass door. She opened it and entered the glazed porch. Frank screwed up his eyes to see her more clearly. As though removing another veil, she opened the door that separated her from Frank. They looked at each other.

Diane said 'Mum just phoned to say she'd given you my address.' Her voice was softer than he remembered it.

'I didn't think she'd let me have it,' Frank answered. He wanted his own voice to sound caressing but it felt loud and coarse.

'I told her a while ago she could, if you phoned.'

'I didn't know,' Frank said. 'Are you alone?'

'Of course,' she said.

'How have you been?'

Diane shrugged and gave a small smile. She turned to go inside, leaving the doors open. Frank followed. The living room was neat and carried Diane's sense of symmetry. He didn't recognize any objects except a picture of Jason in a silver frame. It was an official photograph of Jason in his school uniform, but he had put his tongue out at the last moment.

Frank watched Diane walk through the room in her dressing-gown and felt good again.

'Tea?' she asked at the entrance to the kitchen, holding up a small teapot.

'Please,' Frank said, sitting down on the edge of an arm-chair. 'I've had a bit of a difficult day as it happens.'